D0553659

The Ice House

The Ice House
Nina Bawden

St. Martin's Press
New York

For Niki, in remembrance

THE ICE HOUSE. Copyright © 1983 by Nina Bawden. All rights
reserved. Printed in the United States of America. No part
of this book may be used or reproduced in any manner
whatsoever without written permission except in the case
of brief quotations embodied in critical articles or reviews.
For information, address St. Martin's Press, 175 Fifth Avenue,
New York, N.Y. 10010.

Library of Congress Cataloging in Publication Data

Bawden, Nina, 1925—
   The ice house.

   I. Title.
PR6052.A84124   1983   823'.914   83-9722
ISBN 0-312-40386-0

First published in Great Britain by Macmillan London Limited.

10 9 8 7 6 5 4 3 2

Part One
FRIENDSHIP

I

That summer Saturday in 1951, Daisy Brown aged fifteen, going to tea with Ruth Perkin, also aged fifteen, had an unusual sense of adventure. The invitation, shyly offered, oddly phrased – 'My father says you may come to tea, Saturday', Ruth had said – was unique. No one that Daisy knew had ever been asked to the Perkin house. And although Ruth had been to tea with Daisy, her visits had been arranged more formally than the free and easy Brown household was used to: telephone calls at least a week in advance between the two mothers, the exact time of Ruth's arrival, the exact time she was expected home, always stated and rigidly kept to. Ruth was not allowed out later than seven o'clock summer evenings, six o'clock in the winter.

'Nervous, poor soul, a hen with one chick,' Mrs Brown said of Mrs Perkin, sympathetically dismissing this extraordinary tyranny as acute maternal anxiety. Daisy, accustomed to coming and going as the fancy took her, found Ruth's situation more intriguing. Daisy was popular, she had plenty of friends that she made use of in a casual way, but the restraints imposed on this particular friendship made her value it more. Ruth never complained. Once, perhaps as an excuse, or an explanation, she said, 'My father was a Japanese prisoner during the war. He worked on the railway.' And another time, more mysteriously, 'My mother is always polishing under the mats in the hall.' Otherwise she seldom mentioned her home or her parents, keeping silent when other girls spoke of theirs, and, if they grumbled, smiled in a composed and secretive way that excited Daisy to romantic conjecture of an innocently snobbish and commonplace kind.

Captain and Mrs Perkin, Daisy assumed, must be very superior —'posh' was the word she used in her mind – to be so oddly reclusive, so 'stuffy' and 'fussy'. And rich, of course. Walking Ruth home from school, looking through the tall gates elaborately decorated with iron roses and pineapples, at the hideous, turreted, mock-baronial mansion, Daisy's inward eye furnished it with thick carpets and heavy mahogany tables covered with glossy magazines, like the waiting room of the expensive London dentist she and her brother, Bob, attended twice a year. Everything would be highly polished. A polished hall, a gleaming stairway, and perhaps (thinking now of the photographs of stately homes inside the dentist's magazines), a stag's head with glass eyes among the ancient portraits on the walls.

Expecting this institutional grandeur, Daisy was temporarily discomfited to find the interior of the Perkin house shabbier and less cared for than her own. The entrance hall, gloomily panelled in dark wood, had no pictures or ornaments to catch the eye, and the scuffed, parquet floor showed no sign of the obsessional polishing that Ruth had spoken of. And little Mrs Perkin, hovering behind her daughter – *hiding*, was Daisy's first impression – did not seem at all posh or superior. More like a nervous maid or housekeeper than the mistress of the house. Daisy said, in an encouraging voice, copying her kindly mother's manner with shy people, 'I'm pleased to meet you, Mrs Perkin. How nice of you to let me come.' When Mrs Perkin weakly smiled and held out her hand, Daisy felt it flutter like a frightened bird inside her own, much larger, paw.

Captain Perkin's greeting was heartier. Standing before the empty grate in the large, high-ceilinged dining room (only marginally lighter than the hall, and chilly, even though it was a warm June day) he said, 'Well, it's good to see one of Ruth's young friends at last' – as if Ruth had been deliberately denying him this opportunity for years. 'I'd have come before if I'd been asked,' Daisy said, smiling her bold and cheerful smile, and heard Ruth, behind her, give a little sigh.

Tea was already laid; a white cloth on the table, plates of bread and butter, cakes and biscuits, two big glass bowls of strawberries, a jug of cream. Daisy tucked in. Her appetite was good, her confidence, in spite of her burgeoning maturity, that of a happy, egocentric child. She was only distantly aware that neither Ruth nor Mrs Perkin seemed as comfortably at ease. Mrs Perkin had spoken once, in a low, apologetic voice, to ask if Daisy liked milk in her tea, and Ruth did not speak at all. But Ruth was often silent in company, so her silence now was not remarkable, and Daisy was content to bear the social burden. Unasked, but assuming interest, she told Captain Perkin that she and Ruth were the greatest friends at school, even though Ruth was the cleverest girl in the class and she was such a duffer, unlike her brother Bob, who was going up to Cambridge, and that her father, who had been in the RAF during the war, a bomber pilot, was training to be an Air Traffic Controller and thinking of buying a new car. There was a waiting list for the model that he wanted, but he had put down a deposit. (Whether he would be able to afford the balance was another matter; his children's Harley Street dentist, their riding and tennis lessons, and Mr Brown's extra-marital expenses made it unlikely, but even if Daisy had been aware of these difficulties she would have discounted them. She was merely anxious to establish what she considered social status.) She finished her plate, the last of the succulent fruit mashed pinkly into cream and castor sugar, and said, 'Gosh! What lovely strawberries!'

Captain Perkin passed the bowl. 'Sweets to the sweet,' he said. 'Daisy, the Fair.' His brown eyes, smoothly shiny as conkers, rested on her with the greedy look that she was used to from old men, the fathers of her friends, but there was another element in Captain Perkin's gaze, a bright, brooding intensity, that made her uneasy. Captain Perkin said, 'I daresay you have lots of boy friends, Daisy,' and she was conscious that her last year's summer dress was too tight across the chest. Blushing slightly, she owned to 'quite a few', adding, 'My mother says there is safety in numbers.' She rolled her eyes flirtatiously at Captain Perkin. She couldn't help it. Flirting was as natural to Daisy as breathing.

'I hope your mother knows what she is doing,' Captain Perkin said. 'I am careful with Ruth. But I have seen a bit of the world, you understand. I know what men are, with ripe young girls.' He spluttered as he laughed, as if his mouth was full of juice. And, with a gloating emphasis, 'I know what girls are, come to that!' His eyes were on her breasts.

Daisy hunched her shoulders forward to give her dress more fullness in the front. She glanced at Mrs Perkin, expecting her to intervene and rescue her as her own mother would have done. But Mrs Perkin sat with downbent head, the delicate fingers of one tiny hand pleating the edge of the table cloth. And Ruth was silent still.

Daisy said – she could think of nothing else to say – 'These really are the best strawberries I've ever tasted, Captain Perkin. Did you grow them?'

'The gardener did,' he said – rebuking her, she thought, for suggesting he would soil his hands with menial work. But she was unimpressed. Though the Browns could not afford it, plenty of houses in this leafy suburb employed jobbing gardeners by the hour. Daisy said, 'We haven't had our own strawberries this year but my father grows most of our vegetables. It's good exercise for him, my mother says, and there's nothing like things straight from the garden. And we have a friend who has a farm and we get fresh eggs from him.

Cream, too. Even bacon, sometimes, when he's killed a pig. That's a great help now the bacon ration has gone down.'

'Cream,' Captain Perkin repeated thoughtfully. He smiled at Daisy foxily. He was like a fox, she thought – or a sharp-nosed terrier, rather. He had that kind of skinny, bony strength, that alert and waggish air. She didn't answer his smile for fear of provoking more embarrassing remarks but his next words were harmless. 'Then I should think your mother might appreciate some strawberries to go with it. Ruth, if you have finished tea, you may pick some strawberries for Daisy's mother.'

Ruth folded her napkin and rose at once. Her mother also rose and took a glass bowl from the sideboard. She gave it to Ruth and whispered something that Daisy couldn't hear. Ruth nodded. As Daisy followed her into the hall, she closed the door behind them. She said, whispering like her mother, 'Would you like to use the bathroom? It's first on the left at the top of the stairs. I'll wait for you down here.'

'Aren't you coming?' Daisy asked, surprised. Though she didn't need the lavatory, she was eager to look round the house. When Ruth came to tea with her, they always retreated to Daisy's bedroom once the family meal was over, played the gramophone, giggled, fixed each other's hair. Daisy said, 'I'd like to see your room.'

A little colour came and went in Ruth's pale face. 'I have to pick the strawberries. Besides, it's nicer out of doors. We can go to my work shop. It's only a sort of garden shed, but it's much more private there.'

Daisy shrugged. 'Okay, let's go. I don't really want to pee.'

She said this rather loudly and Ruth's eyes – nut brown like her father's – widened anxiously.

'Sorry,' Daisy said. 'Excuse my French. I don't really want

to go to the bathroom. But honestly, you know, I don't think your Mum or Dad could hear.'

She felt put down, quite hurt, in fact. After Captain Perkin's crude suggestiveness at tea, it was mean of Ruth to make her feel that *she* had been indelicate. She jerked her chin indignantly, tossing back her long, fair hair, freshly washed and ironed for this visit, and said, 'Miss Prissy Perkin.'

This time Ruth's colour mounted from her slender neck and stayed; a painful, burning blush. '*I'm* sorry, Daisy. I was silly. Of course it doesn't matter what *you* call it. Piss, shit, *crap*. . .' She brought out these shocking words defiantly, filling Daisy with alarm. 'Shut up, you dope,' she muttered, glancing towards the dining room. Although Ruth hadn't shouted, she hadn't whispered, either.

Ruth smiled, a sudden, open, wicked grin, but her breath was coming fast. She gave a furtive giggle, like a naughty child, and ran to the front door.

It was pleasant out, a soft and scented day. Ruth led the way round the back of the house to a walled garden where an elderly man was weeding a line of vegetables. Ruth said, 'Hallo, Jessup. I've come to pick some strawberries.'

The strawberries were netted close to the ground. They would have to crawl beneath the nets to pick them, Daisy saw with some dismay, and was relieved when Mr Jessup straightened his old back and held his hand out for the bowl. 'I'll get them for you, Ruthie. You'll spoil your pretty dress. Get your hair all tangled up.'

Ruth shook her head. 'Thank you, Jessup, but my father told me to. He wouldn't like it if I didn't do it.'

'The Captain wouldn't like it, either, if you tear them nets. A fine old mess you'd make.'

'We'll be careful.'

The old man laughed, showing brown and crooked teeth. 'Get on with you. I've nothing much to do this afternoon.

You've got your friend. Run along, enjoy yourself.'

But Ruth still hesitated. A frown, a quite deep furrow, appeared between her brows. Daisy said, 'It's very kind of him to offer, Ruth.'

Ruth sighed and yielded up the bowl. She was silent as they left the kitchen garden and crossed a shaven lawn. Beyond it, a small, wooded hill rose up, a wild thicket of old trees with saplings and dog roses growing round their roots. Like other gardens in this neighbourhood, the Perkin garden had once been part of a large gentleman's estate, sold off and broken up between the wars and developed by a builder who had a more sensitive feeling for landscape than he had for architecture. His houses were uncomfortable to live in and ugly to look at, mock-Tudor grand or quaintly cottagey, but he had designed the grounds around them carefully, sparing the best trees, making a feature of an ornamental pond, a flight of steps, a Victorian folly. As Daisy followed Ruth along a narrow path around the hill she saw a curious, domed structure on her left, half hidden in the trees some way above, and scrambled up to look. The building was twice her height; she looked through the high, open doorway at the arched brick roof above and the dark drop beneath. 'An air raid shelter,' Daisy said. But it was too old for that.

'An ice house,' Ruth said, standing below her, on the path. 'An old ice house.'

'What's that when it's at home? What *ice*?'

'There isn't any now,' Ruth said. 'Not for years and years, of course. It was before they had refrigerators. People used it for keeping meat and game. They chopped the ice off ponds in winter, packed it tight on top of stones, and it stayed frozen all the summer. There's nothing to see now. Come and see my workshop. It's much more interesting.'

'I think *this* is interesting,' Daisy said. 'It's really *huge*. Did they hang the meat, or what? I can't see any beams.' She held on to the bricks at the side of the entrance and peered in. 'I'm not sure that I can see the bottom, either. It's so dark.'

'It's about twelve feet down, I think,' Ruth said. 'Be careful.' She had climbed up now but seemed reluctant to stand as close as Daisy to the drop. 'There used to be a ladder once. But I suppose it rotted.'

'There ought to be a door,' Daisy said. 'It's dangerous. If you fell in, how would you get out again? You could yell and yell, no one would hear you unless they were quite close. Do you know what I think?' She giggled, shedding half a dozen years, retreating to a ghoulish infancy. 'I bet, if we went down there, we'd find a pile of human bones.'

'Only dead birds and squirrels,' Ruth said. 'My father shoots them and throws their bodies in. Otherwise there's nothing there but stones and dirt. I know, because when I was little, before the war, my father used to put me there when I was in a rage. To cool me off.' Like Daisy she giggled, but on a wilder note.

Daisy wasn't sure that she believed this. She said, with some reserve, 'How beastly.'

'Oh, I used to have a dreadful temper,' Ruth said. 'I suppose it cured me.'

She sounded calm. Daisy, recognising that she spoke the truth, felt chilled. She said, uncertainly, 'Bob once locked me in a cupboard. When I broke his train set. That was bad enough.'

'Much worse,' Ruth said. 'I mean, if you're down there, you can see the daylight above you, but a cupboard would be absolutely dark. I think I used to be afraid there would be ice and I would freeze to death, I didn't understand why it was called an ice house then, you see I was so small, but of course there wasn't. So I wasn't cold.'

Daisy shivered. 'I'd have died of fright.'

'No you wouldn't. I didn't, did I? Obviously.'

Ruth smiled, her pinched and secret smile and Daisy watched her curiously. She had always known that Ruth was 'different' but although she usually admired her cool composure she found it uncomfortably disturbing now. She yawned and hugged her arms across her breasts, finding comfort in their soft and bouncy warmth, and said, 'Well, if you want to know, I think this is a dreary, squalid place. Gives me the creeps.'

'You wanted to look at it,' Ruth pointed out. '*I* wanted to show you where I work.'

'So you did. My fault. I grovel. Mea culpa, as the Romans say!' Daisy was glad to see Ruth smile more openly. She laughed herself and smote her brow theatrically. 'Lead on, Macduff!'

The shed, a weathered, wooden summer house, was tucked into the far side of the hill, its windowless back to the wooded slope, its glass door facing south down a long grass walk beside the hedge that marked the Perkin boundary. The hedge, grown tall and straggly, full of cottony tufts of old man's beard, hid the neighbouring garden and provided a greenly shaded privacy lit by shifting gleams of gold where the westering sun shone through it. Inside the shed, dust motes danced and sparkled in the air but the wooden floor was swept, the sofa had recently been covered in red hessian, and there was a tall vase of fresh cut roses beside it, on a stool. 'My private workroom,' Ruth announced with sudden animation, pointing to an old-fashioned treadle sewing machine, a long mirror on a stand, and a dressmaker's dummy, a headless, canvas body with a grey flannel skirt, neatly chalk-marked down the seams, fastened round its waist. 'That's for my mother,' Ruth explained. 'I'm afraid it's dull, but at least it'll fit her when it's finished. Most of her clothes are terrible, bunching and drooping everywhere. I've got much nicer things to show you. The sofa sags a bit, but it's quite comfortable.'

'You're not going to give me a *sewing lesson*, are you?' Daisy said.

Ruth looked amused. 'Don't sound so horrified.'

'I mean, my fingers are all thumbs, it would just be a waste of time,' Daisy muttered, feeling that she had been rude. She sat on the sofa that twanged beneath her weight, making her feel fat as well. She looked on gloomily (she really should not have eaten that enormous tea) while Ruth opened the lids of two oak chests and began to pull out lengths of materials, silks and satins, velvets, chiffons, holding some up for Daisy's somewhat bored inspection, throwing others upon the floor. Most were remnants, Ruth explained, odds and ends, but all were long enough to make at least a blouse or skirt. There were old dresses, too. 'This belonged to my grandmother,' Ruth said, unwrapping a brown paper package and shaking out a full skirted gown of dark green, watered silk. 'It was made before the First World War, by a dress designer called Lucille. It's miles too big for me, but it would fit you, Daisy, if I altered it.' She measured Daisy's body with her eyes. 'In fact, you could almost wear it as it is, if you were going somewhere grand. Though it might be better if I cut some of the flounces off. They make it a bit fussy for a girl your age, you need a simpler line.'

Although the idea of wearing other people's cast off clothes did not appeal to Daisy, it was clear no other entertainment was likely to be offered and so she stood up good humouredly, holding the green dress against her while Ruth pressed the stiff silk against her waist with one hand and held the skirt out with the other. 'Look,' she said, smiling at Daisy in the glass, but Daisy looked with more interest at Ruth's face than at her own reflection. She had never seen Ruth look so eager and absorbed. Her closed and wary look was gone, her eyes were bright, her cheeks were flushed. 'Of course you've got to use your imagination, Daisy,' she said earnestly. 'Think of it fitting you properly and nicely pressed, and with your hair up, perhaps, and wearing different shoes.'

Daisy made an effort, but it remained an old green dress to her, an unlucky colour, a peculiar shape, and probably, after all these years, not very clean. Why didn't Ruth wear it herself if she thought it was so marvellous? She put this more politely. 'It's pretty, Ruth, but if you're going to cut it about, why don't you make it over for yourself?'

'When would I wear it? I don't go to parties, do I?'

Ruth sat back on her heels, the rich stuff tumbled on her lap. She looked up at Daisy, eyes narrowed speculatively. 'If you don't like the colour, there's a Poiret, but it would be harder to adapt, all beads and things. Or a Schiaparelli that my mother had when she was young. I don't know, though. The skirt's cut on the cross.'

'What does that mean?'

'Cut to make it sort of slinky. Kind of sideways. But that means it may have stretched.' She got up from her knees and delved deep in the chests, dragging out more dresses. 'You could wear black, you're so fair. Black silk. Whatever people say, girls can wear black, though perhaps your mother mightn't like it. Violet satin? No, that's for dowagers. And pink is far too babyish. Or there's this taffeta. A sort of toffee colour, very subtle with your colouring, and there's several yards of it, only a bit faded in the creases.'

Daisy said, 'You can't make things for me.'

'But I would like to. Really. Won't you let me? Please. I've no one else.' Ruth's face, above the shimmer of peacock colours that surrounded her, was urgent with appeal. *Weird*, Daisy thought. If she were to tell her other friends that Ruth had invited her to tea to offer this extraordinary choice of ancient dresses – some of them her *grandmother*'s, for God's sake! – there would be incredulous shrieks of merriment. Well, she wouldn't tell them, she decided virtuously. It would not be kind. Apart from not letting boys treat her 'disrespectfully', being kind was one of the few moral injunctions Daisy's mother had imposed on her.

She turned over the jumbled pile, searching for something that would be just faintly possible. 'I suppose I could wear that cream lace blouse.'

She took off her dress and put it on. When Ruth had pinned a deep tuck in the back, hitched up the sleeves, it looked prettier than Daisy had expected. She fiddled with the neckline, a high frill with a threaded, velvet bow. 'No, leave it,' Ruth said. 'It sets off your throat. It looks wrong at the moment because your petticoat is short. You need a full skirt to balance it. Ballerina length. I can make one from the taffeta.' She wrapped it around Daisy's waist to show her the effect, flaring it about her hips. Daisy said, 'My bottom's much too big.'

'Not really. It shows off your waist. If I dart the skirt, you'll see. It's much easier to dress someone who has a proper *shape*. Bones and angles are a bigger problem.' This was a professional statement, not a compliment to Daisy, because she added, thoughtfully, 'Though I suppose a bad figure would be more of a challenge in a way.'

'Sorry,' Daisy said. She slumped her shoulders and stuck out her stomach. 'Better?'

'Don't be silly. See?' Ruth gathered the taffeta again round Daisy's rounded form, tightening the waist behind her. 'Look *now*.'

Amazing, Daisy thought. An old lace blouse, a faded bit of creased up taffeta. She twisted, preening, admiring her suddenly romantic image in the glass. 'It's lovely. You are clever, Ruth.'

Ruth smiled. 'It's just what I like doing best. I'd like to be a dressmaker. Not ordinary clothes for every day but special things. When I want to be happy, I think of women dancing in big, swirling skirts.'

'I think of food,' Daisy said. 'And getting married. You're sure your mother won't mind your giving the lace blouse away?'

'Why should she? She'll be glad I have someone to practise on. You'll have to come again so I can fit you properly. Try and stand still while I take off the blouse. I don't want to move the pins.'

Wincing when a pin scratched, Daisy remembered her mother's warning. Watch the time, you don't want to over-stay your welcome with those funny people. As she buttoned up her dress – seeing it as a Cinderella garment now, a cheap, limp cotton, much too small – she glanced slyly at her watch.

Ruth saw her. 'Must you go?'

'It's half past six. I have to catch my pumpkin.'

'What? Oh, yes, I see.'

'I'll help you clear up first.'

Ruth shook her head and Daisy looked on as she filled the chests, closing the lids and fastening the brass hasps. When she stood up her face was pale again, screwed up and lined, as if she had packed her colour and vitality away with the bright clothes. Puzzled, Daisy said, 'I really have enjoyed myself this afternoon,' but although Ruth responded with a formal smile, she didn't answer her.

They left the summer house, followed the little path around the hill and crossed the lawn. Walking round the house, Ruth spoke at last. 'You don't need to go back in, do you? You didn't have a coat, or anything?'

Daisy thought of the strawberries but it seemed greedy to mention them. 'I ought to say thank you to your mother, shouldn't I?'

Ruth pursed her lips and frowned. She looked like a worried little witch. Daisy said, quite sternly, 'It would be awfully rude, not to say goodbye.' And then, guessing at the reason for

15

Ruth's odd behaviour, laughed. 'Don't worry, I shan't expect to stay for supper!'

The front door was open. As they entered, Captain Perkin called from the dining room. 'Is that you, Ruth?'

Daisy followed Ruth across the hall. Ruth stopped in the doorway, so abruptly that Daisy almost cannoned into her. Looking over Ruth's shoulder she saw the table cleared of everything except the glass bowl, now full of strawberries, and Captain Perkin standing, feet apart, one arm behind his back. Stiffly, he lifted the other arm and pointed at the strawberries. His index finger quivered. He said, 'You disobeyed me, Ruth. Indeed, you would have deceived me, too, if I had not caught Jessup leaving the bowl on the step by the back door.'

Ruth said, 'Jessup offered to pick them for me, Father. He was – I mean, we had to let him. It seemed rude . . .'

'When I give an order, I expect it to be obeyed. Not to have it countermanded by a servant.'

Ruth's voice was very faint. 'He was afraid that we might tear the nets.'

'So he told me,' Captain Perkin said. 'It does not excuse your disobedience. Come here.'

Daisy listened to this exchange incredulously. What a silly fuss over a few old strawberries! But she could see Ruth's narrow shoulders trembling under her thin dress. She said – loudly, because Captain Perkin had not appeared to notice she was there – 'It was my fault, actually. Ruth wanted to pick the strawberries but I was lazy. I'm afraid I ate too much at tea.'

Captain Perkin didn't even look at her. His eyes were on his daughter. He said, as she drew near, 'You didn't think you'd get away with it, did you?' and, in a sudden, violent movement, seized her by the neck, thrust her face downwards on the table, brought out the cane he had concealed behind his back and began to thrash her across the thighs and buttocks.

Ruth grunted, moaned; her body jerked as each blow fell. For several seconds Daisy watched, appalled and paralysed; she had never in her life encountered, or imagined, such a scene. Then a healthy anger seized her, propelled her forward, shouting, 'Stop it, *stop it*, Captain Perkin,' and when he didn't stop, opening her mouth and closing her eyes like a child in a tantrum and letting fly with the full force of her strong lungs. She screamed and screamed, hearing the echoes ringing in her head, and, as she drew breath, his coldly furious voice, 'Shut up, you idiot girl.'

She opened her eyes. His face, patchily red and white and oozing beads of sweat, was close to hers. She was frightened now, her heart was thumping, but she refused to flinch away. She stared into his face and said, 'You shouldn't hit her. It's against the law.'

Captain Perkin laughed. He said, with a terrible playfulness, 'Naughty girls have to be punished, Daisy.' He turned to Ruth, still lying motionless across the table, and yanked her upright. She stood with hanging head and he pushed her, quite gently, between the shoulder blades. 'Get on with you, remember your good party manners. See your friend out. Give her the strawberries.'

Ruth was limping towards the door. He shrugged his shoulders, laughed again, and gave Daisy the glass bowl. She took it. She wished she had the guts to throw the contents in his face. She told herself that it would only make things worse for Ruth. (Though how could things be worse?) At least she wouldn't *thank* him. She said, 'I'll give the bowl to Ruth at school on Monday.'

Once she had turned her back on him, she longed to run. The thought of his eyes upon her made her skin prickle. She walked out of the room, her head held high, and saw Ruth waiting for her at the door with a blank and stony face. Daisy said, with clumsy delicacy, 'You've got a nasty mark on your right cheek, it'll be all colours of the rainbow later on.' Politer not to mention other, nastier marks, elsewhere.

Ruth touched her cheek. 'I do bruise easily,' she said, with a sidelong, covert glance that struck a horrified chord in Daisy's memory. So that was why Ruth had said that her mother was *always polishing!* There had been other bruises to explain away.

Taking in this knowledge as they walked towards the gate, Daisy felt a shocked concern that was quite a new emotion, involving a queer guilt and shame (as if she had been eavesdropping, or seen something she had not been meant to see) and calling on a reserve of tact and gentleness she had never had cause to use before. She looked almost timidly at Ruth and said, 'Can't your mother stop him? I mean, *my* mother. . .' She stopped. Mrs Perkin was not Mrs Brown.

Ruth said, with light reproach, 'I wish you hadn't screamed so loud. It probably upset her. I try not to. . .' She bit her lip. 'She gets so frightened. It's really worse for her.'

Doors opened in Daisy's mind. She knew she must not challenge this absurd remark. She said, 'All right. But if she can't stop him, someone ought to. Someone ought to tell the *police!*'

Ruth said quickly, 'Oh, it's not as bad as that! It was stupid of me to make him angry. I knew he would be.'

'That was my fault,' Daisy said. 'I'm sorry.'

'You couldn't know.' Ruth looked at Daisy pleadingly. 'He wasn't always like it, though he was always *strict*. My mother says it must have been the war. He had such a dreadful time in the Japanese camps, and when he came back, he couldn't get a job, he was too ill. He's got a pension but that's all, and it's my mother's house, you see, she has an income from a family trust, quite a lot of money, really, and when she dies it will all come to me, he won't have anything. There's nothing she can do to change that, it's all tied up, and it makes him jealous, I suppose. He says I am the only thing he owns and he wants me to be perfect.' She sighed and held her hand against her back as if breathing deeply hurt her. 'I love my mother. I can't help it if I don't love him.'

'I don't see how you could.' Daisy thought of her father, cheerful Mr Brown, coming home and shouting in the hall, 'Where's Daisy? Where's my flower?' Laughing at this silly, family joke. Rubbing his rough jowls against her cheek to tickle her. . .

Ruth said, 'We play chess sometimes. He talks to me. About politics, the government, all sorts of things. He says I ought to go to the South Bank Exhibition in the holidays, that it will be an educational experience. He says the Festival of Britain is an important sign that the country is turning its back on the past and looking to the future. His generation made a mess, it's up to us to manage better. He says, it won't be easy, it'll take hard work and discipline.'

Daisy shook her head. 'He doesn't work so hard himself, does he? You say he's ill, but he doesn't look so ill to me. What does he do all day?'

'He reads the newspapers. He shoots the grey squirrels and the pigeons in the wood. They eat the bulbs and vegetables.' Ruth giggled, a high-pitched, unnatural sound. 'The other day he shot the neighbour's cat. He said it was a mistake but I don't think so. The cat was always scratching up the rose bed. Using our garden as a lavatory.'

Daisy didn't think this very funny, but she laughed as if she did. She understood Ruth's need to cover up her shame. For a moment, she even tried – stretching her comprehension with an almost physical effort – to accept the pitiable pretence. But like an untrained dancer, she couldn't hold the pose. She abandoned the attempt and allowed indignation to rise up in her like a warm and healing tide. She said, 'I think you're potty to put up with it, if my father bashed me up, I'd kill him,' and felt better.

II

From Daisy's silence that evening, Mrs Brown assumed that the visit had not been a success. Usually Daisy chattered easily about where she'd been and what she'd done, confident in her mother's interest and to her mother's pleasure. Mrs Brown, who adored her anyway, was especially grateful for this openness. Her husband's chronic infidelities, about which she never spoke to anyone, had left her lonely, and although she loved her dear son, Bob, there was already, at eighteen, a certain lofty patronage in the way he treated her, as if his eyes were fixed on distant, masculine horizons, his mind occupied with matters that she could not expect to understand. Though Mrs Brown often idly dreamed about Daisy's wedding day, the marquee on the suburban lawn, the bridesmaids, her radiant girl in white, a crown of flowers upon her tumbling hair, she knew that when it came (and ripe Daisy was bound to marry early) her own life would be bereft. She was prepared for Bob to fly the coop, it wasn't natural for a young man to stay at home, but the thought of Daisy's chaotically untidy bedroom empty gave her a deeply painful pang. That night she looked in as she always did to say goodnight, tidy up Daisy's royally scattered clothes, scolding just a little as she did so, and found Daisy lying on her back, staring wide-eyed at the ceiling light. When Mrs Brown came in, she didn't move or speak. Her mother picked up the ancient teddy bear, lying on the rug beside the bed, and placed it on Daisy's pillow, saying, first, 'What has poor Teddy done?' and when that elicited no answer, 'Is anything wrong, my lovely? Have you got a pain? Tell Mummy what you feel.'

Daisy looked at her mother, shook her head and smiled. She felt too many things to speak of. Bewilderment, pity, horror, but chiefly a kind of shame. She knew something that her mother's kind imagination would not be able to take in. By saying nothing, she was protecting not only Ruth's secret, but her mother's innocence. And yet she longed for comfort. She sat up in bed, put out her arms, wrapped them round her mother's neck and fiercely squeezed, as if she were a small child still. Her mother gasped and laughed and hugged her back and said, fearful suddenly that Daisy had heard unpleasant gossip about her father as some day she was bound to, speaking the words she had often rehearsed for when this occasion should arise, 'You know, my darling, Daddy loves you.' And when Daisy held her mother tighter still, as if she could burrow right inside her, Mrs Brown was sure that this must be the trouble. She stroked her daughter's hair and said, 'He's always been a wonderful father, he'd never want to hurt you, that's what is important, nothing else.'

Daisy found these words mysterious. What had her father got to do with it? She dreamed of him that night, his big, red, merry face contorted with anger and mounted on the body of a powerful bull. Horns sprouted from his head as he pawed the ground and bellowed and Daisy, screaming silently, ran and ran, thundering hooves behind her, until the ground gave way and she began to fall. And fell and fell, until her heart stopped and she woke.

By Monday, the memory of Saturday had merged with this bad dream. Standing by Ruth in morning Assembly, slyly peering at her friend's pale profile bent in prayer, Daisy felt bemused, quite giddy with sudden disbelief. Then Ruth turned to look at her with an impassive face, no smile, no frown, and Daisy knew she couldn't dodge the issue. What had happened was no dream, not even a single, shocking incident that could be brushed aside, explained away. The truth, the solid, inescapable fact, was that Ruth lived with violence daily, and now she knew that Daisy knew, she was expecting her to shrink away because of it. Part of Daisy wanted to. Unhappiness was 'boring'. She felt its contagion threatening her like a dark and spreading stain. But she had some sensibility and a natural kindness. As they left the hall she offered the only comfort she could think of. She said, 'If you really meant it, I would love you to make up that blouse and skirt for me.'

And was rewarded by Ruth's rare and glowing smile.

Part Two
MARRIAGE

I

Towards dawn, the couple who had recently moved in next door to Ruth and Joe Aberdare began making love. Ruth, already awake, wondered what the time was. The digital clock was on Joe's side of the bed and his bulky shoulder, with the duvet hunched over it, hid the luminous dial from her view. Four-thirty, she judged, from what she could see of the pale saffron sky through the window. Perhaps it would be a fine day. It had been a dull, chilly summer so far.

Behind Ruth's head, only the thin wall between them, the young woman groaned rhythmically, 'Oh God, oh God, oh God.' Ruth smiled at this pious evidence of enjoyment but hoped they would finish before it woke Joe. The newcomers had up to now appeared to be considerate neighbours, scrupulous about bonfires and dustbins and keeping the radio and television turned low after midnight – all the things that were so important if you lived in a terrace of pretty but shoddily built Georgian houses. And yet, here they were, not more than a foot away, bedhead to bedhead, merrily mollocking. Ignorant, perhaps, of how the sound carried. Or too happy to care. But Joe was still sleeping. Ruth fancied she detected a change in his breathing and held her own breath. If he woke he might feel embarrassed. Or threatened.

Most of the time, to speculate on what had happened between them just lately (or, more to the point, on what had *not* happened) filled Ruth with a frozen perplexity, a deep, inexplicable shame that she was unwilling to examine too closely, let alone speak of to Joe. She believed that it must be her fault, but to say this, when he had always started their love making, might seem like an accusation. If he no longer wanted her, it would hurt him to say so. And to bring up the subject herself, tell him that it didn't matter, made no difference to her deep love for him, might hurt him more. She could bear her own feelings of loss, of rejection. She didn't want to hurt Joe.

The cries next door were diminishing. Little grunts and squeaks, a soft, happy chuckling. *Home but not dry*, Ruth thought, titillated by this mildly coarse phrase that had come to her quite unbidden as if another Ruth, a woman of a much cruder nature, had spoken aloud in her mind. The voice was familiar, had acquired over the years a distinct and robust personality that had sometimes alarmed Ruth when she was younger. As a little girl she had thought of this other person, her secret self, as Rude Ruthie, and often, during her terrible childhood, she had feared that in some moment of weakness, or ungovernable anger, she would allow this nasty child's vulgar tongue to take over, shout bad words, scream abuse at her father. After her father had died, Rude Ruthie had vanished – or been replaced by a less threatening companion who amused Ruth and sometimes comforted her. She could say things to her that she could say to no one else. Sometimes she thought that she bore a resemblance to Daisy, who was her only close woman friend, but she had the advantage that she would never repeat what was said. Now Ruth said to her intimate, 'Of course it hurts. I like bed. But poor Joe has been so tired lately. All this last year. Coming home from work and falling asleep in front of the telly. Sitting at the table with his head in his hands. He says his eyes ache. Perhaps they do. But he's worried about himself, I think. He's been reading medical books on the sly. Hypochondria? That's a disease, isn't it? Or, perhaps it isn't that. Perhaps he just doesn't want to make love any longer.' And her intimate answered, 'Why should he fancy you, skinny old hag?'

They were talking next door. The man's voice had a low, peaceful rumble; his wife's lighter tone had a gentle laugh running through it. It struck Ruth that if she put a glass to the wall and her ear to the glass, she might actually hear what it was they were saying. The thought made her blush and her pulses move faster. Remembering the hot day they moved in, how they had looked, sunbathing among the packing cases in their tiny back garden, she had a sudden, clear vision of smooth brown legs lovingly tangled, a girl's long, gleaming hair spread like wheat on the pillow. Ruth felt a pain like a silent, dark groan in her belly. She moved her own legs in the bed, touched Joe's warm, solid rump with her foot, and was comforted. She had had such luck – amazing luck, really. She had never thought she was pretty – 'a funny little stalky girl, all bones and eyes', was what Daisy's mother, Mrs Brown had once called her – and she had been stunned when Joe had asked her to marry him, astonished and delighted by the way his love had made her feel beautiful. She said, to her private friend, 'Of course it's sad when things come to an end, but one mustn't be greedy! Life moves on and you have to accept it. I shall never play the violin now, or be a brain surgeon or a politician, never go wind surfing. There's no end to that kind of catalogue. From the day you are born doors start slamming behind you. And as you advance up the century they slam more often, more noisily. Perhaps that's what is worrying Joe? Avenues closing, life narrowing. Arthritis, false teeth, retirement.'

Stuff and nonsense, she thought – putting her confidante back in her box and addressing herself. She and Joe still had their own teeth (her back molars were capped, but that hardly counted as dentures), their joints were still supple. If Joe was a bit deafer than he had been, that could be an advantage with

those two lusty children living next door. Not that they were
children, really – the girl must be in her twenties, with those
two bouncing babies, the man rather older. Six years, perhaps,
the same gap as between her and Joe. But Joe was still only
fifty-one, and very fit in spite of his hypochondria. Well, he
had asthma, and it had been bad these last weeks, with the
high pollen count. All the same, last night at Luke's farewell
dinner, she had been proud to see how young Joe had looked
among his port-flushed contemporaries, sitting tall in his chair
while they slumped, ash from expensive cigars falling like
dirty snow on their stomachs, while the Chairman launched
into his eulogy.

The gallows speech, was how Ruth thought of it. The wake
before the old horse was sent to the knackers. And this
particular retirement party had been more painful than usual,
because Luke Brett, Daisy's husband, was going unwillingly,
seven years before the normal departure at sixty, a victim of
the recession that was closing down the ecological research
department of the oil company he and Joe worked for. Of
course, research was always the first thing to be cut, Luke
must have known that, but according to Joe he was taking it
badly. 'All his life's work gone for nothing,' Joe had said. 'Not
true, you know, but I daresay that's how he feels.' It was how
Joe would feel, Ruth had thought. He had always been more
ambitious than Luke, more obsessional about his career, about
reaching the top rungs of the ladder. But watching Luke at the
top table, his thin, gentle, bearded face politely turned to the
Chairman, Ruth had suffered for him. If Joe was right, this
occasion must be agony for him.

The Chairman was an old ham, so accustomed to this kind
of duty performance that he sounded almost sincere. A
flattering tribute, spiced up with small jokes, ending on a
throbbingly expansive note, cheeks quivering with what,
heard for the first time, might appear genuine feeling. 'A sad

28

loss . . . an eminent chemist, a colleague, and, perhaps, more important, an old, trusted *friend* . . . one of those rare and exceptional people, a man who knows how to take light things seriously and serious things lightly, a civilised man, a man, you might say, of *bottom* . . .' Pausing then, weaving his heavy head in affected, sorrowful humour, bright, black eyes sunk like raisins in the pale dough of his face, the Chairman had allowed time for appreciative murmurs from the free-loading sycophants (some of them, Ruth noticed, tucking an extra cigar into their jacket pockets) at the top table. Not a bad act, she had thought, if he had not used precisely those words at the last full dress send-off she had attended.

Looking at Joe, to see if he had realised this, taken in the insult to his old friend, she saw he was watching Daisy, seated between him and the Chairman, with frowning concern. Then Daisy, who had been staring into space with a faint smile on her moist, parted lips, like some lovely, spell-bound princess, turned and spoke to him. Joe had nodded, it seemed with bewilderment, and later, driving home, shouted with laughter as he told Ruth what she had said. '*There are a lot of spiders about this summer*. A bit irrelevant, even for her, I thought. What was she thinking of?'

'Spiders, apparently.'

'When old Luke was getting the chop?'

'Perhaps she didn't want to think about that.'

'Hmm. Maybe not. Oh well, I expect you're right. You know Daisy.'

Ruth supposed this was true. And yet, lying restless in the big bed, she wondered. Oh, of course it was true! Daisy was her oldest friend! Even in the early years of their marriages, when she and Joe had lived in the country, Luke and Daisy in London, they had never lost touch. Not many interests in common, perhaps, but so many other things to bind them together, all those years of births and deaths, weddings and funerals, sharing the high and low points of each other's lives. Pictures passed through Ruth's mind, snapshots, entries in a diary. Daisy in the wedding dress Ruth had made her, throwing her bouquet at Ruth afterwards, Daisy clutching Ruth's hand at Mrs Brown's funeral. But friendship, unquestioned, was one thing; 'knowing' another. Other people were always a mystery. (Even Joe, sleeping beside her!) All you can ever really know is what you see and hear. Ruth knew Daisy's measurements (hardly changed in the last thirty years, bust an inch larger, waist a bit thicker), the sound of her laugh, the tone of her voice. She thought she knew Daisy's moods. That air of dreaming absence usually meant she was bored. Daisy never troubled to pretend interest when she didn't feel it. But how could she have been bored last night? No! She had simply withdrawn her attention because she couldn't bear to listen to the Chairman, that old humbug, that arrogant, overweight playboy, trotting out his silly, stale jokes, his bumbling platitudes. Poor Daisy! Poor *Luke*! He had born it so well. Replying to the Chairman he had made such a splendid speech, funny and graceful and modest. But what else would one have expected? Luke was an intelligent, sensible adult. Even if he felt bitter, he would know there was no point in repining, that resentment drained out the spirit. What a fool he would think her, if he knew she was lying here, fuming on his behalf! Why on earth was she? Why was she feeling so *angry*?

Anger was frightening, a dark, hot balloon swelling inside her. But she knew how to deal with it. No point in looking for causes – that made it worse. Instead, she lay still, planning the day ahead. She would go to the shop, spend some time in the workroom above it, find out what auctions were coming up, speak to Danny about the printed silks she wanted to buy from Milan. She had been to the factory last month and given a provisional order, but Danny had told her that the price they wanted for one of the prints was too high. Usually she accepted his judgements but in this case she was sure he was wrong. He couldn't see how rare it was to find a designer whose colours and patterns changed with the light; how in this particular print the grass greens and murky browns would look, how made up, in a dress, on a body, they would flow together as if under water. Although Danny had been her business manager ever since she had opened the shop and had taught her all she knew about costing and buying and marketing, she had never been able to shake his conviction that one of his duties was to protect her from impracticable enthusiasms. Oh, of course he had been nervous at first that she had too much money behind her, that the shop was a rich woman's hobby. But, surely, now he knew better? Well, better enough to indulge her over the green and brown silk. She thought about it, almost feeling it in her fingers as she shook it out of its bale, draped and pleated it. Most of her dresses were made to order now, but she would make this one for a woman she hadn't met yet, a tall woman with light brown hair who would stop when she saw it in the window.

The hot balloon had shrunk and cooled. But she still felt restless. She slipped out of bed and went to the bathroom, poured a glass of water and stood at the window while she drank it, distracting her mind with the view that after nine years in the house still amazed her.

First, the great sweep of sky, apricot coloured now, streaked with long wisps of transparent blue cloud and crossed by a solitary aeroplane, a stiff-winged bird, glinting. Then, the astonishing sky line, from the bizarre, graceful skeletons of the tall yellow cranes marking the site of a new office block near the tube station, to the delicate spires of the small city churches, the gold figure of Justice on the Old Bailey, the solemn, grey helmet of the dome of St Paul's, the ferocious Barbican tower blocks, rearing up like jagged-toothed dinosaurs, the purer lines of the National Westminster Bank, the faint strokes, pencil thin, of more cranes, far away at the docks, beyond the gin factory. Ruth followed this sky line from one side to the other, murmuring the names of the buildings she knew almost reverentially, like a morning incantation or prayer, before withdrawing her gaze to what lay immediately below her, three floors down, the small, sloping gardens of the terraced houses.

The sun had not reached them yet and after the brightness of the huge sky they seemed still dusky with night, a few pale roses and white painted iron chairs glimmering secretly. Beyond them, at a lower level, each small garden having a flight of steps leading down to it, the big communal garden looked even darker and more mysterious, the great trees, beeches and London planes in full leaf, sheltering the birds, in full song at this hour of the morning, hiding the tenement on the far side of them and the litter beneath; the plastic detritus, old shoes, broken baths and toilet bowls, scrumpled up bags containing the bones of Kentucky Fried Chicken.

Ruth and Joe had bought the house for this view, the birdsong, the garden. The eight or so acres belonged to the terrace and had once (according to Luke and Daisy who had lived there since the early sixties) been an agreeably private domain, not maintained as a park, but as a patch of tamed woodland, with wild daffodils and dog roses and bluebells in season. When the Aberdares had moved in, the vestiges of this pleasant privilege still remained. They had allowed their younger child, Marigold, to roam free, strolled there themselves in the evenings, able to satisfy their curiosity about their new neighbours by looking into their lit windows from a polite distance, marvelling how differently each house was arranged, the five floors providing such variations in vertical living that no one was the same. But the invasion from the tenement had already begun. On later walks they discovered piles of foul smelling garbage, used condoms, small, trodden-out bonfiires. And it wasn't long before eight year old Marigold came home complaining that 'rough boys' had made fun of her, broken up the camp she had made with her friends. One of the boys had thrown stones at them.

The tenement had originally been a row of imposing family houses, the backs facing the terrace garden, the stately fronts forming one side of a pretty square. The decline of the houses, starting with bed-sitter lets during and after the war, had been accelerated by the passing of various rent acts to protect sitting tenants, and completed when they were acquired by the local council that lacked (or was unwilling to spare) enough funds to restore them, and had finally scheduled them for demolition at some unspecified date in the future. In the meantime they were let to 'problem families' who had taken over the woodland, dropping down into it from ground floor windows, using it for gang fights, gang bangs, as a rubbish dump, a public lavatory, driving the rightful owners back behind the walls of their small individual gardens that were now protected by sharp pieces of glass, rolls of barbed wire, strongly thorned rambler roses.

Although spasmodic surges, small earthquakes of indignation and fear, still threw up committees, petitions to the Council, aggrieved letters to the local paper, it was more or less accepted that there was no real defence against the shock troops from the tenement. The police, of course, were too busy. They paid perfunctory attention to the burglaries that took place (neither barbed wire nor roses affording sufficient security) but rarely discovered the culprits, the families they came from being not only itinerant but of a kind that closed ranks when questioned. Being broken into was a natural hazard of life and reactions were normally stoic, little sympathy shown to victims who moaned too loud or too long when they lost this or that priceless or irreplaceable object – Aunt Maud's brooch, the family silver. As Luke had said when his cherished stamp collection had been stolen last year, as long as no one was hurt, one should look upon this sort of thing as an unofficial re-distribution of income.

Ruth hoped that if they were burgled (*when* they were, might be more realistic!) Joe would be as philosophical. Even though he agreed in principle that it was a form of bondage to be defined by possessions, the week after Luke's burglary he had ordered an expensive and elaborate alarm, and the week after that, picked up a Sealyham bitch from the Battersea Dog's Home. The bitch was yappy and uncertain tempered and the alarm had a perverse life of its own, going off in the night or when they were away for the weekend, for no obvious reason. But if Ruth complained, Joe grew angry and obstinate. He set the alarm, didn't he? He walked the dog! 'I want you to feel *safe*,' he said.

Ruth, who had felt safe before, smiled as she stood at the window, watching the lovely apricot light fade from the sky and a bulge of spongy grey cloud swell slowly up like a fungus up and around the dome of St Paul's. It was going to be a disappointing day after all. Never mind. She would dress, take the beastly dog out before breakfast. That would please Joe. He liked a long, leisurely shower in the mornings.

The telephone rang in the bedroom. She sped to answer it but Joe had already done so at the second ring, knocking his glasses, his paperback thriller, his asthma inhaler, and a mug of water off the table in his sleepy hurry. He was holding the receiver to his ear and blinking in a dazed, uncomprehending way. Ruth went to the bathroom for a cloth to mop up the water and heard him say, 'Oh, God. Oh, God. Oh, my God!'

She almost laughed. If the young couple could hear him next door, it might sound like mockery; an unkind repetition of their loving cries to warn them to keep quieter in future. But sound only seemed to carry through the wall if you were standing (or lying) close to it, and Joe, as she saw when she returned to the bedroom, was sitting with his legs dangling over the edge of the bed, a good couple of yards from the head rail. His face, red and crumpled with sleep on one side, was deathly pale on the other. His eyes stared at her with a shocked and dreadful expression and Ruth thought, Oh, my God, *Mark*! Their son had gone out on his motor bike to a party. He had still been out when they came home from the dinner and went to bed.

Joe understood. 'Luke,' he mouthed at her silently, and for a second Ruth had a falling sense of relief, of dropping through terrifyingly empty space to safe landing. Then Joe said, 'Okay. Yes. We'll be round at once. Yes, of course. Hang on, darling.'

Darling? *Luke*? Ruth did laugh then. Oh, she shouldn't. Something was wrong. But she was always so fearful for Mark on the bike. She said, still light with gratitude, 'I didn't know you and Luke went in for that kind of endearment.'

'Daisy,' Joe said. 'That was Daisy.' He was bent over, grunting, feeling under the bed for his socks and his shoes. 'Luke's dead.' He sat up, his whole face crimson with effort now. Then, as the blood drained out, white as flour.

Ruth clapped her hand to her mouth. She had been about to say, 'How did he die?' But that was a question in a children's game. *Mrs Maginty's dead. How did she die?*

Joe said, 'Last night, when they got back, he couldn't sleep. He decided to drive up to Norfolk, go to the cottage. The police found him dead on the motorway. They told Daisy an hour ago.'

Ruth thought of the crash. People drive so foolishly fast, frail bodies in fragile cars, crumpling on impact like toys. She said, 'It can't have been Luke's fault. He's so careful, such a good driver. I suppose he had a bit to drink last night. All the same.'

Joe was crossing the room, zipping his trousers with one hand, opening a drawer in the chest with the other. 'There wasn't a crash. It wasn't that kind of accident. He wasn't in the car. Just smashed up on the road. God knows. . .' He was pulling a grey fisherman's sweater over his head. 'Well, maybe He does. If He was awake at the time.'

When his curly, dark head appeared, Ruth saw his mouth quivering, the shine of tears in his eyes. She ran to him and he put his arms round her, holding her head pressed to his chest so that she could hear the rasp of his breathing. She said, 'You're wheezing. D'you want your asthma thing? It fell off the table, I'll get it.'

It had bounced under the bed. She had to lie on her stomach to reach it. Joe emptied his lungs, put the inhaler in his mouth, pressed the spring and breathed in, holding his breath, counting to ten.

Ruth sat back on her heels, watching him. These attacks, that had started ten years ago, could be alarming. His own fear made them worse. Several times, when he had been desperately fighting for breath, she had had to call the doctor to give him a shot of adrenalin. If this was going to be a bad one, she ought to ring Fergus.

But his colour was better. He said, 'It's all right, I'll live. Don't just sit there. Get dressed.'

While she scrambled up, took her underclothes from the chair, he opened the cupboard, rifled through dresses, clicking the hangers. He said, 'This will do, won't it?' A wool skirt, a silk blouse, a tweed jacket. He said, 'Hurry up,' thrusting them at her.

One hand behind her back, fumbling for her bra fastening, she took the garments, dropped them on the bed. She said, 'Tell me what happened. What Daisy said. I ought to know. Please, darling, don't *sigh*.'

'Sorry. It's not clear yet. They hadn't found the car when they spoke to Daisy. Only his body. He must have been walking on the motorway.'

'The car broke down?'

'They don't know. I *told* you. Christ, must you fuss with your hair?'

'No, of course not. But it gets into my eyes.' Trying to be calm, combing her hair back with shaky fingers, she looked at his scowling face in the glass. 'I should have plaited it last night. Only we got back so late. I shan't be a minute. We ought to leave a note for Marigold. I don't suppose she'll wake up, but in case. Why don't you do that? Leave it on the kitchen table. Just say we've gone to Daisy's, we'll explain later.'

Joe sighed again, with histrionic impatience, but he went, thumping down the stairs heavily. Ruth tied her hair back with a ribbon – though she was quicker and neater now he was not here to fuss her, there was no time to put it up. Perhaps she should have it short, she thought, pulling on her skirt, buttoning her blouse, glancing at herself in the mirror. Less trouble, but it was so thick, it would need constant cutting, and she hated to waste time at the hairdresser. Oh, she shouldn't be thinking about her appearance. Not now. Not when Daisy. . .

Her friend's face rose up in front of her, its pink and white smoothness blotched and distorted with tears. But she had not seen Daisy cry for a good many years. Not since her mother's funeral. They had both wept then. They had both loved Mrs Brown. Daisy had loved her father, too, but she had not shed a single tear when he died. She had stood at the graveside in the icy March wind, impassive, a cool, mourning goddess. *That* funeral had been such a short time ago, just a couple of months. Ruth thought – Oh, poor Daisy! Her father. Now Luke. . .

She left the bedroom and ran down the stairs, past the big L-shaped living room that took up the whole of the first floor, to the long, narrow hall. The door of Mark's bedroom, at the front of the house, facing the street, was wide open. He lay on his back, all his clothes on, snoring gently. The Sealyham, on the bed, at his feet, lifted its head and its upper lip. A disagreeable, silent, pink snarl. Ruth stood in the doorway, wishing she wasn't so stupidly frightened, and Joe came up from the basement and looked over her shoulder. He said, 'Good party last night, I should think.'

He touched Ruth's arm, opened the front door, and held out his hand to her. Suddenly, he was smiling, all his irritation gone, a smile so full of pure grief that her own sorrow rose up to match it, a rush of tears, choking her. She whispered, 'I'm sorry, I know you loved Luke. I loved him too. I can't really believe it.'

'No,' he said, 'I can't either. It'll take time. Don't try to think of it now. We must think of Daisy.' He took her hand and held it as he closed the front door, as they walked down the street, their footsteps echoing loud in the quietness, to the house at the end of the terrace that was blazing with light.

II

The front door stood open. Joe marched ahead into the narrow, lit hall. The rooms on the ground floor were empty; Luke's study, Daisy's small sitting room. Joe looked back at Ruth. She whispered – the house seemed so eerily silent – 'Downstairs, I should think.'

The lower floor of the Brett's house was its social centre; what had originally been two poky rooms and a passage knocked through into one large living-kitchen. When Joe and Ruth had moved to the terrace, Joe had been anxious to convert this floor of their own house in a similar manner so that when they had guests there would be no tiresome separation, Joe providing pre-dinner drinks on the first floor while Ruth was cut off from the merriment, cooking down in the basement, but by the time the sale was completed the planning regulations had changed and he had been refused permission to remove the partition walls. Joe had been angry and disappointed and as Ruth followed him down the stairs, she felt as she always did, a faint regret that he had not been able to do what he wanted. The way the Bretts had arranged it, the room was both cosy and spacious, the kitchen area discreetly lit and concealed by a pretty trellis of climbing plants, the long dining table occupying the centre, and a comfortable clutter of sofas and chairs at the other end, round the Swedish wood stove. No wonder Luke and Daisy had always given such marvellous parties, Ruth thought – and then caught her breath. The conscious sadness with which she had used the past tense seemed out of place here. Daisy appeared to *be giving* a party.

She was sitting at the head of her table, in a high-backed Jacobean style chair, wearing a magnificent Chinese robe of heavy gold satin embroidered with silver birds, scarlet roses. Her long, pale hair flowed over this robe, brushed and gleaming. Her daughter, Georgia, stood behind her chair like a lady in waiting, and a man sat on her right, deferentially leaning forward and holding Daisy's rather large hand palm upwards, as if paying homage, or telling her fortune. A circle of warm light from a hanging oil lamp (genuine, converted to electricity) fell on their joined hands. Another man had just placed a green glass goblet in front of Daisy and behind her, a dark haired woman was coming forward carrying a tray – more green goblets and an opened bottle of wine.

For a brief second it seemed no one moved, and except for Georgia, and Daisy herself, Ruth thought she recognised none of these people. Looking over the open banister she had a bewildered sense of disorientation as if she had strayed (or been enticed) into someone else's surrealist dream. Then the woman put the tray down on the table and the picture clicked into focus. The robe that Daisy was wearing was one Ruth had made her from material Daisy's father had brought from Hong Kong years ago. It was shabby now, the glittering embroidery tarnished, and Daisy used it as a housecoat, a dressing gown. And the people surrounding her – the acolytes, servitors – were neighbours who had either been summoned before Daisy telephoned Joe, or who had responded more speedily. Simon, pouring the wine into Daisy's glass, was the retired civil servant who lived next door to her, a spruce, upright widower, rosy and hard as an apple, who regularly exercised two sleek, black Labradors in the communal gardens, and was always ready to act the butler at parties. The dark haired woman was Molly, who kept the good delicatessen and liquor store at the end of the street, and the small, plumpish, rather foreign looking man holding Daisy's hand was her husband. Ruth found she couldn't remember his name. Basil? Bruce? Something beginning with B. How absurd not to remember when it would seem, from the intimacy of his present pose, that he was a close friend of Daisy's, and so Ruth must have met him before in this house. Still, she had *placed* him. And now, as if to establish the reality of this scene, Fergus appeared, emerging from the kitchen beyond the green jungle of plants, with a tall glass of water. He was a neat, chunky, almost bald man; as he bent to put the glass of water next to the wine, his domed head gleamed under the light, a few strands of gingery hair clinging damply to it like seaweed on a pink rock. He took a white box out of his pocket and said, 'Take a couple of tranquillisers now, another at lunch time, and again if you feel that you need them this evening. But they may make you drowsy, so I should try to get through the day if you can, and take a sleeping pill when you go to bed. If you haven't got any, I'll have some sent round.'

Daisy said, 'I don't want pills, thank you, Fergus.'

'Well, that's up to you.' He touched Daisy's shoulder and looked up at Joe and Ruth who had paused on the stair. 'Good,' he said, 'glad you've come,' welcoming them with a gravity that was not assumed for this occasion. Fergus laughed sometimes but he rarely smiled. His normal expression was one of alert and listening seriousness that made him, in spite of his unappealing physical appearance, immensely attractive to women. Certainly he made them attractive to themselves, Ruth thought. Even now, in this tragic moment, she found herself straightening her back, lifting her head high on her neck. Not that Fergus was watching her. He was closing his bag, reaching for his overcoat that was hanging over a chair.

The Aberdares advanced towards Daisy. Joe didn't speak,

simply put his arms round her and kissed her. Then stood aside, leaving the way clear for Ruth who suddenly felt dreadfully agitated, heart beating fast and unevenly, afraid she would say the wrong thing, something stupid, or clumsy, or hurtful. Though to imagine that anything she could say would affect Daisy's dark, dreadful pain seemed a self-regarding presumption. She thought – how would I feel if it were Joe? – and at once her tears spurted, welling up uncontrollably and running down her cheeks like rain.

'Don't cry for me,' Daisy said. 'I'm too angry.'

Her eyes – grey, with flecks of brown round the iris and clear, pearly whites – were quite dry. There was no puffiness round them, no sign that she had, at any point, wept. These eyes regarded Ruth sternly, perhaps with a certain contempt. Ruth felt it, anyway. Abashed, she felt for a handkerchief in her jacket pocket. Wiping her eyes, she glanced sideways and saw that Molly's husband – Bill? Benedict? – had withdrawn his hand from Daisy's and was sitting hunched up, his head bowed. Ruth looked up, beyond Daisy's shoulder, and met Georgia's eyes, grey like her mother's but softer, and with swollen red eyelids above them. The girl smiled at her tremblingly. She gave a little, helpless shake of her head. Despair? It seemed to Ruth more like a warning.

She said, 'Of course, Daisy. Such a terrible accident. You're bound to resent it.'

Daisy said, 'It wasn't an accident, Ruth. He killed himself. Walked straight in front of a truck on the motorway.'

This couldn't be true. Ruth said, 'Oh, darling! It must have been accidental. Luke wouldn't . . .'

Daisy ignored her. She said, 'How could he do such a wicked thing? The policeman who came to tell me said that he walked straight in front of the truck, the driver had no chance to swerve or to stop. Can you imagine how that poor man feels now? Like a murderer. No one has the right to do that to anyone. If Luke wanted to die, if he couldn't face life any longer, he should have shot himself, taken poison, thrown himself over a cliff. Not involved other people. That's the coward's way. Luke was a coward. Weak and selfish.'

She spoke clearly and firmly, making a considered statement, words hard as stones.

Joe said, 'Oh, for God's sake! Daisy! Pull yourself together, there's a good girl. Why on earth should Luke want to kill himself?'

'He was *disappointed*.' Daisy spat this word out with scorn. 'Aren't we all? Aren't you disappointed, Joe? Or is your life perfect? I can't believe that it is. But you wouldn't commit suicide, would you? You're a man, you've got the guts to go on, pick yourself up off the ground, go on fighting. First class people do that. Luke couldn't make that sort of high grade. He was born second rate.'

Georgia said, 'Mother. . .' on a low, moaning note. She swayed, hands clutching her stomach. Ruth went to her and held her. The tall girl leaned on her and Ruth took her weight, feeling like a stake supporting a young, willowy tree. She said, 'Don't *listen*, Georgia. Your mother's upset. She doesn't mean it.'

Daisy laughed. She sipped at her wine and put the glass down. Her face was set calm, only a faint heightening of colour on her cheekbones betrayed inner turbulence. She said, 'Do you know why she's called Georgia? That time Luke went to America, to a conference in Atlanta, he took me along and I was pregnant when we came back. Although we'd had a bit of a holiday after the conference, driving all over, Luke enjoyed Georgia more than anywhere else and so he liked to think his daughter was conceived there. A sweet idea, you might think. But it wasn't original. He got it from brother Paul. When Paul was a medical student he did his midwifery training in Cornwall. So many baby girls were called Heather! Their mothers said, *That's where she was got, doctor!* A good joke, Luke thought, so he took it and used it. That's what I meant by *second hand, second rate*. Paul was always the leader, Luke trailed after him, trying to copy him.'

She picked up her wine, drained the glass, and set it down hard. The pupils of her eyes had enlarged, making her eyes seem much darker. 'I should have married Paul. You remember, Ruth, don't you? Paul was the one I met first. I turned him down. I didn't want to be a doctor's wife, an unpaid receptionist answering telephones. My father told me I'd made a mistake, that Paul was the better bet out of those brothers. The strong one. I needed a strong man, my father said, to look after me.'

Except for Georgia, whose face was hidden on Ruth's shoulder, and Molly's husband who remained huddled up in a bowed, devotional posture, they were all watching her. Fergus thoughtfully; Joe amazed, perhaps angry, his brows drawn together. Simon, unobtrusively offering wine round the company, had flushed up a little, nose and leathery cheeks wriggling with thin, purple veins; otherwise his expression was restrained, almost neutral. Either his age or his dependence on other people for his social life had made him cautious about passing judgement. Molly seemed simply embarrassed, running her hands through her short, dark hair, her lower lip caught between her white teeth.

Joe said, 'Has anyone telephoned Paul?'

'He's on his way down from Birmingham,' Fergus said. He was standing beside Ruth and Georgia. He said softly to Ruth, 'Anger is part of grief. The process of mourning. Call me if you want me. I'll be at home for the next couple of hours. After that, in the surgery.'

Ruth nodded, feeling an invigorating sexual charge from the closeness of his tubby body in the buttoned up overcoat.

Though it wasn't as crude as that. It was the intent way that Fergus always looked at her, as if he understood all about her, even perhaps recognising and approving the other Ruth, the secret companion inside her, that gave her such confidence. The feeling was hard to define, she thought, as she watched him run up the stairs. Fergus believed women to be more complex and braver than men – he had once told her so. That was the time she had wept in his surgery because she had been angry with Marigold. Slapped her face – only a light blow, but it had terrified Ruth, that sudden, small act of violence. A terrible warning. She had told Fergus about her father. Apart from Daisy, Fergus was the only person who knew. All she had told Joe was that her father had been a 'difficult' man. It was all she could bear to say in the early days, when they were first married, and after that it was always somehow *too late* – he would have been hurt to know she had kept it from him, hadn't trusted him. She had been ashamed because she had hidden it, it seemed so dishonest, but Fergus had understood. He had understood her shame. He had said that the need to conceal that kind of childhood experience was perfectly natural, that it was not uncommon for a victim to feel guilty afterwards, and she was right and courageous to put it behind her. Of course she hadn't told Fergus quite everything, but even if she had, he would have accepted it, as he seemed to accept everything, calmly, as part of life. If he had more women patients than men, it was because women particularly needed this kind of reassurance. They were so often caught up in small things, minor, messy female ailments, fears of growing old and unattractive to men. Fergus was not repelled by their ageing bodies. He liked women in a way that was broader and deeper than a simple romantic or sexual interest. She had once tried to explain this to Joe when he had called Fergus 'your funny little doctor'. But Joe had only grinned in a condescending masculine way. When Joe was ill, which in spite of his hypochondria and his asthma was not very often, he consulted Fergus's partner.

They heard Fergus slam the front door. There was silence for a moment. Then Joe said – with an air of relief as if now Fergus had removed his calmly professional presence he could take the gloves off – 'Daisy, listen. If it helps you to rage, well, I suppose that's a natural reaction. But don't attack Luke. Whatever had gone wrong between you, that's destructive and cruel. I'm not reproaching you, Daisy, I love you as we all do, but you should be remembering the good things, not the bad. How Luke loved you and Georgia, built his life round you, supported you, how he took care of your father.' Joe stopped, dabbing his forehead with his handkerchief, watching Daisy hold out her empty wine glass with an imperious gesture. Simon re-filled it. Joe said, 'You were grateful to Luke for the way he helped you look after your father. You told me.'

'Oh, I *was* grateful!' Daisy's eyes sparkled; she spoke with a gleeful, malevolent emphasis as if delighted that Joe had fed her the cue that she wanted. 'Of course Luke was *wonderful*, Joe! Visited Daddy every night in the nursing home, played bezique with him, read the financial news, even though that sort of thing bored him stiff. And I was quite taken in. After the funeral, I thanked him. I thanked Luke for being so good to my father, and do you know what he said? He said that he was only doing his duty. D'you know what that meant? That cold word? The truth is, Luke hated my father. He hated him because Daddy was a real *man*, because he and I were so close, and Luke knew he could never measure up to him. My father had terrible disappointments in his life, *he* lost jobs too, that little business he tried to build up came to nothing, ending up poor, in bad health, but he never complained. Not even when he was dying, suffering so terribly. He was brave while he had breath in his body. He would never have taken the easy way out. Luke knew that. It made him ashamed.'

'You should be ashamed, Daisy,' Ruth said. 'However Luke felt, he was good to your father. For God's sake, he kept him for years! Paid his debts, bought his whisky, had him to live with you.' She was trembling with outrage and a feeling of daring – she had never before spoken so fiercely to Daisy. Her role had always been the listener, the pacifier.

Daisy said, in a satisfied voice, 'Luke moaned to you, did he? About my dreadful, drunken, blood-sucking old father?'

Ruth shifted her hold on Georgia, who was now sobbing quietly, and helped her to a chair. The girl continued to lean against her, face pressed to Ruth's stomach, but Ruth found this position more comfortable. Georgia was a big, bony girl, graceful but heavy. Ruth patted her shoulders, calming herself as well as Georgia, and said, more gently, 'Luke never complained, Daisy. You know that. Luke knew that you loved your father. He did his best for him because he loved you.'

Daisy stared at her. Joe said, in a loud voice, 'This is all quite irrelevant.'

'Raking over dead ashes,' Molly said. 'I don't hold with it.' She put another bottle of wine on the table and started to open it. She was careful not to look at Daisy. 'Bloody damn. This cork's stuck.'

She shoved the bottle across to her husband who stood up obediently and put it between his knees. He filled glasses. Ruth shook her head but he smiled at her and she accepted more wine. His large, dark, liquid eyes watched her appreciatively while she sipped it. His name was Ben, she remembered. For Benjamin? What did he do for a living? He was wearing an elegant, high-necked black sweater and a pale jade medallion on a gold chain round his neck. Oh, of course. He was an antique dealer, selling jade, old jewellery, fine porcelain.

Daisy had shown her a cornelian ring, a pretty, Victorian piece she had bought from him.

Suddenly, Daisy started to cry. Open-mouthed, like a child bawling. Ruth looked at her, fascinated. She was making a strange, honking sound like a goose, but there was no sign of tears. Putting it on, Ruth decided. She had realised that she had gone too far, lost everyone's sympathy.

Certainly she had changed her tune. When she had stopped honking, she looked round almost pleadingly. 'It's only, I think of my father, the courage he had, and then *Luke*, chucking himself under a lorry because he had taken a bit of a tumble. Leaving us. Leaving Georgia . . .' She stood up, leaning across the table, seizing Georgia's chin in her square, competent hand. 'Look at this poor, lost, beautiful child. Why on earth did he do it?'

'You don't know that he did,' Joe said. 'Not for certain, dear. The truck driver may have been lying. If the car had broken down and Luke was going for help, walking along the motorway to an emergency telephone, perhaps he was trying to flag the truck down. The driver just didn't see him in time. Or was going too fast, and skidded.'

His face was strained. Ruth saw that he longed for this to be true. He had known Luke most of his working life – not as old a friendship as Daisy's and Ruth's, but old enough. And close. They played squash together, dined at each other's houses, Luke was Marigold's godfather. If Luke had been at the end of his tether, Joe should have known it.

Georgia had stopped weeping. She was endeavouring to smile at her mother. Though their eyes were alike, her hair was much darker than Daisy's was now – the same dark golden colour as the young Daisy Brown's. She was a lovely girl in a rather droopy, Pre-Raphaelite way, with a very white skin that looked almost translucent now, washed by her tears. She made everyone else look quite shockingly *old*, Ruth thought. Even Molly, who was only in her early thirties, a boyish young woman with cropped hair and small breasts barely lifting the plaid woollen shirt she was wearing, looked tired and faded beside her. And Simon looked ancient. A worried old tortoise, stretching his wrinkled neck, tongue darting out nervously as he prepared to speak.

'I'm sorry, Joe. You don't know. The police rang just before you arrived. After Daisy had called you. I spoke to them. They'd found the car. It was parked on the hard shoulder, about a quarter of a mile back from where Luke was killed. They couldn't find anything wrong with it.'

'That doesn't mean anything.'

Simon said, very apologetically, 'There was a witness. The driver had his mate with him.'

'Even so . . .' Joe stopped, frowning.

Molly said, 'Aw, come on, chaps! Dead, one way or another, what the hell does it matter? It won't bring him back.'

No one challenged this statement. Perhaps its brusque vulgarity offended Simon a little. He winced, jaw and cheek muscles flickering under his taut, reddish skin. But Joe seemed to relax, shrugging his shoulders, smiling ruefully. Ruth thought – a bit of sense, finally. She wondered if she should offer to make them all coffee.

Molly said, 'Sorry, Daisy. Look, I'll put the kettle on. Coffee or tea? Wine goes sour on the stomach at this hour of the morning.'

Daisy sank back into her chair, resting her head on the high back, rolling it from side to side in a negative way, as if rage had exhausted her and numb acceptance had taken over. And yet, to Ruth, anyway, she didn't appear at all pitiable. More like a tired lioness, she thought fancifully, some savage predator gathering herself for the next spring. She felt a curious mixture of awe and excitement and alarmed admiration. Not for the appalling things Daisy had said about Luke (none of which she could have meant, surely!) but for the furious strength that had driven her. It had not seemed like hysteria, but an eruption of power, a force damped down for years, burning a slow fuse of anger.

Georgia said, 'Coffee would be very nice, Molly.' Composed now, controlled, she looked round her. 'I'm sorry if – I mean, this has been a dreadful shock for my mother. She had no inkling, you see. Last night, when they came home, we all had a drink, just quietly together, and Daddy said he felt too restless to sleep, he'd drive up to Norfolk. He often did that, went to the cottage alone, to paint, or watch birds, and though he asked Mother if she'd like to come, he didn't seem to mind when she said no. I mean, they didn't argue about it, or anything. I suppose, well, it's obvious he must have felt miserable, part of his life being over, but it didn't show. He was *cheerful*.' Her voice faltered. She looked down at her hands, clasped in her lap. She whispered, 'He just kissed us goodbye.'

Daisy said, 'I don't suppose anyone really thinks I drove him to his death. All the same, thank you, Georgia. In fact I should say thank you to everyone.' She smiled brilliantly. 'For rallying round me so splendidly.'

She spoke as if they had all come unasked, Ruth thought wonderingly. Had she really called them together at this early hour to witness her fury? To make a deliberate, public announcement? Oh, surely not! She had telephoned in pain and despair and once her friends were about her, she had shrunk from their sympathy. Daisy had always hated people to pity her. Even when her little boy, her first child, had died. She had said to Ruth, on the telephone, 'Don't be sorry for me, I can't bear it, I don't know why but it makes me so angry.' Fergus had said that anger was part of grief. But it took a bit of an effort on this occasion to see Daisy as grieving. All that pent-up hatred and malice. Perhaps, if Fergus was right, if her anger was a natural response to the shock of bereavement, she would break down soon, weep for Luke. *Home they brought her warrior dead.* The widow in the old ballad hadn't wept until they sat her baby on her knee. Georgia was a bit large for that! Ruth said, 'Daisy, don't be brave. We all love you. We know how much you loved Luke.'

Daisy looked at her consideringly. She said, very slowly, 'He was my husband. Georgia's father. I kept house for him, cooked, washed his socks. He paid the bills. That was the bargain. Now he has broken his side of it. I feel he has cheated. That's all I feel.'

Joe cleared his throat. He said, 'Rubbish.'

Daisy didn't answer this. Her eyes were a steely, battleship grey. She sat regally upright in her high-backed chair, in her rich, shabby robe. Ruth thought – like an Empress sending men to their deaths.

Molly put a mug of coffee in front of her, another in front of Georgia. She said, 'Poor old Luke, what an epitaph.' Her eyes were wet. She brushed them with the back of her hand. 'Do you mind black coffee, Daisy? There doesn't seem to be any milk.'

Daisy shook her head. Apart from this slightest of movements she was sitting perfectly still now, gazing into distance, lips parted, as if the devil that had suddenly seemed to possess her had departed as suddenly, leaving behind this graceful *princesse lointaine*, calm, removed, beautiful . . .

Ruth knelt down beside her, took her hand and stroked the veins that stood out on the back of it. She felt tender towards these signs of age in her friend. She said, 'What can I do, darling? Please tell me.'

Daisy looked down and sighed. The sigh brought her to life again. She said, in an ordinary voice, 'Well, there's Luke's mother. If you can bear it. You quite like her, don't you? I don't mean I want you to break the news to her. Paul will ring when he gets here. She doesn't wake up much before nine or nine-thirty. If you could go sometime after that, stay with her a bit?'

Ruth's eyes filled. 'What are you going to tell her?'

'That Luke was killed in an accident. Can you stick to that, Ruth?'

'Yes. Of course.'

Daisy said, 'She's so old. Thank you, Ruth. You're sure it's not the most frightful nuisance. Shouldn't you be at the shop?'

'It doesn't matter. Do you want me to stay with you now? I can of course, but . . .'

Joe said, 'The children can get their own breakfast for once. Or I can get it. Don't fuss, Ruth.'

Daisy said, 'It's all right. I think I shall have a bath.' She gripped the arms of her chair, rose in one, fluid movement, and walked to the stairs. Then she turned and said, 'Perhaps I ought to wash my mouth out with soap while I'm about it.'

When she had gone, they all looked at each other. 'Well,' Molly said, 'she ought to get an Oscar for that performance. Anyone else want some coffee? If not, I'm off. Coming, Ben?'

'Brisk lady, my wife,' Ben said, fingering his piece of jade, sounding edgy. His liquid eyes were resting on Georgia.

Simon said, 'I think I'll hang on a bit. Hold the fort till Paul gets here.'

'That would be kind, Simon,' Georgia said. 'It would be nice to have someone to answer the telephone. That's all there is to do, really.'

She smiled, a little, fixed, polite smile, the daughter of the house taking over, dispersing this gathering, ushering her mother's friends up the stairs. At the door, Molly patted her cheek. 'I'll pop up lunch time, my duck. Bring cold cuts and a salad. Plenty for everyone, so you won't have to worry.'

She set off at a trot, like a smart little pony. Ben embraced

Georgia, kissing her on the mouth rather damply – Ruth saw Georgia flinch – and hurried after his wife.

Ruth said, 'Poor love, this is awful for you. Daisy didn't mean what she said, don't let it upset you.'

'I don't know,' Georgia said. 'They haven't been – I mean, she's been different lately. Perhaps it was Grandfather dying. Or perhaps it started before. I thought it was a habit they'd both fallen into, not talking much, and Dad didn't mind, now I wonder . . .' Her white throat moved as she swallowed. 'I'm afraid he was lonely. If only – oh, I'm sorry, you know what I'm going to say, and it's *stupid*, just what everyone says when this sort of thing happens, how you wish you'd done this, or that . . .'

Joe said, 'Hush, my sweet.' He put his hands on her shoulders and she leaned against him for a second, her head on his breast, then withdrew, smiling painfully.

'Get some breakfast,' Joe said. He closed the door and turned on his heel.

Ruth ran to keep up with him as he strode up the street. She said breathlessly, 'Joe, please don't be angry with Daisy. I know it was terrible, some of the things that she said, but she was rather magnificent, too. Being so open about what she was feeling, not caring what we all thought of her. She was dreadfully wounded, and not ashamed of it, that was what was so splendid . . .'

Joe didn't answer. His silence made her feel foolish – a silly woman, wittering on, saying ridiculous things. Well, not ridiculous, really; she had just expressed herself badly. A curious excitement seemed to have seized her, bubbling up the kind of sentiments that would have been more appropriate if they had just come out of the theatre. *How did you enjoy the play, Mrs Lincoln?* 'Oh, dear,' Ruth said, 'I'm so sorry.'

Joe was opening their front door. As he did so, jerking it sharply towards him as he turned the key because the frame was out of alignment, the young woman next door appeared on her step to pick up the milk bottles. The baby straddled her hip, fat hand clutching her long, yellow hair.

Joe said, 'Good morning,' and she turned, easing her hair out of the baby's grasp, shyly drawing her wrap across her bare breast. Joe nodded cheerfully, ushering Ruth into the house in front of him. As he closed the door, he was smiling.

Ruth said, 'She's so pretty.'

'Yes. Look – I'm not angry with Daisy. I mean, just now, I could have broken her bloody neck for her, acting up like that, but that's something different. I'm bloody sorry for her, if you want to know . . .'

Ruth put her finger to her lips. Mark's door was open. But he was still sleeping, gracefully curled on the bed, one hand under his cheek, the other lying loose on his thigh. Seeing him, so peacefully sleeping, so defenceless, made her heart ache with love. She whispered, 'Should I put a blanket over him? I don't want to wake him.'

'He's all right,' Joe said. 'Let him sleep it off. Nothing to wake up for, has he?'

There was a note of irritation in his voice. Mark had come home, at the end of his first year at university, and announced that he was not going back. He had not yet explained why, except to say he had found his philosophy course 'quite irrelevant'. Ruth had persuaded Joe not to badger him, but she knew he was disappointed, found it an effort to control his anger. Perhaps that was one of the reasons why he had been so glum lately. Silent, even morose sometimes. Oh, poor Joe, she thought. Now he had a new burden to carry.

They went down the stairs to their basement kitchen, a small room opening onto the garden. The Sealyham plopped down the stairs behind them. Ruth opened the door and the bitch ran out in a scamper of white wool. Joe put the kettle on the stove and stood watching it. He sighed, deeply and painfully.

Ruth put her hand on his arm. 'I can't believe it. Why should Luke kill himself?'

Joe shrugged his shoulders and yawned. He was rubbing his chin with his hand, feeling the bristles.

Ruth said, 'I know his work was important to him. But it wasn't the whole of his life. He had so many interests, the cottage in Norfolk, his painting. He loved the theatre. I know Georgia said he was lonely. But I thought he and Daisy were happy.'

Joe said, quite roughly, 'What makes you think that? Christ, Ruth, don't you see anything you don't want to see? Oh, God, I don't mean that. I mean, you're too *nice*, Ruth. You behave well yourself, you believe other people do, too.' He turned from the stove and looked down at her. 'But you ought to know. They were *wretched* together. You heard what Daisy said, didn't you?'

'Yes. But. . .' She saw Joe was right. Safe in her own happy marriage she made comfortable assumptions about other people. She said, 'Well, of course I see now. And perhaps they were never as close as we are. But they never seemed – I mean, they didn't bicker or quarrel.'

'It had gone beyond that.'

He spoke with conviction. She thought – he saw more of Luke, knew him better than I did. She said, hesitantly, 'Had Luke found someone else?'

'Perhaps. I don't know. Daisy might.' He looked into her face with an odd, searching, almost fearful expression. 'Doesn't she ever talk to you?' He gave a sudden, loud, nervous laugh. 'I thought women were always discussing their husbands and lovers.'

Ruth shook her head. 'I don't. I suppose I would feel, I don't know, embarrassed, or disloyal, or something.' She laughed to make this sound a lighter thing than she felt it to be. 'Of course Daisy and I used to talk about boy friends when we were young, at school, and just after. Or rather, Daisy talked and I listened. But then we got married.'

'And that put an end to all conversation?'

'You know what I mean.' Ruth wondered if he did know. 'I mean, I have you to talk to. I don't need anyone else.'

But perhaps Daisy had needed someone. If she had really been so unhappy. Someone to pour her heart out to, a shoulder to weep on. Oh, not to weep! Someone to shout at, more likely!

Ruth said, 'I've been too busy and happy.'

'You sound as if you thought that was wrong.'

'No. Just that I should have made time. I feel that I've failed her.'

'Oh, Christ!' Joe put his arms round her. 'I shouldn't have told you.'

'Silly! What can I do, Joe?'

'Nothing. Forget it.'

'I could go to her. Talk to her.'

Joe laughed. 'You'd hate that. She'd hate it, probably. So just go on being yourself. Don't feel guilty.' His arms tightened, making her gasp. 'Go on being happy.'

III

Comfortably clad in her dead husband's striped flannel pyjamas and thick Jaeger dressing gown (no point in replacing her own worn out night attire when he had left such a good stock of warm garments behind him) Luke's mother, Lady Stella Brett, sat in the kitchen of her Chelsea flat, watching her friend, Walter Scully, polish off a plateful of eggs and bacon and fried tomatoes.

She was glad to see him eat with such appetite. She suspected that except when she cooked a meal for him he fed himself out of tins. Men living alone, as Walter had done since his wife left him, seldom looked after themselves sensibly. When he had turned up this morning after walking his dog in the Gardens, he had looked pinched and cold, chilled to the bone. Food had restored his colour and preparing it for him had helped her over the first, monstrous onslaught of pain. Though it was returning now, gathering in her stomach like a labour contraction, she felt strong enough to resist it. At least until Walter had gone. Old people look so hideous when they cry, pulpy flesh wobbling loose on the bones, and although Walter was old too, a little, shrunken up gnome with large, ill-fitting false teeth, he was a man, and she still had some feminine vanity. If it had not been for Paul's telephone call, she would have been dressed before Walter came.

She drummed her fingers on the table. She said, in her deep, strong voice, 'I could murder that truck driver.'

Tactfully, Walter did not look at her. He wiped his plate

with a piece of bread and gave it to the small, matted old dog sitting beside him. He said, 'Some of them jam the accelerator down with a piece of wood on long journeys. Dangerous habit, but how do you stop them?'

Before he retired, Walter had been a long distance truck driver. Stella had met him, as she met most of the people she considered her friends now, in the Embankment Gardens. He had been sitting on the bench that she usually occupied, the dog at his feet. Stella had spoken to the dog first. A dog is a useful introduction if you are feeling like company, and she always carried a few biscuits with her. The dog had accepted the biscuits and Walter had removed his shopping bag and his newspaper to make room for her on the bench. That had been fourteen months ago. Their relationship had developed at a decorous pace – at least four weeks before he had suggested a drink in a pub, several more before she had invited him home for a meal. She had done so with some hesitation, knowing it was a turning point. Until then she had gone to the Gardens as a man might go to an old-fashioned club, to meet her cronies casually, without pre-arrangement. Now Walter often appeared in the mornings, offering to shop for her and usually staying for breakfast; a couple of times, when he had come for supper, he had spent the night in the spare room. She had seen more of Walter this past year, she thought, watching him fussing over the dog, combing the tangled hair over its eyes with his fingers, than she had seen of her sons or their families. The days he didn't come in the mornings, she looked forward to seeing him in their usual place around noon. The comfort of their friendship lay in its regularity rather than in any shared interest. Unless you counted old age as an interest: their ailments (his eyesight, her rheumatism) providing an unfailing topic. All the same, it seemed to her that she spoke to Walter more freely than she had ever spoken to her husband or to her sons. She felt *more herself*, with him, she decided. All those years of being a wife and a mother had defined and constricted her.

She said, 'I'm glad you're here, Walter. Would you like some more coffee?'

'You ought to have something yourself. You ought to keep your strength up.'

Walter looked at her shyly. He was moving his mouth about, pressing a finger against one side of his jaw. His teeth were hurting him, she could see. Perhaps he had got a tomato pip caught under his plate. But he wouldn't remove it in front of her.

She said, 'I'm all right, don't worry, Walter. I expect Paul will come soon. I'll have to get lunch for him. I'll eat something then.'

I hope Paul drives carefully. Though to lose two sons in one day would be improbable, surely?

She said, 'It's funny, you know. It was always Paul I was afraid for. Driving those fast, sporty cars. Luke was always the cautious one. Paul used to laugh at him, call him an old woman.'

'Well, it's always the way,' Walter said.

Am I glad it's not Paul? The handsome one, the successful one? So much still in front of him? Oh, God, don't make me choose, even in my own thoughts . . .

She said, with a heavy sigh, fretfully shaking her head, 'When I heard Luke had got the sack, I thought, well, at least he'll have some life of his own.'

'He wasn't *sacked*,' Walter said, frowning a little. 'Just an early retirement. It's not the same thing.'

'Retired, made redundant, it's the same thing whatever you call it. Thrown out like an old boot. Kaput, I hoped he wouldn't feel it too badly, that he'd go back to his painting. He used to enjoy it. Painting pictures, that is. I'm particularly fond of that one, the picture on the wall by the dresser. When

Luke got married, I offered to give it back to him, but Daisy didn't like it, apparently. Or he thought she might not. I never knew which.'

As Walter got up, putting his thick glasses on to examine the picture, she felt suddenly anxious, fearing he would say something hurtful. *An inoffensive piece of art.* This was a phrase that came to her suddenly as being about the most offensive thing he could say. Though perhaps it was not one Walter would think of.

'Very nice,' he said. 'Quite artistic.'

'It's the Embassy in Ankara. My husband's last post. We had been hoping for Paris, but it was not to be, and as it turned out we were happy in Turkey. So that may be one reason I'm so fond of Luke's picture.'

To begin with, she had been nervous of telling Walter that her husband had been in the Diplomatic Service. But Walter had seemed quite unaffected. He had not even been put out by the fact that she had a title. (She had been careful to explain that her husband had only been a knight, not a baronet.) Old age, she thought, was a great equaliser. Class, all those stuffy old notions, went out of the window. On the other hand, she didn't really want her sons to know about Walter. Especially Paul. Luke might have understood, but Paul was a stick in the mud. So conventional.

She said, 'We thought Luke had talent. Not a great one, perhaps, or not at that time, but it could have developed. My husband had a good eye for that sort of thing. He was sure the potential was there.'

All wasted now. Frittered away on getting and spending. Such a short time to live.

Pain stabbed her throat as if she had swallowed a fish bone. She said, 'I think I'll get dressed now. Please don't go, Walter.'

She wanted a private weep in the bathroom. But she had held back too long. When she closed the door, turned on the tap, sorrow stayed locked like a stone in her chest, no tears came to dissolve it. She looked at herself in the mirror, shocked as she always was by the sagging age of the face that looked back at her, rubbed her cheeks with punishing fingers, splashed with cold water. *Luke*, she said, *Luke*, forcing a groan, calling on her love for him to assist her. She felt a ridiculous panic. When Paul came, he would expect to find her distraught. But no one could mourn to order.

Nor love, either. As she dressed, taking her heavy under-wear, her tweed skirt, her ancient, shapeless sweater, from the hook on the back of the door, Stella thought of Daisy who had not loved Luke for a long time. She must be careful not to blame Daisy for that, never hint that she knew it. Parents were not supposed to notice these things. Like children, they were expected to accept what they were told, without question. Paul had loved Daisy, but she had married Luke. 'A woman's privilege to change her mind, Mother,' Paul had said; gallantly concealing his hurt. 'Daisy is very young, and though I admit I thought we had something good going, there hasn't been anything, well, of an intimate nature between us. So it's been a fair fight, and as far as I'm concerned, the best man has won. At least Luke has kept her in the family, given you a good daughter-in-law.'

Daisy had been good enough. Too lazy to be anything but kind, Stella had always considered, hoping that this would make her older son's marriage agreeable to him, that Luke would never guess what she so clearly saw, that there was no passion in it. Not Daisy's fault, and perhaps she had not even been aware of the lack – what you don't have you don't miss – but it could be a danger to Paul now. Though he had a wife he seemed fond of, and children, death threw everything into the melting pot. And beneath that appearance of genial apathy, Daisy was a strong, greedy girl. Spoiled by her father. Stella had liked the cheerful old lecher (remembering with pleasure her seventy-fifth birthday, nearly ten years ago now, when he had fumbled her breasts as he kissed her) but he had been a burden on Luke and not only financially. He had made Daisy dissatisfied. Loading her with clothes and jewellery that in the end Luke had paid for, his message had been, *No man is good enough for my daughter.*

Rubbing a powder puff over her face, Stella thought – *suppose Paul leaves Judy and the twins and takes up with Daisy? Gives up his good job in Birmingham and runs off with her to America?* Paul had always said he could make much more as a surgeon in the States than he ever could in this country but Judy hated the idea of leaving the town where she had been born and brought up. A dull girl, Stella thought. If Paul went off with Daisy, would he want to take Georgia, too? Would Georgia go? Surely not. Her uncle in her father's bed!

A bell rang inside Stella's skull. This was a story she had heard before. For a moment she stood, hardly breathing, trying to trace the allusion down the twisty, cobwebbed passages of her mind, but as happened so often now, it whisked round a dark corner and vanished. Oh well, she thought, breathing again, it's common enough. No need to bother to trace the source of an old woman's fancies. You get to my age, there's nothing new under the sun. It was Walter's wife I was thinking of, probably.

Walter had been married for forty-five years. His wife had left eighteen months ago. Walter had come home from walking the dog and the first thing he'd seen when he opened the sitting room door was his brother's naked bottom and his wife's feet, in her old bedroom slippers, clasped round it. Walter had closed the door, left the house to walk the dog for another hour, and when he came back, his wife and his brother had gone.

'She's living in Wimbledon with him. He's got a corner shop, he and my sister used to run it together, but she died, you know, so I daresay he can do with the help. Mind you, I've no choice in the matter.' Walter had grinned when he said this, a bit wry, but quite cheerful. 'When I look at it straight, I've only myself to blame. I encouraged them, really. Turned a blind eye for too long. He'd be there when I came home from a job, sitting in my kitchen having his tea, and I'd get the feeling they'd been up to something but I didn't like to mention it in case I was wrong, and it seemed a bit extra delicate, anyway, him being my brother. There was the boy, too. My son. He was only about seventeen when I reckon it started, and I didn't want to turn him against them. He thought the world of his mother and his uncle had always been good to him, not having kids of his own. Of course he knows now but he's a grown man and it doesn't affect him the way it might have done when he was younger. And I put it to him that his mother will keep the little business in better shape than his uncle could have done on his own. The shop will come to him when they both pass away, so he'll get the benefit.'

Hamlet! Of course! 'You silly old fool,' Stella said aloud. Though if Georgia had been a boy, she would have made the connection before. Poor Walter! So uncomplaining! But acceptance was the only way, really, take what's handed out, grin and bear it. It was a tiresome middle class habit to think there must always be a solution. It struck her with some satisfaction that she had learned more about certain aspects of life since she had taken to spending her spare time in the Embankment Gardens than in all her years in the Service. Situations that would have seemed horrendous or tragic in Ankara, Cairo, Helsinki, were everyday occurrences among her acquaintances there. One old woman appeared fairly regularly with bruises, black eyes – beaten up, not by her husband, but by her orphaned fifteen year old grandson who lived with her. 'He can't help it, he gets sniffing the glue, and he doesn't know what he's doing. I thought of calling the police once or twice, then I thought, well, it won't get you anywhere. Even if they take him to court, they'll just send him back, because there's nowhere else, is there?'

Stella had listened, making no comment. None was asked for and she suspected it would be a blunder, anyway, to offer more than sympathy to the battered grandmother, as it would be a mistake when Walter complained of sore gums, to suggest he should get some new dentures. She was anxious not to appear bossy and superior. She had even worried about wearing her fur coat when the weather was cold, unaware that its great age made her look more like a respectable charwoman than the widow of an Ambassador. Not that she wished to deceive, only to be accepted on equal terms. She sometimes feared that this caution about her social position made her too reserved, that she didn't contribute enough. Or perhaps it was simply that her own life lacked incident of a kind she could easily share. Well, she had something to offer now. Her son was dead! She could pass on her speculations about Paul and Daisy!

The prospect was surprisingly strengthening, set her blood throbbing to an old tune. As a little girl, her talent for mischief had bordered on malice. Her mother had been a profuse letter writer of a gossipy kind. The young Stella had found it an agreeable diversion to open the envelopes, left on the hall table for posting and not always stuck down very carefully, and switch round the letters. Though she listened gleefully to her mother's side of the disturbing telephone calls that sometimes resulted, her main pleasure had been the delicious sense of power that coursed through her. She had made something happen! Now, in her helpless old age, she felt the same need for power, to be active, not passive. When she thought of Paul coming, treating her like a derelict ancient, speaking to her loudly and clearly, as if she were deaf or half-witted, a deep, vulgar desire to stir the pot, shake his complacency, seized her.

MARRIAGE

Combing her hair in front of the mirror, Luke's death for the moment forgotten, she cackled at her reflection, seeing the years fall away and a wicked child grinning back at her.

IV

When Ruth rang the bell, the door opened immediately as if
Stella had been waiting impatiently. Not for Ruth, though.
'What are you doing here?' Stella said, peering at her with
apparent surprise and suspicion. A dim hanging bulb in the
hall behind her shone through her sparse hair, making it look
like a pale, dusty halo.

'Daisy asked me to come. That is, I wanted to. All I meant
is, that Daisy . . .'

Stella said, 'Ha!' She turned her back, leaving Ruth to close
the door, and shuffled ahead into the living room. The thick
velvet curtains were drawn, the room lit by a standard lamp
with a parchment shade, burned in several places. Stella took a
pile of albums and photographs from a low chair and
motioned Ruth to sit in it. She remained standing, her back to
the electric fire in the hearth, her feet, in stout brogues,
mannishly planted apart. Head thrust forward, blue eyes
hawkishly staring, she looked down at Ruth. She said, in a
self-satisfied, sardonic tone, 'So Paul isn't coming. I ought to
have known it. What's Daisy up to? Don't tell me. Got her
claws in already!'

Ruth was mystified. 'Daisy's upset, of course. I'm sure Paul
will come as soon as he can.'

She thought – I should comfort her. Put my arms round her.
But her chair was so low that to rise and embrace the old
woman would be an unnaturally theatrical movement. And
Stella was twice her size, anyway.

Stella loomed over her. She smelled of old clothes. She said, 'Do you want tea? Walter had the last of the coffee. Otherwise there is whisky, or some rather unpleasant sweet sherry. I don't know where it came from. One of the boys brought it, probably. It isn't my tipple.'

Ruth shook her head. Who was Walter? The last thing she wanted was alcohol. But Stella was already pouring whisky into two tumblers. She gave one to Ruth. 'Drink up, you look a bit peaky. Ruth, isn't it? Ruth – let me see, wait a minute . . .' She waved her hands as if to pluck Ruth's surname out of the air. 'Cardiff,' she said, pleased. 'That's it. Ruth Cardiff.'

'Aberdare,' Ruth said, automatically. Oh God, did it matter? She should have introduced herself when Stella opened the door. But they had met often enough. At family parties – Georgia's eighteenth birthday only a few months ago. All the same, she should not have assumed that Stella would remember. She found herself blushing.

Stella said, 'I knew it was some town or other in Wales. You get to my age, you'll be glad to get close as that. Of course I know who you are, my dear. I'm not totally gaga. Cogs a bit rusty, that's all. In the mornings especially.'

'I'm sorry,' Ruth said.

'Sorry? What for? Yes, of course, but it's not my first death and I'm over the worst of it. So is Daisy, I'd guess. Or Paul would be here. How long has it been going on? That's what I wonder. Not that I blame Paul. It's always the woman's fault.'

Rambling, Ruth thought. The shock. Well, not rambling altogether. Paul's mother would know that Paul had once asked Daisy to marry him. But that was a long time ago, ancient history. Stella Brett was going back in time in her grief. As Daisy had done in her anger.

Ruth said, 'I expect Paul is busy. Daisy needs someone to help her. Practical things . . .' Like identifying the body? Her frightened blush deepened. 'That's why I came. To see if I could be any use.' Why had she imagined she could be? What had she expected? Tears. A helpless old woman crumpled in a chair, weeping. Certainly not this terrifying dowager, knocking back whisky.

Stella said, 'Mind you, I don't altogether blame Daisy. I had a low boredom threshold myself when I was a young married woman. Did I say young? Ha! When I was not so young, either. Though I was lucky, of course. I had the two wars. 1914 and the last one. Something real happening. All those years between, such boredom, such greyness! Then the second war – I could hardly wait for it. Listening to Chamberlain on the wireless, I thought, now we live again! Though it wasn't the same, my boys were growing up, you fear for your children. Not like the first war. I was only a child then. I remember my brothers in their beautiful uniforms and I wasn't afraid for them, it was all honour and glory, the sound of the drums. I met my husband when I was sixteen, my parents kept open house for young officers home on leave, and I fell head over heels in love, seeing him blinded and maimed for his country, and my devoting my life to the hero, nursing him nobly and sweetly. All young girl's nonsense, but it was fire in my blood. I wrote to him at the front, burning up with excitement, a load of lies, how I thought of him, prayed for his safety, when it was just the other way round. I wanted him martyred. I couldn't make up my mind whether he should lose a leg or an arm – two limbs, I thought, would be going too far. In fact he sat in some mustard gas and one of my brothers told me he would have a tin bottom. That took some adjustment, it was hardly the romantic wound I had thought of, but by then I was committed. I married him for his tin bottom. I couldn't envisage it, what kind of contraption, and I looked forward to my wedding night with a certain gruesome excitement. But it was only skin grafts, an elaborate tattoo on his arse. I was fond enough of him but out of his uniform he was ordinary. A long time before I allowed myself to admit it, ten years or so before I recognised how much he bored me. I used to look at him and think, if you're going to die, why don't you die now and give me my freedom while I'm still young enough to enjoy it. He was a good man. I see now that was the trouble. I resented his goodness. It showed me up, even to myself, in my thoughts. I never let him know how I felt by a word or a look because what I felt was quite unacceptable. I wanted excitement and violence, pillage and rape, and what he offered was peace and kindness. So you see, I understand Daisy.'

Ruth gazed at her glass. Throughout this extraordinary statement she had not dared look at Stella. Perhaps it was not so extraordinary, she thought with trembling wonder. She had pictured herself holding Luke's mother's hand while the old woman muttered sad, broken cries. Perhaps this response was more natural; anger at Luke's life cut short, the waste, the futility.

Stella gave a long, groaning sigh. 'Luke is like his father. Kind, clever and ordinary. That is, Luke *was* like him.'

Ruth raised her eyes from her whisky and saw that Stella was sitting down now, leaning back in an armchair. Her head rested against the padded wing, her blue eyes were closed. It was almost impossible to connect her tired face, her tubby, soft, elderly body, in shabby, jumble-sale clothes, with the words she had spoken. Ruth could hardly believe she had heard them. She said, 'Lady Brett – this is terrible for you.'

Stella opened her eyes. They shone with a cold, hostile light. 'I don't feel what I should. I'm not a nice woman. I was trying to tell you. I suppose you can't understand. Can you contemplate your son's death? What's his name? Matthew?'

'Mark,' Ruth said, trembling.

'Yes. Yes, of course. An Apostle. I can't see Luke any longer, *that* is the terrible thing. Not as a grown man, anyway. Only as a fair haired little boy, running after his brother.

Though Paul was the younger one, he was always the leader.
You know Paul, don't you?'

Ruth remembered Paul at Luke's wedding. A large, healthy
young man with a flower in his buttonhole; competent,
confident, boyishly masculine. After the ceremony, posing
for photographs, he had towered over slender Luke, arm in
arm with his Daisy. She remembered another thing. Daisy had
said, when Ruth was helping her off with her dress, 'Luke
won't boss me about, that's a good thing. I couldn't put up
with a marriage if I had to play second fiddle.' Had she
regretted Paul, at the last moment?

Ruth said, 'We haven't seen much of Paul lately. Only when
he's been in London, staying with Luke and Daisy, and he
doesn't come very often.' She stopped. Luke's mother needed
to talk about *Luke*. She said, 'Luke wasn't ordinary. He has
been our dear friend for a long time. He was sensitive and
gentle and good. A marvellous person.'

'He and Daisy weren't suited.'

'They were different. That doesn't mean . . .'

'He should have married a soft girl. Someone he could have
looked after. Not that rampaging rogue elephant.'

'I wouldn't call Daisy . . .'

'Oh, I daresay you wouldn't.'

Ruth laughed. She said, 'I'm sorry.'

'I'm glad my description amused you.'

'I shouldn't have laughed though. I know what you mean,
but it isn't fair, really. Daisy likes her own way and she takes
what she wants, but she's open and honest and natural.' A pure
natural force, Ruth thought suddenly, a clean wind. She said,
'She doesn't lie, or cheat, or pretend.'

'Ha! Well. I suppose you feel you have to be loyal to
her.'

'No. I mean, I do feel that, but not in a forced way. I love
her.'

Ruth was surprised to hear herself saying this. She meant it, but usually she found it hard to speak so straightforwardly.

She said, 'I've known Daisy so long. We were friends at school, she was my only friend, really, and then, when my father died, her parents were so good to me. I almost grew up in their house.'

'Oh, I know about that!' Stella sat very upright, looking suddenly lively and interested. 'I remember who you are now! Poor little rich girl, ghastly parents, father dying in some bizarre manner, mother mad as a hatter. Some scandal. Luke told me, or Daisy. Years ago. Can't remember the details. What happened, exactly?'

Ruth felt her whole body tingle. 'It was a kind of shooting accident. My mother was shocked, of course. But she didn't go mad.' She made herself breathe deeply and calmly. 'No scandal, really. Nothing worth talking about.'

Stella looked at her, drumming her fingers on the arm of her chair as if playing the piano. She said, in a disappointed voice, 'You mean you don't want to talk about it! Decent, middle class reticence! My friends in the Gardens are much more communicative. Still, never mind. None of my business. Put the inquisitive old woman back in her box. No one tells an old woman anything. I don't suppose they'll ever tell me what really happened to Luke. I expect that lorry driver will get away with it. Accidental death, that's how it'll come out at the inquest. No blame attaching to anyone. Always simpler that way, isn't it?'

Astonishingly, she was smiling. It seemed to Ruth that her smile held a terrible knowledge. A vengeful clairvoyant. A Fury. Oh, of course that wasn't true. Stella was a sad, half-demented old lady. Her smile was the crazed smile of grief. She wanted to hit out at someone because Luke was dead, because she felt his life had been unhappy and wasted.

Ruth said, 'I'm so sorry. There's no comfort, I know. Except – I think Luke and Daisy were happier, perhaps, than you think.'

Even if one of them had been unfaithful, that could still be true, surely? She forced herself to think about it. Suppose Luke had found someone else? That wasn't uncommon. Middle-aged men felt their youth slipping by, needed reassurance and comfort. Set against years of shared happiness, shared loss – their dead little son – that meant almost nothing. But perhaps it hadn't meant nothing to Luke. Any honourable man would feel shame. In the ordinary way, shame was something that you could live with, but if other factors came in, other pressures, then it was bound to be harder. People didn't kill themselves because their careers came to an end. They didn't kill themselves because of some stupid, sexual entanglement. Luke had had both to endure. He loved this other woman (who was she? His secretary? Some girl he had met on a bus, at a party?), had loved her a long time in a sweet, anguished way (for Luke such an affair couldn't be casual, a quick fuck in the bushes, in the back of a car) but he had loved Daisy too, and it had torn him apart. Perhaps, in the end, he had told Daisy, hoping for sympathy, for forgiveness, a new start? A foolish hope, he must have been deeply deluded, far gone in despair to have entertained it. Daisy was the last person to put on a false front, play the understanding wife, lock up her anger, allow it to fester inside her. She would scream, shout, bellow her rage from the rooftops until she had purged herself of the poison. Much the most wholesome way to go on, taking a long view, but time had run out for Luke. He had lost his job, his girl, his wife, been left with nothing . . .

Ruth gulped at her whisky. *I am making this up*, she thought, *I can't know*. Joe had said they were wretched. But he didn't really know, either.

She said to Luke's mother, 'I really do believe that Luke was quite happy with Daisy. If he hadn't been, Joe and I would have known. We saw such a lot of them.'

Stella said in a grumbling voice. 'That doesn't prove anything. The closer you are, the less you see sometimes. All the same, I shouldn't have ranted on at you. I apologise.'

'No . . .'

'I suppose I was angry because Paul hadn't come. Luke would have done, he would have come to his mother instead of rushing to comfort that spoiled, greedy, young woman. If I have anything to do with it, Paul won't comfort her long. I shan't pussy foot about, keeping my mouth shut, pretending . . .' She beat her clenched fists on the arms of her chair, her blue hawk's eyes suddenly blurring with tears. Ruth got up and knelt in front of her, taking her hands, holding them.

'Hush,' she said. 'Hush . . .'

Stella snatched her hands away. She heaved herself up, pushing Ruth aside, and marched across the room. She threw a photograph album and a large brown envelope onto Ruth's lap. Pictures spilled out of it. Ruth tried to gather them up. Pictures of Luke as a boy, as a young man, looking serious, smiling, holding a tennis racket, sitting in a chair in a summer garden, glancing up from his book at the camera.

Stella said, 'Take them with you, give them to Georgia, she might like them, they're no good to me. As far as I'm concerned, Luke isn't there.'

She stood, head thrust forward, breathing roughly and raspingly. 'It makes no sense, an old woman like me still lumbering up the earth.'

Ruth said, still on her knees, the photographs clutched to her chest, 'Please. Let me do something. Could I make you a cup of tea? Get you a sedative? Have you got anything? Shall I phone for your doctor?'

Stella smiled at her kindly. 'Oh, I don't bother with doctors. I'm all right. Just need time. You're a good girl, thank you for coming. But you can't understand. Old people need other old people for that. Thank God I've got Walter! You're too young and too happy to help me. You are happy, aren't you?'

Ruth nodded. She felt the foolish tears coming.

'Good,' Stella said. 'Hang on to that while you can. Make the best of it.'

V

Alone in the workshop above the boutique, Ruth was sewing a triangular piece of lace onto the bodice of a cream silk wedding dress. The silk was new, made in Italy, the lace old and delicate, part of a lot Ruth had bought several years ago from a bankrupt fabric firm in Stepney. Ruth employed two excellent, middle-aged seamstresses (both out at lunch at the moment) but this was the kind of work she liked to do herself, taking pride in her minute, beautiful stitching, the clever concealment of a pulled thread in the lace, an almost invisible iron mould mark as she joined the old to the new. Although her dresses were all original, Ruth thought of herself as a crafty copyist rather than a creator. Poring over Victorian and Edwardian prints and photographs, choosing the flattering lines, keeping the romanticism of the designs without the discomfort, she paid no attention to fashion. She built her clothes to last, was always delighted to re-fit a dress she had sold years ago, renew lace, repair a torn hem, cover a stain with a neat piece of embroidery. Her success pleased her for the pleasure it gave. She was happiest when she was able to turn a plain woman into a beauty for a special occasion, disguise awkward hips, scrawny necks, choose a subtle shade for an ageing skin, persuade a shy girl to show off her pretty arms, her young shoulders. The money she made was only peripheral to this sweet satisfaction. She knew that her work was good, she had never doubted her talent, but she didn't rate it too high. Making clothes for rich women wasn't *useful*. To be a good dressmaker was a frivolous occupation set against a doctor's, or a politician's, or a social worker's, but at least it did no harm, gave employment, and she was proud to know she did it well.

She put a last stitch in the bodice, fitted the dress on the dummy, and stood back to look at it. The silk ruffles of the long sleeves, fitted at the narrow wrists with a smaller ruffle and gathered into a fairly wide shoulder, balanced the deep Vee of the Edwardian lace, sweeping down to the waist at the same angle as the slight lift of the skirt in the front. The girl wouldn't trip as she walked to the altar. A pity that her veil didn't match up with the Stepney lace, but it was a family piece that had been worn by her mother and grandmother and sentiment was more important than perfection on this sort of occasion. Ruth said, under her breath, superstitiously, 'Wear it in health.' She would not see the completed dress on the bride. That was a small self-denial to keep the sales staff happy and confident. Besides, though Ruth saw customers when they first came, to assess what she could do for them, she was happiest in the workroom.

She felt calm and happy now, looking at the cream dress. Perhaps it had been a bit selfish, though, to have sought solace this way, to have come to the shop at all after she had left Stella. Either Ida or Beatrice could have sewed on the lace just as well. (Indeed, Ruth sometimes felt that the two women indulged her, leaving her little tasks, finishing touches.) On the other hand, there had been nothing else more immediate. When she had telephoned Daisy, Georgia had said she was out with Simon. Paul had been and gone – was now in Chelsea with his mother. Molly had brought food from the delicatessen as she had promised, and was keeping Georgia company. In Ruth's own house, the daily housekeeper, Mrs Costello, would be looking after Mark and preparing the evening meal. She was a bustling Sicilian who more than earned the good salary that Ruth paid her, polishing silver and furniture as lovingly as if they belonged to her, sweeping under beds, inside cupboards, with a huge, heroic appetite for order and cleanliness that still left her time to fuss over Mark in a thoroughly sexist, old-European way – young men, where Maria Costello came from, were treated like princes. Late breakfast, an enormous, rich lunch, warm towels when he wanted a bath, cups of coffee. Even though Ruth deplored this kind of behaviour in principle, she hoped that it comforted Mark. She longed to comfort him herself but she guessed that at the moment she was quite the wrong person, as perhaps any parent would be. However loving she was, however considerate, she couldn't heal or even help the bleak sense of failure and disappointment he must be feeling. The best she could do for him was to leave him alone for at least part of the day with someone who did not pity his situation or in any way worry about it. And the rest of the time, try and reassure him by her quiet, waiting presence, that she was there when he needed her.

She must do the same thing for Daisy, she thought. Wait quietly, let Daisy know somehow that she would come the moment she called her. Now that she knew the cause of Daisy's bitterness, her terrible sense of outrage and loss, she might be able to help her, coax her to look back on her marriage with tenderness, weep for Luke with the love that must, deep down, still be there. It might be hard to begin with, to break down the barriers, but Ruth was sure she could do it. She felt, at this moment, unusually confident, physically extremely well, and filled with a deep, peaceful, wondering happiness. It was odd, even shameful, perhaps, that the shattering events of the morning should have had this effect on her. Perhaps it was true that the contemplation of other people's misfortunes sometimes made you count your own blessings.

She counted them now with a sense of awed and reverent

wonder. Her job, this innocent craft that gave her such innocent pleasure. Her children, her sweet son (sadly troubled just now but that would surely pass soon) and her daughter. Marigold could hardly be called 'sweet', she was too awkwardly adolescent, sulky and stormy, but she was a kind girl at bottom, strong, loving-hearted. And, of course, Joe. Her dear Joe! When she thought of the numb, cold, careful girl she had been – not shy, exactly, but a little sharp-tongued, wary, defensive, locked up inside herself like a girl in a tree or a statue, she felt gratitude, as well as love for him. Joe was the first man, the only man who had loved her; he had been father, brother and husband in one, setting her free with his love, filling and possessing her with a wild torrent of feeling that astonished, amazed her.

Until she met Joe at a party Luke and Daisy had given just after they married, she had believed herself to be 'in love' with Bob Brown, Daisy's brother. But that was only because Bob was so much like Daisy in his lovely, bouncy high spirits, his easy conviction that the world was designed for his happiness and well being. That had been the time when Daisy and Bob had seemed like gods to her, or at least beings of a high, aristocratic order. Lordly Bob could not be expected to love her. She was his sister's sad, plain little friend who had had such an unhappy time and must be looked after. When Ruth was at design school in London and came to spend weekends with Daisy, Bob squired her about, saw she was never without a partner at tennis club dances. Though Ruth had suspected that his kindly behaviour was prompted by Mrs Brown, it hadn't detracted from it – indeed it had made Bob seem more noble in her eyes, a very perfect, gentle knight. She had nursed a few dreams but they were private indulgences; shy, secret companions like little mice in a prison cell. To have shown Bob by a word or a look how she felt, would have been a fearful embarrassment to him. Once, a few days before

78

Daisy's wedding, when they were clearing up supper together, Bob had suddenly seized her and kissed her behind the kitchen door. She had stood perfectly still in his arms, afraid that if she moved some spell would be broken, and he had laughed, tweaked her nose gently as he let her go, and said, 'Little, funny, ice-maiden.'

She had wept that night, scalding tears. Bob was right, she was cold, nothing could thaw her, make her an ordinary, lovable, human girl. But Joe was several years older than Bob. A lusty, grown man who knew what he wanted and went straight towards it and took it. No action on Ruth's part was needed. Joe had simply picked her up, swept her along like a twig on a fast-flowing river, refused to take no for an answer, told her how lovely she was until she had felt herself changing from a plain girl into a beauty. And he had borne her up ever since, carrying her along on the warm tide of his love. Even if the river ran slower now, it was still deep and strong; she floated in a safe boat on its smooth water.

This image, that came to her now, made her feel profoundly emotional. Though after twenty-one years of marriage 'love' was no longer a simple emotion, she had never doubted that she loved Joe. What she had forgotten – or not thought of often enough, even though she relied on it, trusted it – was how much his love had done for her. A kind of fear seized her. *All he has done for me*, she thought, *love and trust, comfort and safety, what have I done for him?* Practically, of course, her money had changed his life. Joe's schoolmaster father had died unexpectedly young, in his thirties, and his boyhood, alone with his mother, had been if not poor exactly, a bit pinched and narrow, counting the pennies, his education a struggle, hard work and effort, long nights of study for his university scholarship. Ruth, whose own tastes were frugal, was happy to see Joe able to spend as he wanted – good clothes, a new car every year, first class travel, private schools for his children, generous help to his mother, to friends who were down on their luck. But this last year, when he had been so withdrawn, apparently too weary or too depressed to turn to her in bed, she had been too caught up in her own selfish fears of seeming demanding, importunate – or, worse, by an even more selfish fear of rejection – to ask him what was the matter. Perhaps he was afraid of losing his job, like Luke. Or feeling old and tired, inadequate, even impotent, and too humiliated to tell her. Oh, if that were so, she had let him down terribly! Perhaps his hypochondria had some real cause after all. Maybe he had some mortal disease he was keeping from her. Cancer. Failing kidneys. Liver. His heart!

Ruth closed her eyes and counted, very slowly, to ten, a device she had always found useful when this kind of irrational panic assailed her. Mark, on his motor bike, struck by a lorry, bleeding to death in a gutter. Marigold, attacked by some evil lout in the subway, terrified, screaming . . .

She opened her eyes. She said, aloud, 'I must talk to him, we must talk to each other.' Joe had cherished her, protected her when she was weak and he was strong, now it was her turn to protect and cherish him, lead him through the dark wood into broad sunny uplands. She musn't rush into it, fly at him in a heroic frenzy of sentiment; she must find the right time, be gentle, reassuring, explain slowly and quietly that she hadn't questioned him before about how he was feeling because she had been afraid of intruding, foolishly and crassly and selfishly afraid of hearing him say that he no longer desired her, but now, even if that was true, he could tell her and she wouldn't be hurt, only remember the years he had loved her, be content now to be his dear, trusted companion.

She thought – suppose he laughs at me? Would he be right to laugh? She said, to her own, private friend, 'Is this just sentimental twaddle?' but though she thought she heard a distant, coarse giggle, she didn't wait for an answer. She

mustn't allow herself to be inhibited. What did it matter if she
made a fool of herself? And perhaps it wouldn't be so difficult
to choose the right moment. Joe must have been stirred,
churned up as she was, by Luke's death. What had Luke's
mother said? *Something real happening, now we live again.* She
had been talking about the war but there was a kind of deep
truth there. Most of the time people just carry on, one foot in
front of the other, the high point of the day a situation comedy
on television, the low point a traffic jam on the North Circular
Road. It takes a catastrophe to wake them up out of limbo.

Ruth said, to her intimate, 'A bit over the top we are at the
moment. No breakfast. That huge tumbler of whisky. Light-
headed if not actually drunk. What do I really mean? That
violence is sexually exciting?'

All the same, looking at herself in the mirror, a small,
shapely woman, skin glowing, dark eyes glittering, a feeling
of excited resolution still held her. When had she last told Joe
that she loved him? She would tell him this evening.

When the telephone rang, she was smiling. Danny, ringing
about the silk from Milan, said when he had given her details
of prices and dates for delivery, 'You m-must have just
finished something you're p-pleased with.'

Ruth laughed, cradling the telephone receiver between chin
and shoulder, scribbling figures on a pad. 'A wedding dress,
with some of the Stepney lace, how did you know?'

'You s-sound happy. You always sound happy when you
are working.'

She thought, conscience stricken, I shouldn't sound happy!
But there was no point in telling Dan about Luke. He didn't
know Luke. Indeed, he barely knew Joe! They had met early
on, when she had first opened the shop, but Joe had been put
off by Danny's appearance. 'My God,' he had said, 'I believe
the chap perms his hair!' Now, on the rare occasions that she
mentioned Danny, Joe called him, 'Your poofter friend' – on

no evidence, Ruth thought, apart from Danny's crinkled hair, his flowery bow ties, and the fact that he was unmarried and lived with his mother. Not that she had any evidence to the contrary. Nor was it her business. She felt comfortable with Danny but it was a working partnership only. And yet, in a way, she found it easier sometimes to talk to him than to Joe. . .

She said, curiously, 'Don't I sound happy at other times, Dan?'

'N-not always. N-not in the s-same w-way.' She heard him sigh. His stammer was always worse when he said something personal. He said, 'S-sorry.'

'What for? I suppose I like working, that's all. Especially when I feel I've done something well. It makes me feel, I don't know, not *happy* exactly. . .'

Safe was the word that came to her suddenly. She felt safe in the workshop as she had felt safe when she was young, in her shed in the garden. For some reason her father had never come near her when she was there. But she didn't need that kind of safety now, did she?

'Confident,' Danny said. 'So you j-jolly well ought to be. I've been looking at the sales figures for last year and I think there s-seems room for a small act of f-folly. That green and brown design that you wanted. I hope that makes you h-happy!'

VI

On her way home, Ruth stopped at Molly's delicatessen. Mrs Costello would have prepared the main course for supper, chicken on the spit, vegetables cleaned and ready for cooking. Ruth selected two tins of smoked oysters (she didn't much care for them but Joe loved them), half a pound of ripe Brie, deliciously runny, and a jar of peaches in brandy. She went to the liquor shelves and picked out three bottles of Veuve Cliquot.

'Going it a bit, aren't you?' Molly said. 'That fizz is bloody expensive.'

'Well, if you want to keep it,' Ruth said, in a bright, brittle tone, responding as she thought Molly expected.

Molly raised her almost non-existent eyebrows. She had plucked them out several years before in obedience to a passing fashion and only a few had grown back again. The brown line that replaced them today was uneven, giving her round face an artless look, like a child's drawing. She was wearing a cotton shepherd's smock the colour of oatmeal, a nuclear disarmament badge pinned slightly askew on the yoke, and huge, dangling, multi-coloured glass ear rings. This curious garb made Ruth feel affectionate towards her. Keeping a small shop of this kind in what was, except for the gentrified terrace and a few pretty squares, a semi-derelict neighbourhood, must be a continuous struggle with the competition from the new supermarket. Molly kept some local trade, old age pensioners with bad legs who couldn't make it to the main street, other more affluent customers dropping in for last minute purchases. But it was a brave venture to keep smoked oysters, vintage champagne.

'I'm not planning a celebration, exactly,' Ruth said, uncomfortably conscious that something of the sort was what she had in her mind. She blushed. 'I was thinking of Daisy. I thought she might . . .'

'Daisy's had enough under her belt, I should think. She had a merry old time down the pub with our Simon. When I left Georgia, lunch time, I met them both reeling back. God, he's a creep, that man.'

'What do you mean?'

'Don't you know? Oh, well, I suppose it shows you've a nice nature. It's hardly a secret to most people round here. Simon is our very own Widow's Comforter. It's by way of being his retirement career.'

'Oh, Molly, I'm sure. . .'

Molly's ear rings flashed like strobe lights as she shook her head warningly. A man had come into the shop, an ageing, undisguised homosexual with a long, sad face surrounded by lank, greasy hair. Ruth had often seen him in the street, mincing along with tiny steps like a Chinese woman with bound feet.

Molly said, 'Hi there! How are things, Dickie Bird? Feeling better? If it's only a quickie, the lady will wait. She's buying the place up.'

Ruth took out her cheque book while Dickie Bird bought two ounces of pâté, a small rye loaf, and two cans of beer. Molly was a frightful gossip, what Marigold called a 'gabbage', she mustn't encourage her to say unpleasant things about Simon, she would just pay and go. But when the man had left and Molly had rung up her cheque, Ruth still lingered out of politeness. If she rushed off, Molly might feel she had snubbed her.

Molly said, 'Poor old Dickie, he got a bad thumping last week. Bloody National Front thugs. He may not be much of an ornament on the face of the earth but they're even less so, to my way of thinking. Filth. You'd think the police would do something, wouldn't you? But they don't want to know. Tarred with the same brush, I suppose. They just laughed at poor Dickie Bird when he went sobbing down to the station.'

She leaned her elbows on the counter, ear rings tinkling as she shook her cropped head in sorrowful resignation. Then grinned at Ruth. 'Now,' she said. 'Where were we?'

Ruth blushed. 'I was just going to say that I had always thought Simon such a nice man.'

'Did I say that he wasn't? He's fond of those dogs. I always like a man who likes animals. All I said was, if he sees a chance to dip his wick he's quick off the mark. When my Ben went off with that floozie, couple of months ago now, Simon was round in a jiff. A few beers at the Pheasant and Firkin. No shorts – he may have done Daisy better, but in the usual way he doesn't exactly push the boat out, old Simon. So after the beers, it was coffee and sandwiches at my place. Into the old fumble routine pretty sharply. I must be missing 'certain things' was his enticing suggestion.'

Ruth felt weakly appalled. 'I'd no idea, Molly.'

'Why should you? Simon only tries it on with the lonely ladies. And, mind you, though I didn't take up his offer, I don't suppose it would have been too bad an experience. He's a clean, healthy old man, keeps himself fit and exercised, not an ounce of flab on him. I should think he'd put on quite a fair performance. A matter of pride to see you enjoyed yourself too.'

'I meant. . .' Ruth lowered her voice, glancing over her shoulder. Suppose someone else should come into the shop? 'I mean, I didn't know about Ben.'

Molly shrugged her shoulders and sighed. Ruth guessed

that she was more distressed than she cared to admit to. She said, 'Are you sure, Molly?' She thought of the way Ben had looked at Georgia, how he had kissed her. 'After all, lots of men like flirting with pretty young girls.'

'The bastard picked up pubic lice and passed them on to me.'

Ruth felt her skin crawl. 'Molly! How dreadful!'

'Oh, well. Not the first time, and I daresay it won't be the last. He always comes home to Mother and I take the bugger back, more fool me. What puts me off really, what *gripes* me, is that they get younger and younger. *I* get to feel about a hundred and five. I've even thought of going in for a face lift. This one was barely over the age of consent, though I'm not even sure of that. At least I taught her a lesson.' She picked up a cloth and started wiping the counter.

Ruth waited. She ought to go. Later on, Molly would regret these shameful confidences. On the other hand, perhaps she needed to unburden herself. So, however distasteful she found it, she ought to stay. 'Oh, come on, dear,' her inner voice whispered, 'don't kid yourself you're being a martyr. Rooted to the ground is what we are! Fascinated.'

Molly said, 'I didn't intend to do anything, I don't tangle with scrubbers, but this was only a silly kid, someone had to do something. I happened to catch her in Marks and Spencer's, buying her knickers, and I slapped her face for her. Six or seven times, I should think. Very hard.'

Ruth felt her knees buckle beneath her. 'Molly! How could you? What *happened*?'

Molly smiled reminiscently. 'She bawled. Scared out of her wits, poor little cocker. It caused quite a commotion. People came bustling up. I just said to them all, loud and clear, *This girl has been fucking my husband*, turned my back and stomped off. No one followed me, luckily. It gave me some satisfaction but it was a grubby thing to do, really. Undignified. I'd have done better to hop in the sack with old Simon.'

'Oh, Molly!'

Molly looked at Ruth and sighed. She said, 'Christ, I'm sorry. Why I had to bore you with this, I don't know. It just came over me all of a sudden. I've been brooding all day. Worked up. It's Luke, I imagine.'

Luke? For a dizzying second Ruth thought she was about to hear more revelations. Of course, there couldn't be much going on in this area that Molly wasn't aware of. She was here all day in the shop, a receptive ear, a sharp eye, people came in and out, most of them – or so it seemed to Ruth at this moment – heavily engaged in some form of sexual activity. (Except me, she thought, except me!) But surely – *surely*, if Luke had had an affair, if Joe was right about that, he would have been careful to keep it off his own doorstep. Discreet, for Georgia's sake, if not for Daisy's.

'Dying like that,' Molly said. Her voice had grown husky. 'Honestly, you know, he was one of the last decent people. If I wasn't a Marxist, I'd call him an old-fashioned gentleman. I've been thinking – oh, just small things, how he used to come into the shop Sunday mornings, that's always a busy time, but he always waited his turn, so polite, not just good manners, you know, but kind of generous and graceful. God knows how he put up with Daisy!'

Molly took a man's red and white spotted handkerchief out of the pocket of her smock and trumpeted into it. 'Hell, I'm sorry, Ruth. I don't usually run on like this. But Luke was your friend, so you understand, don't you?'

'Yes,' Ruth whispered. 'Yes, Molly.'

The two women looked at each other with tears in their eyes. Both smiled shakily. Ruth wondered if more was required – if she should take Molly's hand. Or kiss her cheek. But the counter was between them.

Molly said, 'Well, that's that, then.'

Ruth nodded. 'Except, do you think – I mean, should I warn Daisy? If Simon . . .'

'God, no. Daisy can cope with Simon if anyone can, both hands tied, no problem. Besides, Luke's brother is here, he came in about an hour ago, trying to pay for the few bits and bobs I took up to the house, silly fellow. He said he is staying till after the funeral. So Daisy has got better fish to fry.' She gave a sharp laugh. 'Sorry, that was a crude thing to say. Though you must admit, after this morning – God, wasn't that ghastly?' But her round eyes were sparkling.

'I think we should all try to forget it.' Ruth heard her own voice, repressive, rebuking, almost insultingly ladylike, and was ashamed. Not that it mattered. The important thing was to put a stop to this dangerous nonsense. She said, 'Of course it was shocking, but in such a sad way. Daisy was hurt, she was just lashing out.'

'All guns firing, I'd say.'

'If you like. But there's nothing between her and Paul, I'm quite sure. There was, years ago, but she chose Luke instead and that was the end of it. Paul is married. Daisy would never . . .' She thought of Paul's mother and stopped, her pulse quickening. She said, 'We shouldn't be talking like this. It's unfair to Daisy. Oh, Molly, you know that, you're her friend, aren't you?'

Molly said, in a neutral voice, 'You know her better than I do.'

'I'm sorry. I didn't mean to suggest . . .'

'Oh yes, you did, quite right, too. One track mind, that's my trouble, though it's not my fault entirely. But I'll keep my trap shut. I would have done, anyway.'

'Of course. I *am* sorry.'

'Aw, come on!' Molly grinned at her suddenly. 'D'you know, Paul Brett bought champagne, too, not the stuff you've got, a couple of bottles of the cheaper variety, but you've helped to pay the rates for the week between the pair of you. Christ, what a thought! Making a profit out of Luke's death. Oh, my God!'

'Life has to go on,' Ruth said. The truth of this trite remark struck her with sickening force. Battered word currency newly minted with meaning. Molly nodded, biting her lip. She opened the counter flap and came up to Ruth. For a moment, Ruth thought she was going to put her arms round her. She tried not to stiffen. Molly was such a warm, natural person, she mustn't rebuff her! But Molly just looked at her with a sad, earnest expression and said, 'Let me give you a hand with those bottles.'

Ruth got into the car. Molly put the champagne on the passenger seat. She said, 'Take care, now.' Ruth said, 'You, too,' meaning it, hoping that Molly knew that she meant it. Driving off, stopping to turn at the next intersection, looking into her mirror, she saw Molly standing at the door of the shop, arms folded, hugging her little breasts under the shepherd's smock, gazing after her with screwed up eyes, a pursed mouth. Ruth thought – I was right, she really is gallant, how can she bear it? The feeling of gratitude for her own happy life that had been growing within her all day, swelled to almost painful proportions, a joyful ache in her stomach.

VII

Daisy sat on the sofa in her ground floor sitting room; Paul sat beside her; Joe on the swivel chair in front of her writing desk. Both were big men, their dark suited bodies heavy and out of place in the small, pretty room; bulky intruders in a feminine boudoir. They made Daisy, who was wearing a high-necked white cotton dress, patterned with summery flower sprigs, appear quite frail and Victorian. Her face was pearly pale, the skin stretched tight over her jaw and cheek bones, a little soft and puffy under her eyes. She looked at Ruth in a vague, out of focus way, as if she were still slightly drunk from her boozy pub lunch with Simon. Or perhaps she had, after all, taken the tranquillisers that Fergus had given her. Paul held her hand on his knee. Joe was twisting the swivel chair, pivoting on his heel restlessly. As Ruth came in (the front door was on the latch) he said, in an irritable voice, 'There you are! I wondered where you had got to!'

'I went to the shop.'

'You might have said you were going.'

'I thought you would know.' Ruth smiled at him. Why was he so cross? She said, equably, 'I wouldn't have gone if Daisy had needed me. I did telephone Georgia.'

'All the same . . .'

Daisy said, 'Don't bully her, Joe. You went to work, didn't you?'

Joe sighed. 'Sorry,' he said. 'Okay, I'm sorry.' He didn't sound it.

Paul gave Daisy back her hand, patting it in a brotherly fashion as he put it into her lap. He stood up, smiling, a tall, ruddy man with receding hair and sharp, blue, hawkish eyes, like his mother's. He said, 'Ruth, my dear,' put his hands on her shoulders and kissed her formally, first on one cheek then on the other. His skin pricked her – he must have shaved very early this morning before setting off in the dawn – otherwise he seemed fresh and uncrumpled as if he had just showered and dressed, scenting himself with some brisk, male cologne. He had never kissed Ruth before; presumably he considered it the right greeting for this solemn occasion. Paul would know what was appropriate in all circumstances, Ruth thought, feeling wild, guilty laughter bubbling inside her. In some societies it was the done thing for a man to take his deceased brother's wife into his home and his bed.

Paul said, 'Thank you so much for going to visit my mother. The dear old soul was enormously grateful.'

Paul's confident manner, his pleasant, calm, authoritative voice, had a curiously hypnotic effect upon Ruth. The picture of Stella Brett that she had in her mind seemed to fade, replaced by the piteous image of a dear old soul, sobbing brokenly, allowing herself to be comforted with cups of strong, sweetened tea. With perhaps just a small dash of medicinal brandy.

She said, 'I really was glad to go, Paul. I'm fond of your mother.' This was the proper, expected answer. Paul nodded, with such a deeply approving sigh that Ruth was tempted to mischief. 'Though I don't know that I was as much help as I would have liked to be. Was she all right when you left her?'

'She seemed to be bearing up quite remarkably. I would have stayed longer, but she was busy cooking, apparently expecting someone to supper.' Paul frowned – that his mother should calmly proceed with her social life after such a catas- trophe didn't quite fit in with his view of things. Then his brow cleared. 'That generation believes in the stiff upper lip. A matter of training and discipline. Carrying on, that's the thing, one has to admire it. Of course she has only had to cope with what one might call an edited version. A straightforward accident – that's what we must stick to. To complicate it with what, after all, is only conjecture, would be wantonly cruel, at her age. We have to remember she is an old woman.'

He spoke as if old people were a different species, Ruth thought. She felt that to keep the truth from Luke's mother was to insult and degrade her. But she was Paul's mother, too. 'I suppose you're right, Paul,' she said meekly.

Daisy said, 'Ruth, I ought to apologise to you. I behaved very badly this morning.' She spoke in a faint, demure voice, her eyes lowered, her large, competent hands clasped in her white cotton lap. Ruth looked at her. Was this contrite act Paul's influence?

Joe said, 'Don't be an ass, Daisy darling. You didn't say anything . . .'

Daisy shook her head helplessly. Joe glanced at Paul and cleared his throat. 'That's to say, nothing that wasn't absolutely forgivable.'

Ruth said, 'How is Georgia?'

'She's gone to a film with your Mark,' Paul said. 'Nice lad, that. Good idea to get Georgia out of the way for a bit. Give Daisy a chance to let go.'

Ruth caught Joe's eye. A swift, private, wry smile would not have been out of place. But Joe looked away, staring into distance, scowling thoughtfully. Suddenly he clapped his hands on his knees and leapt to his feet with a great show of energy. He said, 'Well, now. Do you and Paul want to eat with us, Daisy? I expect Ruth has something laid on. And since Mark is out, we can easily feed the five thousand.'

Paul said, 'I'd planned to take Daisy out. I thought a quiet dinner alone might be the right ticket. And you and Ruth have been quite splendid enough. You've earned a bit of a rest, both of you.' He sat down beside Daisy and put his hand on her shoulder. 'Come on, old lass, buck up a bit, say thank you to these good people.'

'Thank you, Ruth,' Daisy said. She spoke flatly, like an obedient child. Then her voice wobbled a little. 'Thank you, Joe.'

Joe sighed. He bent over Daisy, took her hand for a moment and held it while she smiled up at him weakly.

Simon was walking his dogs in the communal gardens. It was growing dusk now and they bounded before him like shadows, black, graceful hounds of the night. They were strong, healthy young animals but Simon carried a stout walking stick as an extra protection and prided himself on being ready to use it. The growing lawlessness that had taken over the gardens was shocking, but it had given him a role to play that appealed to the romantic side of his nature. He liked this time of the day, watching the lights coming on, his neighbours moving about while he was out here alone, on what he thought of as his Evening Patrol, keeping an eye on the terrace. Especially on the houses where there were women alone.

Simon was sensual, sentimental, and deeply chivalrous. All women to him were frail creatures, weaker vessels, and it hurt him to think of them locking their doors, listening for stealthy sounds in the night, trembling in their beds without the comfort of a strong, male protector beside them. Sometimes he indulged in a sweet, boyish dream in which he met a marauder, made a Citizen's Arrest – it wouldn't be difficult, those sort of criminals were all cowards and bullies – rescued some terrified widow or spinster or maiden. Not a married woman, unless her husband was away, or unfaithful. Even in his fantasies, Simon had principles.

This evening he clasped his stick with more relish than usual. He had had a good, fulfilled day. The morning's dreadful excitement (though one should not think of it like that, it was how he did think of it, and being an honest man he admitted it) had been oddly invigorating. Terrible about Luke Brett, of course, a terrible thing, and he grieved for him genuinely. Luke had been a good chap, a good host, free with his liquor, even if some of his conversation had been a bit above Simon's head. Simon liked a good read, spy stories, adventure, but the books he liked best were his boyhood favourites, Dornford Yates, Buchan and Henty. These authors were not intellectual enough for Luke, probably. A dry stick. Too dull for Daisy, who liked to enjoy life. Poor girl, Simon thought tenderly. He was pleased that he had been able to calm her down lunch time, tell her that she had nothing to blame herself for, all women were liable to fly off the handle at times of emotional stress. They simply didn't have the control that men had. It was a biological difference. Daisy had listened very attentively, he was sure he had comforted her. If Luke's brother hadn't turned up, taken over, he might have been able to comfort her rather more thoroughly. Still, there was time. Once the funeral was over, she would need a man's arms about her. Why not *his* arms?

'Lucky in love', his wife used to say. Dear old Muriel. She had known he would never be unfaithful to her, he despised married men who betrayed their wives in that way, but his thoughts and his eyes had wandered from time to time. And he couldn't help it if women still found him attractive. 'You're such a naughty boy, still,' Muriel would say, stroking his hair when he had confessed some small peccadillo, 'my own, darling boy.'

A wife in a thousand. He missed her quite terribly, his old friend, his chum, his lifelong companion. Nothing had been the same since she'd gone, carried off by that wicked cancer, but he had kept his spirits up, never burdened anyone with the deep, hollow sadness that occasionally visited him. If you wanted to keep your friends, you had to bear up, be agreeable company. Tears were all right in a woman, indeed, they sometimes raised the old pecker, but a weeping man was attractive to no one. Passing the Brett house, he thought of Daisy and felt his loins stirring. But her windows were dark. A bit foolish, he thought, advertising that the house was empty. Better to leave a light on here and there, fit a few time switches. He would look in on Daisy tomorrow and tell her. He marched on, whistling to his dogs and they came at once, fawning about him. 'Heel,' he said, in a crisp, military voice, '*heel*,' and they fell back obediently.

Mrs Costello had left a pot full of cold tea on the side of the sink. Emptying it round the roots of the white camellia at the end of her garden, Ruth saw Simon go past. He brandished his stick at her cheerfully, and she acknowledged his wave, smiling and blushing. Fortunately, it was too dark for him to see her face clearly. Silly to blush, anyway. Simon didn't know what she knew, what Molly had told her. Perhaps she should not have listened. On the other hand to turn a deaf ear to what appeared to be common knowledge was not necessarily virtuous. It might even be priggish. And it had not been just vulgar gossip, since Molly had been talking about herself mostly, such painfully intimate details, baring her hurt soul not only bravely, but easily, naturally. I should not have been so embarrassed, Ruth thought. Although she could never have spoken so freely, perhaps that was a failing, a kind of ingrained, stupid shyness that she ought to get over. Next time she met Molly she must make a true effort to respond with more open friendliness, be more outgoing. Not that there was much in her life of great interest to Molly, certainly nothing to match the appalling confidences Molly had given her, but that didn't matter. A readiness to reach out, to share, was the important thing. She thought, we are all members one of another, that's what I must remember, and went back into her house, smiling happily.

Marigold and Joe were sitting at the table. Ruth arranged the smoked oysters on a dish, decorated them with parsley. She had already cut brown bread and butter.

'What's this for hell's sake?' Marigold said.

'Smoked oysters.'

'Yuck.' Marigold put her hand on her stomach and affected to retch. Joe raised his eyebrows at Ruth.

'Your father likes them,' Ruth said. She sat down and unfolded her napkin. The table looked pretty, she thought. Mrs Costello had picked a bowl of red roses and set out new candles. Ruth had replaced the ordinary glasses with crystal goblets in honour of the champagne. Joe had opened one of the bottles without making any comment. Ruth wondered if he thought it odd of her to have produced it this grief-stricken evening. Would a cheaper wine have been more in keeping? But Joe had not even looked at the label. He sipped from his glass, nodded approval, and started eating his oysters. In silence.

Ruth said brightly, to Marigold, 'You like champagne, don't you, darling? Just one glass for you, so don't drink it too quickly. I'm sorry about the oysters. But there's chicken, and strawberries.'

Marigold smiled at her. She looked beautiful when she smiled, Ruth thought. Mark took after her, but Marigold was like Joe, his full mouth and heavy features fined down in her pretty face, made touchingly feminine.

She said, 'I thought the champagne would relax us a little. I bought it from Molly. She's such a nice woman.'

Neither husband nor daughter seemed to have heard this

remark. Well, of course, there was nothing to *answer*! But the silence seemed loud to Ruth, a boom in her head. *Talk*, she thought, *try and be natural*. Though what could she say? She couldn't tell Joe about Molly's husband in front of Marigold. Nor about Simon. She said, 'I'm glad Paul is here to look after Daisy. He's so solid and competent.'

'Paul's a pompous ass,' Joe said.

He was looking so pale and unhappy, so crushed by his sadness that Ruth was ashamed of what now seemed a frivolous urge to 'make conversation'. She longed to put out her hand to him, put her arms round him, hold his dear head. But it seemed intrusive, impertinent, to try and soothe his pain away as if it were little more than a headache. He was mourning for Luke. His friend's death had hit him much harder than she would have imagined if she had thought about it beforehand. They had been good friends but not soul mates. Luke was not interested in sport and Joe did not care for painting or music. Clearly that sort of thing didn't matter. The bond that held people together was much more mysterious, you couldn't define it.

Marigold said, 'I don't see why I couldn't have gone out with Mark and Georgia. I'd done my homework.' She gulped her champagne and looked mutinous.

Ruth shook her head at her. 'Darling, I'm sorry. But Georgia is so unhappy. Easier for her to have just one person to talk to, don't you think?'

'They're not talking if they go to the cinema. Besides, Luke was my godfather! I'm upset, too!' She looked at Ruth sternly. 'Why did he have a crash? Was he drunk? Mark wouldn't tell me. I don't see why I shouldn't know. I'm not ten years old.'

'It was an accident, Marigold.' Ruth was watching Joe who had pushed his plate of oysters away only half eaten, and was prodding between his teeth with a gum massage stick. She said, 'No one really knows how it happened.'

'If he wasn't drunk, it can't have been his fault, can it? Will the driver of the truck go to prison?'

'I shouldn't think so.'

'Well, I think he ought to.' Marigold's sudden, thunderous scowl made her look even more like her father.

'Accidents happen,' Ruth said, getting up from the table, removing the uneaten oysters. She fetched the chicken and served it, with baked potatoes and salad. No one spoke for a while. By the time Marigold had cleaned her plate, Joe was still pushing his food about. Marigold said, 'Mum, can I take my strawberries to eat in front of the telly? There's something I need to see.'

When she had gone, Ruth said, 'What a child she is still. Children always say I *need* instead of I *want*!'

Joe looked at the ceiling. 'Must she turn that thing on so loud? She isn't deaf, is she?'

'It's her generation. They've got used to a certain level of sound. Shall I ask her to turn it down?'

'Oh, for God's sake. What the hell does it matter?' He looked at her, his eyes bright with anguish. 'I'm sorry, I can't finish this chicken.'

'Would you like strawberries? Or Brie? I bought a nice piece of Brie from Molly. And some peaches in brandy. I could open those if you like.'

'Brie, I think. What came over you? Fancy peaches? Champagne?'

'I don't know. Yes, I do.' Her heart began to beat very fast. She sat straight in her chair. 'I felt, suddenly – well, not *suddenly*, I've been thinking all day, since this morning, how lucky I am, how lucky *we* are, so lucky and happy to be here, safe together, loving each other, so much of our lives still in front of us. So I wanted to celebrate that. I don't think Luke would mind if he knew. In fact, knowing him, I think he'd be glad. He'd know it doesn't mean we don't *care* . . .'

Joe said nothing. He poured the last of the champagne into their glasses, giving Ruth a little more than he gave himself. Then he put his elbows on the table and looked at her with a strange, deep, serious expression, as if he were trying to read her face, trying to see her more clearly. She thought – Of course! He feels as I do! We are both suddenly more aware of each other!

She felt such love for him, it was a huge, aching, joyful pain filling her. Then a sharp, shaking, sexual need. She wanted to say, 'Please, my love, take me to bed.' But he was looking so sad. And Marigold would know what they were up to if they rushed upstairs, leaving the remains of the meal on the table. Children were so embarrassed by that sort of thing. She might be nervous of going up to her room in the attic, passing their door. *Wait*, Ruth told herself, *there is plenty of time*. She felt faint at the thought of the long night before them.

She said, 'Joe, darling, I know how dreadful you must feel about Luke. I'm so sorry.'

'Oh, God!' He put his head in his hands. 'I don't want to talk about it.'

'It might be better to talk. I know that it's difficult. But it helps to share things sometimes. I loved Luke, too. Maybe not as deeply as you did, but enough to understand.'

Joe groaned. He said, in a muffled voice, 'You can't possibly. Oh, my dear Christ! I feel so bloody responsible.'

'Darling, how can you be? Except in the sense that we all are. All his friends. If we'd known he was feeling so desperate . . .'

Joe was moving his head up and down in his hands, tugging at his hair with his fingers. He mumbled, 'Leave it alone, do you mind?'

Ruth unwrapped the Brie. It was running creamily at the edges. She pushed it towards him with a clean plate, a clean fork. Joe ate cheese like a Frenchman, without bread or biscuits.

He lifted his head from his hands and looked at her. Although his face was ravaged, his rumpled hair made him look young and vulnerable. He said, rather abruptly, 'You're so good, Ruth. Such a nice person. I don't deserve you.'

She laughed nervously. 'I'm not really nice, Joe! I'm a mess, really. A lot of untidy bits and pieces. It's only with you I feel whole.' The truth of this seemed suddenly awesome. She said, 'I owe you so much, besides loving you.'

He stared at her – again with that long, solemn, searching look. This time it puzzled her. Why didn't he respond to her, say something, speak? The love and joy she was feeling was so immense. Couldn't he feel it, bursting out of her, reaching out to him? Perhaps not. Men were different from women. Love and sex meant much less to them. One thing at a time. He was grieving for Luke. She must respect that, allow him space to grieve quietly.

She got up from the table, took the dirty plates to the sink. Mrs Costello would put them into the dishwasher tomorrow. Returning to the table she stood beside Joe who was eating his Brie, gazing in front of him. Very gently, she touched his untidy hair, meaning to stroke it lovingly back into place, but he jerked away from her hand. An instinctive, flinching movement.

She said, 'Oh!'

'Sorry!' He smiled at her, an odd, effortful smile, his eyes watching her sorrowfully. He looked guilty, ashamed. She felt suddenly cold, a sweaty chill breaking out all over her body. She said, 'I didn't mean to make you jump.'

He took her hand and squeezed it. 'I was just miles away.'

'Thinking of Luke?'

'Well. Luke. Daisy, too.'

'Poor Daisy, we must do all we can.'

'Yes.'

'I mean, nothing can really help, I suppose, not in any deep way, but we can just try and be there whenever she wants us, make sure that she knows that we love her.'

He nodded. He said, yawning, 'Christ, I'm so tired. It's been such a long day. I hope Mark has remembered to take his front door key. I really must sleep.'

Mark and Georgia sat in the Gate cinema in Bloomsbury, watching an Hungarian film dubbed into German with English subtitles. Mark was holding Georgia's hand, stroking the palm with his finger. On the screen a black girl, playing the part of a dancing teacher, was writhing naked on a rug with a handsome young actor. Georgia closed her eyes. It was dreadfully embarrassing to be watching this kind of scene with Mark sitting beside her. People shouldn't be allowed to make films like that, really. Sex was disgusting. Not holding hands, the way Mark was holding her hand was gentle and comforting, but *more* was quite horrible, the way people went on, moaning and clutching and fumbling. She had heard her father and mother in their bedroom one night. She hadn't wanted to listen but she couldn't help it. Her mother was refusing to make love with her father and her father was moaning and weeping. Now he was dead. A suffocating feeling rose up in her as if her throat was filled with dry, fibrous material. *Oh Dad, oh my Dad!* Her foul mother, she thought. Yet she loved her, if not quite as much as she loved her father. How could her father have been so weak and so feeble? He shouldn't have stood for it. He should have bashed her up, beaten her. No, he would never have done that. He was such a gentle man. He could never have hurt anyone. This film she was watching, that Mark said was 'tremendously brilliant', was all about people being cruel to each other, about the Nazis in Germany years ago, before the war. The Nazis had beaten people up, Jews, and black people, and gypsies, buried them alive, put them in gas ovens. It would serve her mother right if something like that happened to her! Oh, she mustn't think that, it was wicked, she loved her mother. Could you love people if you felt this huge, dark rage against them? She must stop feeling it. It was terrible, frightening. . .

Mark was offering her something. 'Like a cigarette, Georgia?'

'I don't smoke. It gives you lung cancer.'

'Not for years and years,' Mark said. 'Anyway, we all have to die sometime.'

Georgia started to cry, very softly. Mark made a grunting sound in his throat. He cradled her close and said, 'What is it, baby?'

She rested her head on his shoulder. She whispered, 'I can't tell you.'

Mark's fingers were stroking her cheek. He said, 'You can tell me anything. I love you. You know that, don't you?'

Ruth was standing in the shower when Stella Brett spoke to her. Stella's voice was quite unmistakable – clear, incisive, in an old-fashioned, upper-class way. It appeared to come from the shower tap. She said, 'If my husband couldn't bear me to touch him, if he hadn't made love to me for over a year, there is only one question I'd want to ask him.'

Ruth soaped her breasts and her belly, feeling for the moment merely startled and curious. She must have been thinking of Stella. But she hadn't been – or not consciously. She reminded herself that Rude Ruthie had sometimes startled her by speaking in a loud, common way, an impish street child, shouting insults. And her grown up companion had often assumed other voices, merrily teasing or sharp, particularly when speaking thoughts Ruth did not care to acknowledge. But this was a new development. Ruth said, 'So we're turning into a ventriloquist, are we?' She turned off the shower tap. 'That's enough of that, thank you.'

She stepped out of the shower and dried herself carefully. This must not happen again. She said, to her intimate, 'Don't play funny games, please. And speak when you're spoken to in the future, if you don't mind. And try not to be so crude and naïve. That remark was both, wasn't it?'

She dropped the towel and looked at herself in the mirror. Her cheeks were flushed, her body white and still pretty, her small breasts neat and firm. She pulled off her shower cap and her long braid flopped down. She unfastened it with her fingers, letting her hair fall loose on her shoulders. She smiled cautiously at her reflection and picked up a lipstick. With it, she drew a line round her nipples. They stood up at once, like hard, pinky brown buds. She opened the door of the bathroom and listened. No sound from Marigold's bedroom above. Ruth drew a shaky breath and walked naked across the landing.

Joe was sitting up in bed, reading. He looked at her over his glasses and felt under the pillow on her side of the bed. He said, 'Want your nightie?'

Ruth shook her head. She sat down beside him. He gave her a vague smile, thrust her nightdress towards her, and went back to his book.

Ruth said, 'Darling . . .'

He looked up again, frowning. 'What is it?'

Her mouth was dry. She said, with great difficulty, 'Am I so very ugly?'

This time he looked at her suspiciously. 'What an odd – no, of course not. I just thought you'd catch cold.' He patted her knee.

'Listen,' she said. 'Please. Just for a minute.'

He put his book down on the table, dog-earing the page, took off his glasses and placed them in their leather case slowly and carefully. Then he lay back on the pillows and smiled at her in a kind, resigned way that made her resolution falter. It would be easier, perhaps even wiser, to put her nightdress on, get into bed, pick up her own book. She was enjoying it. The latest Saul Bellow. She was probably tired, though she didn't feel it, but with luck she would sleep. With luck, even the merry making of the couple next door wouldn't wake her.

She said, 'Would you like a brandy, Joe?'

'I don't think so. No. Do you want one?'

She nodded, slipped off the bed and went down one flight of stairs. There were two large, gilt-framed mirrors on the wall of the stair well, and another outside the drawing room door. She saw her white, naked body, pale as moonlight in the mirrors and, as she went into the drawing room, the Ultra Sonic movement detector, positioned above the arch, facing the balcony window, took note of her presence. The burglar alarm was not on, she had refused to let Joe turn it on at night, turning the house into a prison, but the detector still clicked, flashing little red dots of light as she passed it. A not un-friendly, watching eye. Ruth poured a large brandy, went back to the bedroom and said in a bright and sociable voice, 'I hadn't realised how many mirrors we had in this house until now.'

'Perhaps you don't look at yourself as often as I do.'

'Why do you?'

'I don't know. To reassure myself that I exist, I suppose.' Joe spoke in a tone of rueful self-denigration.

Ruth swigged at her brandy. Dutch courage. She said, 'I love you, Joe, that's the first thing. You seem so unhappy. I do want to help you. Is it just Luke? Or is something else worrying you?'

'I don't know.'

She said, slowly, 'I really mean, I suppose, is there someone else?'

He moved his head fretfully, side to side on the pillow. 'You ought to know better than to ask such a question.'

He sounded angry. She said, 'I didn't mean to upset you. It's just that you haven't, I mean, you don't seem . . .' She stopped. There were some things too hard to say. She compromised. 'Do you love me?'

'I think so.' He dragged the words out, watching her. She couldn't read his expression. Sly or shy? Shamed? Regretful?

She said, 'Do you love someone else more?' Terror seized her. 'Oh, I'm sorry, so sorry to ask, I don't want to know, but please tell me. I mean, I *must* know.'

'Oh, God! Well, perhaps. I don't know. Not love *more*, I think. Only differently.'

She finished the brandy and put the glass down. She couldn't look at him. She had gulped the brandy too fast and it made her belch. She said, covering her mouth, 'Sorry!' And then, very carefully, 'Why didn't you tell me?'

'I didn't want you to be hurt. You're my wife, my dear friend.' He sounded almost comically mournful. 'I do love you.'

'But you don't want to – to fuck me?' This was the first time in her life she had used this word. She said, blushing, 'Is that the difference?'

'Oh, I don't know. I don't know.' He took her hand, fondled it. He said, 'It's more complex than that. I can't explain. I really *don't know*, as I said. I'm so tired. And, though you may not believe me, so *sorry*.'

She wanted to snatch her hand away. Instead, she removed it quite gently, touching his cheek with her finger. She stood up to put on her nightdress, covering the hideous body that he found so repellent, disgusting. She fought back her tears. She said, 'How long has it been?'

'Oh, Christ! Must you?'

'Please tell me.'

'It won't help.'

'I want to know, all the same.'

His sad eyes reproached her. She was merciless. A cruel torturer, applying thumb screws, the rack. 'Eighteen months. Two years, maybe.'

'Who is she?'

'I can't answer that. What can I say? Name, rank and number? Just a girl. Well, a woman.'

'Younger than me?'

'Does that matter?' He looked at her ruefully, with such evident pain now, that she started to cry. He reached out for her, gathering her close, rocking her, pressing her head down on his shoulder. He said, 'I'm so sorry, so sorry.'

Tears eased her a little. She longed to stay in his arms but it seemed undignified since he didn't want her. She withdrew, got into the bed on her own side and lay on her back, legs stiff, arms stiff at her side. Joe put out the light. Headlamps from passing cars patterned the ceiling.

'How often do you see her?'

'I don't know.'

She laughed faintly. 'Well, you know how often you see her better than I do.'

'Three or four times a week, maybe. Something like that.'

'Where do you meet?'

'Oh, here and there. Pubs. The Tate Gallery.' He sounded as if this was all infinitely tedious. Boring. Ruth felt sorry, and angry.

She said, 'Why?'

'I wish I knew. Oh, dear God, I didn't want this to happen. I feel as if my head was a rusty tin, perched on top of my body. That's why, I suppose. Middle-aged man, male menopause, old age galloping towards me like an express train. So shabby

106

and ordinary. Just one thing. She has always known I would never leave you.'

'You told her that, did you?'

'I think so.'

'How kind!'

'Don't sneer. Oh, I'm sorry, sneer if you want to, you have every right. Only not too much, please. It will only alienate me. Push me away from you.'

'You've done that already.'

'Don't sound so desolate.'

'I can't help it. I feel so . . .' What did she feel? Cold, she thought, *cold*. As if some vessel inside her had cracked, spilling out icy water. Her heart broken. She wondered who had first put those two words so felicitously together to express how she felt now. She wished she knew how to behave, what to say. Should she scream, rage, wail, cry? Would that be the natural thing to do? More natural, surely, than this strange, stilted conversation. But there were small babies next door, the other side of the thin wall, and Marigold was sleeping above them. She said, 'I feel scared. Sort of physically frightened.' That was near enough. If it were only that, she could bear it. She had borne it before.

'I won't leave you,' Joe said. Not heroically or resentfully, but quietly and calmly, stating a positive fact.

'That's what they all say,' her voice said inside her. 'That's what they all say to begin with.' Stella speaking? 'Shut up, stay out of this,' Ruth answered silently. Of course she believed Joe. She had always trusted him. She must continue to trust him. Or there was nothing.

He said, 'Unless you want me to go, of course.'

Was there hope in his voice? No. It was something he had to say, the polite thing, the courteous thing. For form's sake. He didn't really imagine she could live without him. He was such a wonderful, desirable person. *Well*, she thought, *he still is, to me.* Though perhaps not for very much longer.

He groped for her hand. His hand was warm, a bit sticky, very familiar. A broad palm, long fingers, with little, gingery hairs growing on the backs of them. If she felt a hundred hands in the dark, she would know which was his hand, the moment she touched it. This hand, this same hand, had held another woman's – in pubs, in the Tate Gallery. Three or four times a week. How had Joe found the time? He was always so busy. The Tate Gallery would have been *her* suggestion, presumably. Joe was not interested in art. Somewhere else, somewhere more private (at her flat? An hotel?) this hand had stroked breasts, tickled ear lobes, pushed thighs apart. She thought, *I don't believe it, it isn't happening, it isn't true, I am not believing it, in a moment it will not be true. Please God make him say it's not true . . .*

She said, 'No. I don't want you to go. I love you.'

'Thank you. I do thank you for saying that.' He sighed very deeply. 'Now I can tell you. It's over. I mean, I think that this other thing's over. If you had asked me to leave, I wouldn't have told you, it would have been blackmail.'

She wondered if she believed this. Her mind seemed suspended above her body, like a bird hovering. Poor, silly bird, not knowing which way to fly. She thought – the thought came from nowhere – *Sins come home to roost, this is my punishment. He has waited all this time to punish me through Joe, a worse punishment than a stick or a strap. But I have tried. I have tried to be good. It's not fair.*

Joe said, 'The stupid thing, the incredibly stupid thing is that you need never have known. If you hadn't forced me to tell you, I would almost certainly have given her up. I was moving towards it. We would have been spared this. You would have been spared it.'

'I don't want to be spared. I'd only want not to know if it hadn't happened. But it has, and I do know, so we have to start from there, don't we? You must tell me more. Everything. What she's like, how you felt when you started. . . Well, perhaps I can guess that. But I want to know how you feel now. What you mean when you say that you *think* it is over.'

'I don't know.'

'You must know.'

'Please,' he said, 'don't. Don't force me any more, don't strip me naked. Leave me some pride, for God's sake. Just accept it if you can, give me time. Oh, I know you must feel bitter, hurt and resentful, I deserve that, but don't. . .' A deep, groaning sigh. He said, 'I'm so desperately tired.'

She said, sharply, 'I'm sorry you're tired. But there's this other − person. Just a shape, a shadow to me, a kind of unknown enemy, don't you see? It isn't just curiosity, though I suppose that's there on one level. Fairness, too. After all, she must know about *me*. But it's more than that. As the children say, I really do *need* to know.'

'What good would it do? Oh, dear God, I've told you it's almost over. Just let it be now, don't push me. If you really do love me.'

'*That*'s blackmail,' she said. She felt a restless energy pulsing through her, stomach churning, heart racing. There was a hard lump in her chest. Indigestion. Her body had its own life, her mind had no control over it, had burst through the top of her head, was flapping about distractedly, beating its wings against the walls of the room. She said, 'I'm sorry. I want to be calm and sensible. I love you, I don't want to hurt you, but you can't just leave it like this, turn over and go to sleep. It's not fair.'

'Not fair? Christ alive, of course it's not fair, life isn't fair, what can I do about it? For pity's sake, Ruth, I'm as shocked as you are.'

He was trembling, the whole bed was shaking. She said, 'Please tell me. Not everything, if you really can't bear it, but something, a crumb or two. After all, you've had all this time to get used to something that is quite new for me. It may be ending for you. But it's just beginning for me, don't you see that?'

It amazed her that they were still holding hands. Disgusted her, too. But when she tried to pull away he laced his fingers tighter. He said, in a helpless voice, 'All right, if that's the way that you want it. I warn you it will only make things much worse. As long as you understand that. What exactly is it that you want to know?'

VIII

Ruth stood behind Paul in the second pew from the front in the crematorium chapel. Paul's back, in a dark, cashmere jacket, hid the coffin from her, hid the ramp along which Luke's body would slowly jerk in a minute, through the blue curtains at the end, into the furnace. Stella Brett stood beside Paul, leaning on his arm, her head slightly bowed in the correct posture for a broken old mother. (Wily old thing, Ruth thought. Or had Paul imposed this act on her?) Daisy was on Paul's other side, erect in a dark purple cloak Ruth had made for her years ago, her gleaming head hatless. Then Georgia, wearing white. 'In the East,' she had said to Ruth before they entered the chapel, 'white is the colour of mourning.' Paul's wife, in a navy suit creased across her plump back, stood with her children, a boy and a girl, in a pew on the other side of the aisle. Behind them were Ben and Molly and Simon, and further back, on both sides of the chapel, other friends, colleagues, men from the Company.

Ruth observed all these placements as if from inside a transparent balloon. She had drunk (secretly, quickly) a large glass of brandy before leaving the house, finishing, she had been surprised to see, a bottle that had been almost full a few days before. Well, she'd had need of it. *Brandy*, she thought now, *the natural anaesthetic*. You could build up a good advertising campaign on those lines. Luke, so the autopsy had shown, had been anaesthetised, too. His blood had been swimming in alcohol, the equivalent (Paul had told Joe) of at least a bottle of whisky. It made his death, if not totally accidental, at least only half deliberate. Luke had lost his job, his marriage – for whatever reason, his fault, or Daisy's – lay in ruins about him. He had got drunk, drowning his sorrows, then perhaps knowing he was unfit to drive, scrupulous about that even in his deep, drunken misery, had staggered along the motorway, trying to clear his head, or get a lift to a telephone. Or perhaps he had hoped to die. Perhaps he had felt as she did, Ruth thought, that the past was negated, cancelled, rubbed out, the future hopelessly dark.

Did she feel that? Words, she thought, words. What she felt above all was physical shock, an inward chill spreading from her heart and lungs outward, like some rampant illness, a rampaging cancer. And yet she had moved about, cooked, smiled, walked the dog, helped Daisy prepare the food the guests would eat after the funeral, ironed Joe's black tie, looked through her children's closets for suitable garments. She would go on like that, she assumed, no one would notice there was anything wrong, smiling, talking, a peripheral person, an animated shell. Perhaps Luke had not been able to face that kind of half life. I am stronger than Luke, Ruth thought, I have been taught by a master. She didn't equate Joe with her father, but these last three days she had begun to fear him in a way that was not altogether dissimilar, watching him, judging his words and his silences, summoning up the endurance she had learned in her childhood, preparing herself for the next cruel assault, knowing that she could and would somehow live through it. She would live through this, she supposed. For the children's sake, perhaps even for Joe's, if he wanted or needed her.

She loved Joe, she told herself, nothing could change that. If only he would talk to her about how he was feeling, about what he thought had gone wrong between them. Perhaps shame and guilt held him back. But it seemed to her that he resented her questions, answering only a few of them, grudgingly, like a sullen adolescent caught out in some misdemeanour.

Eunice Pilbeam was his mistress's name he had finally, very reluctantly, told her. She was a physiotherapist with a surgery 'somewhere in Harley Street'. He had been vague about the exact address and since he had so loudly and often voiced his disapproval of private medicine, Ruth wondered if he were ashamed that Eunice was not working in a National Health hospital. When she had asked if they had made love in her consulting room (picturing Joe's plump, freckled behind bouncing up and down on a hard, narrow, orthopaedic bed) he had denied it indignantly as if she had accused Eunice of professional malpractice. She was an Englishwoman who had spent most of her working life in Canada, divorced her 'brute of a husband' after a long, childless, unhappy marriage, and come home 'very bravely' to make a new life for herself. She had no family and few friends in London. She was no longer young, in her mid-thirties, and very lonely. 'She is more alone than you can imagine,' Joe said, rather reprovingly.

This was all he had been prepared to say. 'Do you talk about me?' Ruth had asked, feeling exposed, invaded. He had shaken his head. Had he told her that his marriage was unhappy, that he and Ruth no longer made love? 'Oh, Christ, I don't know, I may have done, I can't remember.' Was he still seeing her? 'Oh, for God's sake! I've told you it's *over*. But she's so distressed, I can't just *dump* her, it would be horribly callous. So give me a bit of time, don't ask me about her, don't *ask*. It's destructive. Destroying *our* chances.'

Well, perhaps he owed this lonely woman some loyalty. But Ruth was greedy for knowledge. On the one hand she saw it as greed and deplored it. On the other, since Eunice presumably knew about her, seeing her as the unwanted wife, a duped enemy to be cheated, outwitted, why should *she* be kept in the dark? Was it so wrong to be curious? In what she had begun to think of as her 'other world', the world that now seemed to hold more than one intimate, a whole sisterhood, speaking in a variety of voices, angry, vulgar and bitter, Ruth hated this stranger who had spied on her life, had no doubt she was right to. She couldn't have loved Joe, watching him grow older and wearier all this last year, drained by the double life she was forcing upon him, blackmailing him with her loneliness, her vulnerability. She must be cold, grasping. In some countries, women like her were stoned in the market place, was what Stella, who had a wide knowledge of such foreign customs, had said. Other, unattributed voices said cruder things, aching cunt on the prowl, thief, wrecker, snatcher. But Ruth rationed the time that she spent with these allies as she rationed the cigarettes she had begun to smoke secretly, hiding the pack from Joe, opening the windows when she heard his key in the door. Most of the day she held on to herself, the real Ruth, alone, a committed non-smoker, steadied just a little with brandy, trying to hang on to her love for Joe, her true, if now painful love, telling herself that if Joe had been (or still was) in love with this Eunice, then she couldn't possibly be all the hateful things that Stella and all the other Ruths called her. Joe would never love a cold, grasping creature, not even an amiable tart. Eunice must be all the things Ruth was not – generous, open-hearted, more beautiful, a much better lover. Though it wasn't the sexual side that hurt so much as the length of time Joe had loved her, keeping his love a sweet, precious, untarnished secret, for so long, all these *years*, sitting in pubs, wandering round the Tate Gallery, holding hands with this clever, amusing and beautiful woman, gazing into her eyes with glorious, free, gleaming affection. *Looking at her the way he once looked at me*, Ruth thought, at Luke's funeral, and felt the hot tears on her cheeks. She let them fall. It didn't matter if anyone saw her, it was right and proper to cry at this moment. *I ought to be ashamed*, she thought, *to be using dead Luke in this way, pretending to be weeping for him when I am weeping for my own loss, my own disappointment.* But she felt no real shame. Guilt of that silly kind had quite left her now.

Joe was nudging her. He slipped her the handkerchief out of his breast pocket – a generous gesture, since he disliked his 'good' handkerchief being blown on, keeping an inferior rag for this sort of use in his trouser pocket. He smiled at her with tender encouragement, put an arm round her and squeezed her briefly against him. He whispered, 'Hang on, soon over now.'

Did he really imagine that her tears were for Luke? It would be convenient for him to believe that so he probably did. Perhaps she should be grateful for Joe's surface simplicity, for his practical nature, even for his somewhat insensitive kindness. As long as she didn't question him about Eunice or about his own feelings, he was kind and considerate. He had written her a short, loving letter, left it on her pillow with a red rose. She was his dear wife, his companion, he was sorry he'd hurt her, but she was in no way at fault, it had been nothing to do with any failure of hers. The letter had made her cry but it had not consoled her. Better if he had berated her for something done or not done. For not taking enough interest in his job, in the legal complexities of mineral rights, in the amount of compensation paid to men injured through their own carelessness on the oil rigs? Well, Joe was not interested in women's dresses! But to be without guilt left you powerless.

All the same she had thanked him for his letter, sobbed in his arms, been grateful when he had finally, gently, made love to her. She had had an orgasm and thought, I ought to feel humiliated by this husbandly favour, that is the natural thing, I ought at least to be angry. But she was too afraid that anger would 'alienate' him, that he would leave her. Afterwards, he had kissed her so sweetly, holding her lovingly, whispering to her, making plans for their future. They would go the theatre

115

more often, spend more time together, dine out alone at least one night a week, drive into the country for weekends. Marigold was quite old enough to leave now, and Mark was responsible. In the autumn, or next spring, when things had 'settled' a little, they would have a really good holiday. A trip down the Nile? Egyptology had always fascinated her, hadn't it?

The energy with which he was making these plans alarmed her. He seemed to be bouncing ahead of her like a light rubber ball, while she felt so heavy, limbs leaden with sadness. She had said she would love to do all these things. But she dreaded them, really. Could she keep it up, her smiling, calm acquies-cence in the new life he saw them as making? Could she believe he was honest? She was afraid, not only of Joe, but of her own turmoil. Disbelief, sorrow, rage – the chaotic fragmentation inside her own head frightened her. Could she bear it?

Of course I can, I am strong, she thought, proudly, drunkenly, as the piped organ music began to play and the coffin (peering round Paul she could see it now) began to move down the ramp. Then, at that moment, Daisy looked round. Dry-eyed – but her mouth was slack with despair. *Oh, Daisy, poor darling*, Ruth thought, *if we do go to Egypt, she must come with us*. Georgia, too; she and Daisy could share a cabin. If Daisy would like that. It would be something to offer her, some small, practical comfort. Daisy would be quite badly off, Joe had said, only half of Luke's pension, though perhaps the Company could be persuaded to make some adjustment as she had Georgia to look after still, send to college. Joe thought there was some special fund, had promised to look into it for her. They could easily pay for her holiday, Ruth thought, if she'd let them, and surely, *surely* Daisy would not deny them this pleasure.

Ruth was weeping, with a kind of happiness now. She couldn't bear to make plans for herself, but she could make plans for Daisy. As the congregation began to file out of the chapel, Paul, turning round, saw Ruth's tears. Walking down the aisle at her side, he grasped her arm in a comradely fashion. He said, in a husky voice, bending down to her, 'Bless you, Ruth, you really did love him!'

She hoped he couldn't smell the brandy on her breath. She smiled up at him weakly. They walked up the aisle into the chilly June sunshine. At the door he released her and said, 'I think, the form is, we have to look at the flowers now.'

The congregation stood in little groups, looking at the wreaths, the bunches of roses, laid out behind a small notice. Luke Arthur Brett. Ruth had not known his middle name until now. This was a formality to be got through, somehow lacking the comfort of gravesides. The flowers would go to the hospital, or an old people's home, a pity to waste them, of course, but they should be left on the heaped earth, to wither and die. Ruth put on a bright face, a fixed smile. Molly, wearing a long, black, granny dress, was talking to Marigold, saying something, making the child laugh. Ben put a hand on her shoulder and she turned to him. Ruth saw him touch Marigold's chin with his finger, tilting her face up to his, smiling down at her. Ruth moved towards them, intending to rescue her daughter from Molly's horrible husband, but Stella Brett, looking weary and ravaged in the clear sunlight, appeared at her elbow. Ruth was startled to see this old woman whose sharp, disembodied voice played such a lively part in her 'other world' standing beside her, wearing a mangy fur coat, quite bare in places, and an old, knitted, mauve turban a little too large for her, cobbled up on one side with a diamond clasp. For a moment she half expected to hear her speak as she did in her mind. But all Stella said was, 'Ruth, my dear, let me introduce my friend, Walter. Mrs Aberdare, Walter Scully. Walter was kind enough to drive me.'

Ruth shook hands with a small, elderly man who said,

'Pleased to meet you,' with a slight *clack* of loose dentures. And then, nodding towards the flowers, 'Beautiful floral tributes. Of course, it's the right time for roses.'

Paul said, behind them, 'Time to get into the car, I think, Mother. You'll catch cold in this wind.'

Stella said, 'I'm going with Walter, dear. He'll bring me back to the house for a little while but we can't stay too long. Walter borrowed his son's car and he has to return it. Besides, there is the dog to consider.'

Paul blinked. 'All right, Mother. Thank you, Mr Scully. Ruth, would you like to come with me? There's a seat in my car.'

'If you like. Though what about Daisy?' Oh, of course, Paul wouldn't want to take Daisy, not if his wife was in the car with him. Ruth blushed. She said, 'Thank you, Paul.'

She followed him towards his car, a low, beautiful, silver Porsche. His family were crushed in the back, his wife's knees almost under her chin. 'You remember Ruth, don't you, dear?' he said as he helped Ruth into the passenger seat, courteously tucking her coat inside before he closed the door.

'Judy,' his plump wife said, smiling. A firm smile, a tough, confident face with sharp eyes like polished black buttons. In Ruth's head, Stella spoke with a chuckle. 'Daisy will have hell's own job winkling Paul out of that marriage. Judy would make minced meat of her. Beat her to a pulp, shouldn't wonder.'

Ruth murmured, 'I ought to tell Joe . . .' But Paul was already in the driver's seat, starting the engine. She saw Joe with Georgia, Marigold, Daisy. He looked like a cheerfully contented middle-aged man with his harem. He saw her and waved. Paul said, 'Put your seat belt on, Ruth, do you mind? I'm afraid I always insist on it.'

She buckled her seat belt. Through the window, the sun was quite hot, making her sleepy. She heard Judy say, from a distance, 'Who is that funny, common little man with your mother, Paul?'

'God knows. Some old crony. She's a bit of an eccentric, is Mother. I wish you'd speak to her about her clothes, Judy. I wish she wouldn't wear that diamond clasp. She'll get mugged if she isn't careful.'

'No one would think it was real, Paul. Not on that terrible hat.'

Ruth closed her eyes, feeling her chin nodding forward. Well, why not doze a bit? This was a tiring occasion. She must gather her strength for the funeral party. Luke's family, his friends from the Company. At once, she was wide awake. How many of Joe's colleagues knew about Eunice? Joe had said no one knew, speaking with absolute assurance, as if when together they had worn invisible cloaks. He, of course, had told no one, and Eunice had been discreet too, for his sake. Noble Eunice! Naïve Joe! No, not naïve, deliberately denying reality. Of course people must know. Men at work. His own secretary. Joe had been late home sometimes but not all that often, so presumably the assignations had been during his lunch hour. Friends would have noticed he no longer joined them in the club bar, drawn the obvious conclusion. Old Joe is having a bit on the side. Winks and nudges. Though perhaps this sort of entanglement was so common among men of his age, no one bothered to comment. But they knew, all the same. At Daisy's house, in a minute, they would smile at her kindly. The betrayed, poor little wife. Well, not *poor*. Was that why Joe wanted to stay with her? Oh, God, she thought, trembling, palms sweating, that's what they all will be saying. *Canny old Joe knows which side his bread is buttered!*

'You all right, Ruth?' Paul said. The car had stopped. He was opening the passenger door, looking solicitously at her. She nodded, unable to speak, swung her legs out, stood up, put one foot in front of the other. She had always disliked parties, and her dislike now had an extra dimension. Though it was trivial, really. What mattered was the *fact*, the horrible *fact*, not who knew about it. The awful thing was that trivial fears, minor pains, were so hard to sort out from the real grief, the deep, the heart-clutching anguish. Joe did not acknowledge this anguish, that was the most hurtful thing. He had said, in his practical way, 'You have nothing to worry about. I have elected to stay with you, doesn't that show that I love you?'

Elected, she thought, *what a word! So vulgarly pompous!* And then, suddenly, childishly, *Joe should be here with me now, he should know how scared I am, meeting these people* . . .

She was talking and smiling quite normally. Daisy's basement room was crowded, the back door open onto the garden. Molly was pouring tea, passing sandwiches, bright and alert and youthful in her dark granny dress, the bodice unbuttoned now, to show her white throat and the swell of her breasts. As she passed Ruth she winked at her. 'Who is that pretty woman?' someone said. Ruth looked up at the stranger beside her. No – not a stranger, one of the men who had been at Luke's farewell dinner. Did he know about Joe and his physiotherapist? Ruth smiled at him, not answering his question becuase he was already moving away. In pursuit of Molly? Ruth kept her smile fixed on her face, looking round for her children, for Joe. No sign of Marigold (she hoped Ben hadn't got hold of her) but Mark was with Georgia, out in the garden, the girl's white dress billowing. She heard Joe's laugh, though she couldn't see him. A lot of people seemed to be laughing. The relieved hilarity that follows a funeral.

Simon said, 'Ruth, you look as if you could do with this.'

She took the cup he held out to her. Sipped at it. He laughed at her surprised face. 'That's right! Whisky! Looks like milk-less tea, an old dodge. Come and sit down. I think you feel a bit groggy.'

His hand was on her arm, shepherding her, his eyes watching her earnestly. Sympathetic hazel eyes, very kind. Widow's Comforter, she thought, longing to laugh out loud suddenly. Well, what had happened to her was a kind of bereavement. Even if Simon didn't know, perhaps he had sensed it. Perhaps bereft women gave off a scent, a kind of chemical odour. She said, with a faint, breathless giggle, 'I shouldn't, you know, I had a simply enormous brandy before the funeral,' feeling his breath on her cheek as he sat down on the sofa beside her, his shoulder and arm touching hers, exerting a light but unmistakable pressure, wondering if he *did* know, but at this moment, not caring.

Simon said, 'Hair of the dog, then, don't suppose it'll hurt you.' And then, searching her face, 'You look lovely, Ruth, but then you always do. Always elegant!'

Simon's lowering tone turned this innocent compliment into a declaration. Leaning against him, drinking her whisky, Ruth felt herself opening to him. If they were alone, she would let him tear her clothes off. What would it be like? Joe was the only man she had ever made love to. Joe was circumcised. Once, when she was waiting to see the dentist, she had read an article in a woman's magazine that said it was more exciting to be made love to by a man with a foreskin, that the foreskin 'caressed' the vagina. Did Simon have a foreskin? Would it caress her? Would he be violent, or gentle? Whatever she wanted, she guessed. According to Molly, he was a skilled operator. A good stud. But surely he wouldn't suggest such a thing, not at a *funeral*! Nor would she listen, of course! She sat up straight, so they were no longer touching, and said, 'Thank you, Simon. For the whisky. I suppose funerals always make one act a bit oddly. I wasn't sure whether Marigold ought to go, really. Luke was her godfather. But she gets so emotional.'

'Is there anything wrong with that?'

'She's only sixteen.'

'Girls of that age are always testing their feelings, I think. I suspect, in a way, she'll have enjoyed the experience. Even if she is grieving for Luke, truly and deeply, the ritual will have helped her. It's very important to know how to mourn.' He looked at her gravely. 'Why are you smiling?'

She said, flustered, 'Just because you're kind, Simon. I really spoke, oh, I don't know, without thinking, and you answered me properly.'

'Didn't you expect me to?'

'People don't always – I mean, they make conventional noises.'

'So do I, sometimes. I'm a conventional bloke, straight up and down. But you're not a girl for party chatter, I think.'

He took her hand, looked at it thoughtfully, and set it down on her knee. Then he sprang up, clicking his heels to attention. 'D'you want any more milkless tea? I'd be happy to get it.'

'No thank you, Simon.'

'If you change your mind, send me a signal. Meantime, I think I ought to go and help Daisy a bit. Pull my weight. Even though I'd much rather sit here with you, out of the old hurly burly.'

She watched him, moving round the room, collecting tea cups, passing sandwiches. Looking after the lonely ladies, she thought – and then, I ought not to laugh at him! He was such a nice man, so amazingly easy to talk to. It would really, she thought, feeling all at once uncomfortably tipsy, the room spinning round her, be wonderful to tell him how she was feeling. An understanding but sensible *man* – so different from the female harpies raging inside her head – would help to put the situation into perspective. With him she could be sensible too; a little sad, naturally, but rational. 'Lord, what fools these mortals be,' was the line to take. Simon was probably the sort of man who knew his Shakespeare.

The trouble was, she could not really imagine herself talking to Simon. What she needed was someone to speak for her, a mediator, a go-between. Someone who was on her side but could sound objective; a kindly, worldly-wise, older woman. Someone who had known her a long time.

'Of course,' this mediator might say, 'this is a commonplace and ordinary event, but then death is a commonplace and ordinary event. But as you know, Simon, one is never prepared, one has to learn how to mourn. What has happened to Ruth is like a death. Even worse in a way. If her husband had died, even suddenly, tragically, she would feel a deep and abiding sorrow, but the memory of all the years they had spent together would have sustained her. She believed they were good years. Now when she looks back at them, at the years of bringing up children, looking after Joe's mother, furnishing houses, planting flowers in the garden, living happily, hopefully, she sees nothing but desert. All spoiled and wasted. You may feel she is exaggerating her feelings of loss and despair. One has to put them in context. Ruth had a difficult upbringing. Except through her friendship with Daisy, she had no contact with what might be called normal life. She was never safe in her childhood. She believed she was safe with Joe; she trusted him absolutely. The breaking of that trust has damaged her terribly; outside what she had thought of as her safe life lies chaos, and Joe has let it in. She isn't mad (or not yet) but she is broken, bewildered. And the situation Joe has put her in *is* bewildering, Simon. If Ruth could be sure that her husband really did want their life to continue, their real life together, not just some empty formality, then she would know what to do. She would say to herself, it is selfish and stupid to be too hurt and jealous, if Joe needed this love affair she must have failed him somehow; marriage is a terrible thing if it locks people into boxes, into tight, narrow coffins. But it seems that Joe is still seeing this woman and he won't tell Ruth why. She doesn't know if, in a crude sense, he is still keeping his options open. Or if (and perhaps this does show a streak of madness) there is something so appallingly shameful that he cannot bear to tell her. Perhaps Eunice Pilbeam is pregnant. Joe's child. Or has had an abortion. Or perhaps she is threatening suicide. (She does, just between you and me, sound a bit of a blackmailing whiner!) Since Joe is being so secretive about this unhappy creature, Ruth is becoming obsessed by these fantasies. And, on a practical level, she doesn't know how to behave. Should she cry, scream at Joe, threaten to leave him? Oh, Ruth can't do that, it's not in her nature. But she resents the demands Joe is making – that she should ask no more questions, accept the unacceptable, be a compliant, sweetly waiting, good wife. Ruth is *angry*, Simon. And there is a point at which quiet people like Ruth become dangerous when they are angry. Ruth's mother was a quiet woman. Weak and afraid. And yet, at the end, when she was driven too far, she became merciless . . .

Ruth stopped. So far this was a good script, a clear statement. It was important to keep it clear, stick to the point, not muddy the waters. She put down her empty tea cup and smiled. 'You could help Ruth if you wanted to, Simon. In one department anyway – one in which her husband has been deficient just lately. You may feel you are a little old for her, but she does find you attractive, and with a bit of encouragement . . .'

Marigold said, 'Are you all right, Mum? You look a bit funny. Simon said . . .' She was standing in front of Ruth, her face crimson, whispering.

Simon appeared beside her. Their concerned faces, one young, puzzled and flushed, the other old, smiling and kind, seemed to wave above her like flowers. Ruth said, 'I'm all right, Marigold, darling. What do you mean, *I look funny?*'

'You were talking to yourself, I saw your lips moving.' Marigold compressed her own lips, rather sternly.

Simon said, 'That's a bad sign!' He widened his eyes and laughed. 'I think your mother is tired, Marigold.'

Marigold picked up Ruth's empty tea cup and sniffed. She said, 'Honestly, Mum!' She sounded more amused than censorious.

Ruth stood up. She said, 'Actually, it was Simon who led me astray. But I'm perfectly competent.'

'Bet you couldn't walk a straight line, though. Hang on to me.' Marigold drew Ruth's hand through her arm and held it protectively. *She is enjoying this*, Ruth thought, *the child becoming the parent* Then – *she doesn't know, does she?* They had kept their voices down, their bedroom door closed. Or sat in the living room after Marigold was in bed. Please God, don't let her have guessed, she's so young.

Ruth said, 'I'm sorry, love. Forgive your drunken old mother.'

'You're not drunk,' Simon said. 'Nor old, either.' His smile was delicately conspiratorial. Almost, Ruth thought, as if she had actually had that ridiculous conversation with him! She found herself wanting to giggle.

'I think I had better go home, all the same,' she said. 'I do feel a bit tottery. Do you mind, Marigold? If you want to stay, I'm quite all right, really.'

'Don't be daft, Mum.'

'We should say goodbye to Daisy.'

'She's busy,' Marigold said. And, for some reason, looked stern again. Her firm, nursemaid's grip supported Ruth, leading her round the back of the sofa, up the stairs. Out in the street she said, sounding serious, 'You haven't got a *problem*, Mum, have you? I mean, a *drink problem*? I know it's something that happens to middle-aged women but I never thought you . . .' Her face was fiery red. 'I'm sorry, that's awful, but I couldn't help noticing. Glasses all over the place. And I smelled your breath. Only this last week, so it can't be serious, really. It's just that if you catch it early on you can get help and I thought . . .'

'I'm not ready for Alcoholics Anonymous yet,' Ruth said.

'No. I just thought you should speak to Fergus. I suppose I'm being silly. It's just Luke dying, of course it upset you.'

'Yes,' Ruth said meekly. 'I suppose it is that.'

Marigold sighed – a huge, relieved sigh. 'Sorry, Mum. I'm sorry I mentioned it. I wouldn't have done if it hadn't been for – oh, never mind.' She bit her lip, frowning. 'I mean,' she went on, 'getting drunk at a funeral, what were you thinking of?'

'I don't know.'

'I didn't mean you shouldn't get drunk. That was prissy. But you were thinking of *something*. You were miles away, honestly!'

Ruth looked at her sweet, anxious face. Marigold was so innocent. She cherished her innocence. Nothing must be allowed to disturb it. *Joe* must not disturb it! She felt suddenly faint with an access of anger so violent that it made her limbs tremble. How dare Joe do this frightful thing, threaten Marigold's happiness in this careless, unthinking way. To betray a wife was not easily forgivable (at least by the wife!) but to destroy a child's happy security was utterly wicked. Hadn't Joe thought of her? No, of course not, he had selfishly gone his own way without caring how it would affect his adolescent daughter who needed a father she could love and look up to. If he had to pick up a dirty whore to flatter his menopausal masculine vanity, why the hell couldn't he have waited until Marigold was a bit older when it wouldn't split her world apart? She didn't know, of course she didn't really *know*, but a kind of half-knowledge that something was wrong was already there, in her troubled face, in her frown . . .

Oh, damn Joe, Ruth thought, *I could kill him!* And yet, though the fury that shook her was righteous (being on her child's behalf, not her own) she was ashamed and afraid of it. Marigold was watching her uncertainly as if she could feel her mother's anger and was afraid of it, too. Ruth thought – I must say something! Words came to her and she used them. She said, 'I was remembering, I think. Looking back. I can't tell you why, what started it off, because I don't know myself, but I was remembering that when I was a little girl, we had an ice house in the garden.'

IX

Physically, Ruth was walking with Daisy, both of them carrying baskets, through the Sunday fruit and flower market. Mentally, she only saw herself walking, breasts, waist and hips covered by pin-striped cotton in two shades of grey, feet in pink sandals. Since the funeral three weeks ago she had not touched any alcohol and yet she still felt in that odd state of drunken detachment in which the mind is removed from the body. *At least, for the moment*, she thought, *I am out of pain*. There was only a weird sensation of total suspense, of absolute powerlessness. She was a minor character in a thriller, waiting for the page to turn, for something to happen.

In her mind, she was writing a letter.

Dear Ms Pilbeam,

This is your lover's wife speaking. I don't know who you are, what you are, nor do I expect you to care what you have done to me. The damage you have done to our marriage, to our long and loving relationship, is entirely my husband's affair and mine. But I think you should know the damage you have done, and are doing, to him. As Goethe said, *Love is an ideal thing, marriage a real thing, a confusion of the ideal with the real never goes unpunished*. My poor Joe is an honest man who has been brought face to face with his own dishonesty and deceit and cannot bear what he sees. Naturally, I have assured him of my love and support, we have discussed

the whole situation fully and freely and we are both . . .
Dear Eunice Pilbeam,
        I cannot talk to my husband, he cannot talk to
me, you are the broken bridge, the missing link between
us, I can only reach out and touch him through you . . .
Dear Eunice,
        Hi, there! I imagine you are as curious about
me as I am about you. He must have told us both quite a
few lies! It might be interesting to meet and compare
notes sometime! For one thing, I cannot believe that you
are such a sad sack as he makes you out to be! *Poor thing,
she has had such an unhappy life!* Etc, etc. As if your little
affair were merely an altruistic rescue operation on his
part! And I wonder if you know what an old hypochon-
driac he is! Perhaps you do, though I suspect he keeps his
more unromantic fears for domestic consumption. It was
bowel cancer last week. Flecks of blood – he actually
called me into the bathroom to make an inspection. Only
bits of tomato skin, as he would have seen for himself if
he had put on his glasses . . .
Dear E. P.
        You are a black bat with a wicked face. In my
dreams you fly round my house, beating your hideous
wings. You are splitting my life into pieces. My mind is
fragile as an egg, a parcel of broken glass . . .

'Tomatoes,' Daisy said. 'Heavens, Ruth, don't they look
lovely.'
She spoke in a tone of wondering enthusiasm. This market,
a local institution for over a century, stalls and barrows
turning what was, in the week, a dead boring street of cut price
stores and supermarkets into a noisy clutter of colour and life,
was patronised by the middle-class newcomers to this area of
the city with a certain self consciousness. The prices were not

very much lower, the vegetables no fresher than if they had been bought from Marks and Spencer or ordered from Harrods. What made it enjoyable, everyone said, was the feeling that shopping there, you were belonging to a community, taking part in the life of a village. Buying a cauliflower from a stall that had probably been run by the same East End family for more than a hundred years was a 'real life experience'.

Daisy was bargaining, flirting with the stall holder. She was laughing excitedly, shaking her hair back. She had been like this all the morning, caught up in nervous euphoria, turning up when Ruth and Joe were breakfasting in the garden (it was the first really hot day of the summer) with the news that Bob had telephoned from Australia to say he was coming to England in three weeks' time, for four months. This was a genuine happiness, she had not seen her brother for years, but it was almost too much to bear. She was radiant, edgy, febrile, sitting in the beautiful sunshine, twisting a handkerchief between her large hands, looking from Ruth to Joe, from Joe to Ruth, with quick, restless, almost shy glances.

'You haven't seen Bob – oh, Lord – since Mother died, have you, Ruth? That one other time he came, you and Joe were away somewhere, or was it before you moved here? I can't remember. Georgia was quite little, I've got a photograph somewhere, her sitting on his shoulders, clutching his hair. He sent you his love, he said he was looking forward so much to seeing you. Thank God he's coming alone, he's left that ghastly bitch he was living with, I told you about her, didn't I? The one after the dancer, or the one after *that* – you know Bob, rather like Dad in that way . . .' And then she had given a huge, gasping, dry sob. 'Oh, I wish Dad was here, oh, I miss him . . .'

At the time Ruth had been too frozen up, too nervous of Joe who sat listening, glum-faced, melancholic, to be moved by this sad remark. Now, standing beside her friend in the market, Ruth's heart went out to her, a lovely warmth thawing her. Oh, it was good to have Daisy to think about, care for! She and Joe must put aside their own selfish concerns. Their unhappiness was such a petty thing beside Daisy's loss. Perhaps it might even be the best way, the safe path to take out of their own private darkness. They must put Daisy first, comfort her, cherish her. They would have lunch in the garden, a long, leisurely lunch in the sunshine, and walk on the Heath, or in one of the parks, in the afternoon. Occupation was the important thing, keep her moving, stop her from brooding.

'*Eggs*,' Daisy said. 'Let's go to the egg stall. I have a sudden *passion* for eggs. Do you know the best way to make scrambled eggs? Between the stove and the table you break a raw egg over the cooked ones and stir it in quickly. It fluffs the whole mixture up, makes it *perfect*.'

'Why don't you cook eggs for lunch, then?'

'May I? I'd like to. You know, it's absurd, but it's one thing I'm going to miss, I've just realised! Cooking! Luke was never as greedy as I am, but he liked food, and Georgia, well, she's into lentils, the whole faddy fashion. Brown rice and beans. Meat makes her feel faint, apparently. She says she can smell the slaughter house. Paul says I shouldn't put up with it. He wouldn't put up with it from *his* children, even though they have more excuse to be fussy. Judy's a rotten cook. Poor old Paul!'

'You can cook for us whenever you want to,' Ruth said. 'And you'll have Bob to cook for quite soon.'

Daisy nodded. She was looking at Ruth with an air of puzzled concentration. Had she been hoping for something more, some deeper response? Did she want Ruth to speak about Luke, ask her how she felt about Paul, say something that would open the floodgates? Ruth thought – I should be able to help her, we should be close, talk and weep freely together, best friends sharing secrets. But she would be a false friend to Daisy if she did nothing but listen, keeping her own secret hidden, pretending *her* life was perfect! She felt ashamed suddenly, a liar, a cheat! That was what Joe had done to her, turned her into . . .

Daisy said, 'You're so good for me Ruth. So calm and so sensible.'

On the main road, at the entrance to the street market, Georgia and Mark were watching the National Front, a group of about twenty men, wearing Union Jack T-shirts, handing out leaflets. On the opposite pavement, the Anti-Nazi League, fewer in number and most of them younger, were asking passing shoppers for their names and addresses, to sign a petition to the Home Secretary. The National Front should be kept off the streets, their presence here, every Sunday, was an insult, a threat to all decent citizens. Mark and Georgia, holding hands, regarded these two groups with interested disdain. 'They're both pretty thuggish,' Mark said. 'Though the National Front are the worst, I suppose.' He had taken a leaflet. He glanced at it, screwed it up in a ball and chucked it down in the gutter among the vegetable refuse, the cabbage leaves, squashed tomatoes. He said, 'Just the usual filth. The blacks are undermining British society, the Jews are encouraging them, and the Government is secretly behind the Jews, it's an international Jewish conspiracy. It would be funny if it wasn't disgusting.'

Georgia said, 'We ought to love one another.' Young and serious, her high, pale brow slightly wrinkled, she said this with perfect conviction.

Mark squeezed her fingers. 'Some of us do.'

Georgia sighed.

Mark said, 'I'm sorry. I won't say it again if it upsets you.'
He dropped her hand.

Georgia said, 'I don't mind your holding my hand. I mean, I
like it. It's the rest that's so difficult.' A warm rose coloured
her cheeks. 'How can you be certain? I mean, I thought my
father and mother . . .'

Her voice, wispily soft, trailed into nothing, a puff of smoke
fading.

Mark said, 'When people get old, it's probably different. So
many other things crowd them – boring stuff, kids and
mortgages. Jobs.' He caught hold of Georgia's hand again,
swinging it lightly, and shook his head, sighing. 'Not that a
job seems likely to happen to me. I shall stay incorruptible.
Though I must say, I sometimes wish someone would try to
corrupt me. It would give me something to offer.'

A sure way to grab Georgia's attention. She said, turning
her earnest, grey eyes upon him, 'Don't give up, Mark. You'll
get a job. But it's who you are, not what you do that matters.'

'What I am isn't much. Pretty useless. Sometimes I wish
there would be a war.'

'No you don't. You don't want to kill people.'

'I could join the Red Cross, or the Quakers, or something.
Or one of those Third World task forces. I could go off and die
of dysentery in some Indian village.'

'Don't tease.'

'I'm not. Or not altogether. I suppose, what I mean is, when
you get these long stretches when there seems to be nothing
except sleeping and eating, just keeping alive, when you can't
even make love to your girl . . .' He stroked her palm with his
forefinger to take the sting out of this, though he meant it to
hurt her. 'Then you begin to long for something to happen,
almost anything, however horrible, to wake you up, make
you feel real.'

Georgia said, 'My father died.' She was very white. 'That

makes me feel less real, not more.' She leaned her head on Mark's shoulder. 'Sorry. I didn't say that to make you feel bad.'

'Well, it does, of course. D'you think I'd forgotten? Poor little love. But it didn't happen to *me*, that's all I was saying, oh, I don't know what I meant, really. Just frustration, probably. Here I am, at the height of my sexual potency, and you . . .'

She wasn't listening. It was the kind of thing she would have tried not to listen to, anyway, but at this moment she was watching the scene in front of her. Several men from the National Front had crossed the road. One of them was carrying a shopping trolley with metal spikes wired round the wheels. He waved this weapon about in an idly menacing way, more of a game than a threat. Even when someone laughed and shoved a plump boy in jeans and a leather jacket who was holding the Anti-Nazi League petition, the gesture still seemed almost playful. The boy shook his head, turning away, protecting his piece of paper, thrusting it inside his shirt. His companions were backing away and the men from the National Front surrounded him, the chosen victim. Still laughing, they pushed him from one to the other, grabbing at his shirt front only half-heartedly.

Georgia said, 'Why aren't the police here? They're usually here, Sunday morning. Oh, *Mark* . . .'

The boy had twisted out of the circle and they let him go. This was what they had wanted. They had started the hare. As he ran, head ducked down, into the market, the hounds gathered, shouting at each other, setting off in pursuit, knocking people aside, yelling 'Sieg Heil'. There was a splintering crash as someone fell into a shop front. Mark seized Georgia and stood with his arms round her, legs braced, protecting her with his body.

At the egg stall, Ruth and Daisy heard the crash of glass breaking, the shouting. Looking in the direction of these sounds they saw at first only an eddying movement, shoppers swept into the stalls at the sides of the street like muck on a river by a sudden surge of the tide. Then the boy broke through, staggering, gasping, face ashen and sweating. He stumbled and fell at their feet, curling up in a ball, hands and arms over his head. A split second later the hunt was upon him, the pack, laying into him with their heavy boots, kicking and screaming, rocking the egg stall, sending the piles of eggs, carefully sorted in sizes (Jumbo, Large Farm, Free Range, Pullet) tumbling and smashing. The stall holder shouted 'Bastards,' and rushed forward, arms wildly waving. An unthinking, brave, foolish act, but they didn't turn on him. They ran off, whooping with laughter, back down the market. No one tried to stop them, no one could stop them; strong men with nailed boots.

The boy lay on the ground as they'd left him. He didn't move. Ruth knelt and put her hand on his chest, felt the rigid muscles of his neck. Daisy said, 'Dear God! Ruth, he's not breathing!'

'I know,' Ruth said. 'It's only . . .' She was cradling him with one arm, feeling in his jacket pockets. She found what she was looking for and held it to his mouth, forcing his lips apart. 'Breathe,' she said, 'breathe in deeply.' She was pressing the button on the inhaler. 'Now,' she said, 'hold your breath, keep it in, I'm counting to *ten*, can you hear me?'

His swollen eyes opened, stared at her. He was whistling, wheezing. She said, 'That's right, that's *good*. Now again . . .'

His chest moved. He lay quiet in her arms. His face was bruised, cheeks split and bleeding. Blood, mixed with slimy egg yolk, bits of egg shell, trailed from his mouth. Ruth wiped his face with the skirt of her dress. She said, without looking up, 'Daisy, don't let them crowd him.'

135

She sat like that, perfectly still, watching him, monitoring his short, snoring breaths until the ambulance came. Two men with a stretcher. They were deft, quick and gentle. 'Let yourself go, laddie,' one of them said. 'It's all right, we've got you.'

Ruth gave this man the inhaler. 'He may need this again, do you know how to use it? Tell them that he's an asthmatic as soon as you get to the hospital.'

He nodded, a brief glance at her face to reassure her, before they lifted the stretcher. A policewoman in a white shirt with a walkie-talkie strapped round her, said, 'Make way please, stand back.' Ruth got to her feet, smoothing her dress down. It was covered with blood and smashed eggs. She said, 'What a mess!'

Daisy said, 'Are you all right?'

'Fine,' Ruth said. She felt this was a huge understatement. She felt astonishingly, wonderfully alive. Her mind was back in her body again, in control, capable, and miraculously whole. The splintered feeling in her head had quite left her. As if the violence coming from outside, that had nothing to do with her, had bound her and healed her. She looked at the gawping faces around her, smiled apologetically at the stall holder, saw how white Daisy was, and said, 'You look shocked, though. I suppose we'll have to speak to the police. Then we'll go to a pub. There's quite a decent one on the corner.'

The police were moving up and down the market, asking questions, looking for witnesses, but not very seriously. This was a common occurrence, even if someone had recognised one of the thugs and was willing to swear to it, that kind of identification was unlikely to hold up in court. If the boy were to die, that would be a different matter, which was why they were taking names and addresses. Ruth was surprised to find she accepted this. She thought – I should be indignant.

She said, to the policewoman, a severe, pretty child – so

young, Ruth half expected her to lick the end of her pencil before she wrote in her notebook – 'That was a very serious assault. The young man could have died. He's asthmatic.'

'Do you know who they were? Any one of them?'

'Not to be certain. It was over too quickly. But the police must know who they are. Where to find them. They're here every weekend at the end of the street. They ought to arrest the whole lot of them.'

The girl did lick her pencil then, looking at Ruth with wide, honest eyes. 'We can't do that, can we?'

Ruth said, 'If the police had been here, this wouldn't have happened.'

'We usually have someone to cover the market. I don't know what happened today.'

Ruth said crisply, 'The police failed in their duty. Please put that down.'

'I'll make my report. That's all I can do.' The policewoman hesitated. 'If you like, you could ring the station. King's Cross. There will be someone in charge of this incident.'

Filed away, put aside and forgotten. There were more important things to be dealt with. Terrorists. Arsonists. The Royal Wedding – checking the roof tops, the sewers. Bombs. Last time Ruth had been to Oxford Street there had been a bomb scare. The police had cordoned off the area with white ribbons.

Ruth said, 'I'm prepared to give evidence.'

'It doesn't seem – that is, we know what happened, some-one will see the young man at the hospital. Thank you, all the same. Not everyone is prepared to come forward.'

Witnesses to this sort of affray were beaten up. They could come, one evening perhaps when Marigold was alone in the house, she and Joe out somewhere, banging on the front door, storming in at the back, from the tenement, from the jungle. Nowhere was safe. No one's house, no one's life. Mine is under threat anyway, Ruth thought, seeing this with absolute clarity for the first time, as if this attack, this sordid, minor street crime under the blue sky of this beautiful Sunday had suddenly made everything vivid, explicit. Violence came out of the blue. There was no safeguard, no permanence, no possible reassurance. Joe had made promises, why should he keep them? The only security lay in reducing one's expectations, in hoping for nothing. Perhaps, at this very moment, Joe's resolve had broken, he was packing his bags, telling the children.

The policewoman was putting her notebook into her shirt pocket, speaking into her walkie-talkie, moving away.

Daisy said, 'I think we should go home, Ruth. You ought to clean up. Honestly, you look. . .' She started to laugh, snorting into her hand.

'I don't want to go home,' Ruth said. 'Daisy, something has happened. Terrible – well, no, not *terrible*, or only to me, but I . . .'

Daisy was watching her, hand still over her mouth, fingers splayed out across it. 'Oh, Ruth, darling . . .'

'It won't take long,' Ruth said. 'We'll go to the pub. I have to tell someone.'

Green light fell upon Daisy from the stained glass window behind her. It made her grey eyes look iridescent, like the inside of a shell. She said, '*What* did you say her name is?'

'Eunice Pilbeam.'

'Oh, God!' Daisy groaned. She seemed more dismayed than Ruth had expected. 'I can hardly believe it. Do you believe him?'

'He couldn't invent a name like that.'

'No. I suppose not. But that's not what I meant.' Daisy's colour rose. She said, 'The old *dog*! I'm sorry, Ruth, how

138

absolutely vile for you. For Christ's sake, why did he tell you? If he wanted a bit of a fling, because that's what it sounds like, why the flaming hell couldn't he keep his mouth shut?'

'I made him tell me.'

'Oh.' Daisy sat very still, fingers curled round her glass of gin. She said, very slowly, 'You mean, you'd guessed something?'

'Not quite. No, I don't think I had, to begin with. It was just, well, I thought he was ill, and I wanted . . .' Ruth looked down at her lap, picking bits of egg shell off her dress, scraping with her finger nail at a fleck of dried yolk. How it happened, the sudden surge of love she had felt for him that had shamed him into confession, was too painful to speak of. She said, 'I think it was Molly.'

'That bitch! The common old *hag*! You don't mean she *told* you?'

'No, no. She was telling me about her husband, carrying on with young girls, she was so upset, I think she had to tell someone. And other bits of local scandal . . .' Thinking of Simon, Ruth blushed. 'Nothing important, simply things I'd no idea about, going on all the time under my nose. It made me feel, oh, a bit stupid, not knowing what it seemed everyone knew. I don't mean I suspected that Joe. . . But I suppose it did make me wonder. Not immediately, not even consciously. But he'd been so distant. I'd thought it was my fault.'

'Little saint.' Daisy was frowning. Then she said, leaning forward, serious, urgent, 'Look, Ruth, it isn't your fault. You've done nothing wrong. What Joe has done is something quite apart from you, separate. His failure, not yours. I know you must be quite frightfully hurt, but don't let it hurt you that way. Oh, for God's sake, darling, don't cry!'

'Only because you're so kind, Daisy. Thank you, Daisy. Of course I do blame myself, I can't help it, but thanks all the same.'

'I was not being kind,' Daisy said. And then, in a different voice, 'Watch it now! Mark and Georgia.'

Ruth turned and saw them, coming into the pub, hesitating in the doorway. Georgia was clinging onto Mark's arm, her head on his shoulder. The two mothers smiled at each other. Love birds! Daisy said, quickly, 'I really am sorry. What can I do, Ruth?'

'Let me talk,' Ruth said. 'Let me talk to you. Joe would be so cross if he knew, but it helps me. I've been feeling so . . .'

Daisy was looking over her shoulder and smiling. She said, 'Hallo, you two, want a drink?'

Their children stood beside them. 'Thank you, Daisy,' Mark said. 'Beer for me, Perrier water for Georgia.' He looked at Ruth, at her tear stained face, her blood and egg spattered dress, eyes widening with horror. 'Mum, you look ghastly, what on earth's happened to you?'

Ruth said, 'I'm sorry, Fergus. I'm quite all right, really. Joe shouldn't have called you.'

She was in bed, Fergus on one side, Joe on the other. Fergus was holding her wrist with his firm, stubby fingers. Ruth looked at the fringe of coarse, reddish curls peeping out from his shirt cuff. Fergus was almost bald but his body was hairy. Thinking of his hairy body under his clothes excited her; she smiled at him shakily. He acknowledged her smile with a grave nod and gave her wrist back to her. 'Pulse a bit fast, that's all. Why shouldn't Joe ring me? He was worried about you.'

Joe had been appalled. His shocked face had made her hysterical; she had trembled and wept. He had put his arms round her and held her so close she could hear his heart thumping. He had helped her off with her dress, held a warm towel for her as she stepped from the shower, insisted she went to bed, plumped up the pillows behind her. His conern, his tender solicitude, seemed quite genuine. But, in an odd way, it had hurt her. He was trying too hard. She thought – he wouldn't make all this fuss if he really loved me! She was ashamed of this treachery. She ought to be grateful, and touched.

Fergus said, 'You're bound to feel shaky. It'll pass, I don't think you need medication. Tell me something, is your rash better?'

Several weeks ago she had gone to Fergus with a skin allergy. He had given her antihistamine but it hadn't helped. She had gone on itching and scratching. Then it had stopped – had vanished completely, she realised now, as soon as she knew about Eunice. She said, surprised, 'Oh, that's gone.'

'Shock,' Fergus said. 'If a rash is nervous in origin, a sudden shock often cures it.' He was regarding her thoughtfully. 'Nothing else wrong, is there? You've lost quite a bit of weight, haven't you?'

'She's not been eating properly lately,' Joe said. 'Picking at her food. I keep telling her.' His tone was sternly reproving.

Ruth said, 'I haven't been hungry.'

'I can give you a tonic,' Fergus said. 'A magic bottle. Though it may not help much. It depends on the cause.' He looked at Ruth with one of his rare smiles. 'Anxiety makes some people eat. Others lose their appetite.'

Silence. Joe was staring into distance and frowning. Then he said, abruptly, 'She's been upset about Mark. No job, sitting about the house all day, brooding, a sort of lassitude seems to have taken him over. I worry, too, but it's worse for Ruth, probably.'

Ruth looked at him in astonishment. He glanced at her briefly, and looked away. *Shifty*, she thought, that's the only word, *shifty*! Oh, she wouldn't tell Fergus what the real trouble was, wouldn't have told him even if they had been alone, but Joe's fear that she might give him away, spill the beans, made him seem mean and small suddenly. Not her husband but a contemptible stranger who just happened to be living in the same house. Oh, she mustn't let herself think that! He was still Joe, whatever he'd done, she still loved him. But her love had to change, she thought. She must give up the foolish and trusting love she had always felt for him, try and see him as a separate person, human and fallible, lovable for his humanity and his failings, but not to be used as a safe cushion, leaned on, relied upon. She had relied on him too much, been too dependent, felt too safe with him. That was her fault, her mistake. Well, she could rectify that, make herself over, teach herself to stand alone, hide her feelings. She had done it before. She had gone to school, smiling . . .

Joe said, 'Ruth has always been a bit of a worrier. Mostly about the children, of course. Scared of leaving them alone in the house, that sort of thing. Burglars. Intruders. Not altogether foolish in this kind of neighbourhood. That's why we got a burglar alarm. And the dog. A bloody nuisance they are in some ways. But some security, too.'

Ruth thought – how comically obvious! A man steals the most precious things from his home, trust and loyalty, and then installs a burglar alarm! Locking the stable door after the horse has bolted! She saw he was scowling at her anxiously, fiercely. She laughed rather wildly and said, 'Joe's right, Fergus. I suppose I've been worrying about Mark more than I realised.'

Joe nodded. The relief on his face, his quick, grateful, shy smile, made her feel protective and tender towards him. She had meant to tell him she had told Daisy, ask him not to be angry, explain how much it had helped her, how it had helped push away the nightmare cloud that seemed to threaten her sanity. But it was clear now that Joe's guilt was too deep and painful. Knowing that Daisy knew would shame him quite dreadfully . . .

She said, 'I shall have to try and stop worrying.'

'If you can't,' Fergus said, 'come and see me.'

When he had gone, Joe sat on the bed. He said, 'I'm sorry about the burglar alarm. I know how it must look to you. I think it meant something else to me. A symbol. I wanted to keep you.'

'Safe in the house? In my *place*?'

'Not quite like that.' He traced her face with his finger and smiled.

She said, 'Do you want me to give up the shop? I don't say that I would. I just want to know if you want it.'

'Why should I?'

'Because it separates us. Comes between us.'

Rubbish, she thought. *She did that. Eunice Pilbeam. That bloody tramp.*

She wanted to scream at him, hit him. But he was shaking his head, smiling at her so fondly, in such a good mood she was afraid to disturb it. 'I don't know,' she said. 'I was just being silly.'

X

Daisy had an aching tooth. At breakfast, the gold cap had come off a back molar in a spoonful of Georgia's home-made muesli, exposing the nerve. This was the morning Ruth had arranged to take Daisy to the shop to fit a new dress, part of the almost bridal trousseau she was preparing for Bob's arrival, and Daisy's dentist in Harley Street was not much out of the way. Nor would a temporary filling take long.

All the same, after ten minutes' wait in the car, Ruth was fretting, uncomfortably restless with the furious energy cooped up inside her, mind tumbling, heart throbbing. Ruth knew what was wrong, though not how to cure it. Adrenal glands, those emergency messengers, respond to emotional stress by working over-time, pouring their secretions into the blood stream, mobilising the body for struggle or flight. Adrenalin increases blood pressure and pulse rate, restricts the small arteries, makes the hair stand on end, enlarges the pupils, inhibits digestion. (In love, or in war, most people lose weight.) It is also the best drug for stopping a serious asthma attack. This is why Ruth knew what was happening. She knew about asthma.

The battered young man had been given an injection as soon as he had arrived at the hospital. When Ruth went to see him, the ward sister told her that he would probably have died in the market if she had not found his inhaler. 'My husband has asthma,' Ruth said. 'Otherwise I wouldn't have known what to do.'

'Lucky you were there, then,' the ward sister said. 'I hope he has the grace to be grateful.' Ought to be grateful, too, for a bed in her hospital, was what she clearly felt. Little sympathy for the victims of street fights. 'Six of one and half a dozen of the other, if you ask my opinion,' she said.

The boy's face was a mess, bruised and cracked, his mouth painfully swollen. Ruth hoped he would be able to eat the grapes she had brought him. He recognised her when she appeared at his bedside and managed a twisted smile but closed his eyes almost at once. His father, sitting beside him in a low hospital chair, thanked Ruth grudgingly when she explained who she was; then, after a short tight-lipped silence, vented his anger. 'I told him,' he said. 'If I had a penny for each time I've told him, I'd be a rich man by now. Keep away from that lot, keep off the streets, it means nothing but trouble, you can't do nothing, only get hurt, who d'you think is going to help you? But he knew best, didn't listen.'

'He was only collecting names for a petition,' Ruth said. 'He didn't start the fight.'

'I'm not saying that. No business to put himself in such a position, *that*'s what I'm saying.' The man's nose, a large nose that dominated his otherwise small-boned, narrow face, reddened alarmingly. 'Books,' he said, with sudden venom, 'books, books, books, that's always been his trouble. Putting ideas in his head.'

'Best place for ideas, perhaps.' Ruth laughed, trying to divert him with this old, innocent joke.

'Wrong ideas,' he said. 'That's what I'm meaning.'

'Someone has to stand up against those Fascist thugs. I think it was brave of him, you should be proud of him, really.'

'That's your way of looking at it.'

'If he was my son, I'd be proud. As well as upset and angry.'

'Would you now? Well.' He looked at the silent boy in the bed and was silent himself for a moment, his expression softening a little. Then his rage gathered steam again. 'Weeks off work, who's going to pay for it? When he gets out of here, he'll be back and forth to the dentist. Smashed his mouth up, broke his teeth. He may get laid off from the factory. Jobs aren't two a penny now, are they? I lost a day's pay coming here.'

'He could apply to the Criminal Compensation Board.'

The man smiled at her, quite kindly; the tolerant smile of experience. 'He wasn't set on for no reason, was he? Asked for it, that's what they'd say. We wouldn't get anywhere.'

'You don't know. If you don't try . . .' Ruth began, but felt helpless. She touched the boy's hand, lying limp on the covers, smiling at him when he opened his eyes and turned his head towards her. She said, 'I hope you enjoy the grapes. They shouldn't hurt your mouth too much. I'll come again, if I may.'

She wondered now if she should have said more. Tried to comfort him more. But not with his father sitting there, glowering. And she hadn't kept her promise, she hadn't gone back.

Not that he had expected her to come, probably. What could she have done for him, anyway? Her own life such a muddle, how could she help other people? Except in small, immediate things, driving Daisy to the dentist, making a dress for her . . .

Daisy opened the passenger door. She was holding a handkerchief over her mouth. 'That's over. Bloody painful. Bloody man! His father never hurt me. Though, to be fair, I suppose he never had cause to. Getting down to bedrock with my old teeth by now.'

'No reason why it should hurt. Didn't you have an injection?'

'It would have taken too long.'

'I didn't mind waiting.'

One-handed, Daisy fumbled clumsily with her seat belt. Ruth fastened it for her. She said, 'You know, she works somewhere round here.'

Daisy looked at her over her handkerchief.

'Eunice Pilbeam,' Ruth said. Just to speak the name started the adrenalin flowing again. She touched the accelerator, racing the engine, and her heart seemed to race with it. A curious, thumping excitement. It was odd that the situation affected her this way, when it seemed to make Joe merely tired. His first outburst of affectionate energy had subsided. Now he sat at meals, yawning and rubbing his eyes; went to bed early, fell at once into a deep, snoring sleep. A retreat, perhaps? When she had suggested this, he denied it resentfully. 'I'm dog tired, that's all. I have a job to do, I know it means nothing to you, never has meant much, has it? If I can't get a decent night's sleep I shall have to resign. Is that what you want?' Blackmail, Ruth thought.

She said, 'Joe hasn't told me her address, of course. I suppose he's afraid I'll confront her.'

'Would you?'

'God knows! I have insane fantasies. Seeing her suddenly – as I might now, for example! Leaping out of the car, bawling insults. Or being quite cold, playing the lady. *Do me a favour, Miss Pilbeam, leave my husband alone!* I drive up Harley Street most days on the way home from the shop, crawling along, looking for her. Sometimes I wonder if I might track her down in one of the pubs she and Joe go to, chuck my drink in her face, make a scene. That's a wild dream, of course. But I would like to see her – just watch her, you know, from the other side of the bar. The only trouble is, I've no idea what she looks like!'

'Large strong lady with a moustache, I should think.'

Daisy sounded weary, muttering into her handkerchief. Ruth, glancing sideways as she stopped at a traffic light, felt a

slight disappointment. This was the sort of game she had
hoped Daisy might enter into. She said, 'I suppose it's vulgar
to speculate. Childish, anyway.'

'Not like you, somehow. God, my tooth hurts! What I
mean is, this sort of *silliness* isn't like you! You were never
silly, even at school, you never even listened to gossip, you
were so smug and superior!' Daisy spoke with a sudden,
remembered irritation that seemed strange to Ruth. After all,
it was a long time since they'd been at school.

She said, 'I didn't *feel* smug or superior. If I was a bit
standoffish, it was only because my father hated giggly girls
and I was always trying not to annoy him. That was really the
worst thing, trying to keep him in a good mood, you could
never be sure what would set him off.'

'I know what your life was like,' Daisy said. She was
looking out of the window. Her voice sounded strained.

Ruth felt ashamed. Poor Daisy, her mouth was hurting her!
How could she be interested? She said, 'Sorry, Daisy. Prat-
tling on like this. It's just that I have no one else to talk to.'

'I'm listening,' Daisy said. 'I didn't mean to put you down.
Talk all you want to.'

'Oh, it's so *boring*,' Ruth said. 'Boring for you, it's even
boring for me, to be so taken up with this woman. I wish she'd
get out of my mind!'

'Is Joe still seeing her?'

'I don't know. I've stopped asking him, it makes him so
angry. He says if I push him too hard, deliver an ultimatum,
something of that sort, everything will just fall apart. I don't
know what he means. I suppose, if I try to put myself in his
position, I can see that if he really did love her, still loves her,
perhaps, then he can't break it off just like that. I try to tell
myself – though I know that I'm looking at it in the best way
for *me* – that it's *she* who won't let him go, that she's ringing
him up, pestering him. The other day, we came home, that

evening we'd been having a drink with you, and Mark said some woman had rung. Thought he was Joe – they do sound alike – but when he said he was Mark, she put down the telephone. Joe said it was probably a girl from the office but Mark didn't think so. I thought he looked at Joe a bit oddly . . .'

'The bitch,' Daisy said. And then, 'Joe won't leave you.'

'He says he won't.'

'I'm sure he won't,' Daisy said. 'I know he's behaved like a shit, but then lots of men do. He wouldn't have been so keen to keep it quiet, for God's sake, if he wanted to leave you.'

'But it's out in the open now. That changes everything.'

'Only for you. Not for him, necessarily.' Daisy was silent while Ruth drove round Marble Arch and into the park. Then she said, hesitantly, 'What I don't really understand, is why it was such a shock to you. Oh, I suppose I do know. You're so straightforward yourself, you assume other people are, too.' She sighed. 'You believed in Joe, didn't you?'

'Yes. I thought he was my friend. Closer than that. I didn't think of him as a separate person. He was part of me, like an arm or a leg.' Driving through the park, across the Serpentine Bridge, slowing to join the traffic queue at the gate, Ruth laughed sharply. 'I shan't be so stupid in future! I don't mean I will never trust him again, if I felt that was out of the question I'd be packing my bags at this moment! But I don't intend to slip back into being the good little wife, trusting him *absolutely*, though I think that's what he'd like, what would suit him. He's terrified that I'll tell everyone what a deceitful old bugger he is. He'd be horrified if he knew I'd told you! What he wants me to do is sweep it under the carpet, go on as before, as if nothing had happened, going out, having people to dinner. It makes me want to throw up!'

'You don't have to do that,' Daisy said. 'I think, if he knows that it hurts you, it's cruel of him to expect it.'

'Not if he really does want to hold us together. Joe is very conventional. He'd hate to admit it, but he cares what things look like to other people. If I made roaring great public scenes, rang him up at the office, yelling and screaming, it would split us up because he couldn't endure it. I suppose I don't want that. So I have no choice except to carry on as he wants me to, lying, pretending. If I can think of myself as acting a part in some kind of shadow play – or perhaps bedroom farce would be better – I expect I can manage it.'

'Oh, Ruth,' Daisy said – rather reproachfully. There had been a reproachful note in her voice rather too frequently lately, Ruth thought. It perplexed her a little. Since she first confided in Daisy, she had been working hard on this new Ruth, this cheerful, cynical, bright personality. A calm and competent lady who would send all the other Ruths packing. She had even adopted a new voice, a light, amused tone. She hadn't expected Joe to notice she was in any way different. Even if he did, he would simply assume she had decided to be 'sensible' – no more tears, no more questions. But she had expected Daisy to recognise and applaud the line she was taking. Instead there was this faint disapproval, these odd, withdrawn silences.

Daisy didn't speak as they drove along Knightsbridge. Ruth found a parking meter a few yards from the shop and said, 'Good timing, I think. Ida's day off, and Beatrice should be out at lunch, so we'll have the place to ourselves. Apart from the dress, there are some other things I'd like you to look at. A printed silk, and a beautiful, very fine cotton. First of all, though, I think you need coffee and aspirin.'

Beatrice had made coffee in the Cona. Ruth gave Daisy a mug; produced soluble aspirin, a glass of water. Daisy sat, watching Ruth shake out bolts of material, put the new dress on the dummy. She said, suddenly, 'Ruth, I want to know something. What do you really feel about Joe?'

Ruth shrugged her shoulders. This wasn't a question she wanted to answer; couldn't answer, except with tears. She fiddled with Daisy's dress, a flame-coloured chiffon, a floating dress for dancing, and called on the new Ruth to help her. She said, a bit breathlessly, 'I don't know. I suppose I would like to have the Joe I used to know back. But since that isn't possible, I can't really tell you. I'm waiting to find out how I feel. It will be up to him, I imagine. I'm the one who's been hurt.'

Daisy shook her glass of water, dissolving the aspirin. She said, 'Don't you think he's hurt, too? He's a man who likes to think well of himself. He can't, now.'

New Ruth laughed. She said, 'Oh, he's enjoying a bad time. He goes into the tortured soul routine, how unspeakably guilty he feels, how worthless he is, but mostly to avoid answering awkward questions. How true it is, I don't know. Nor do I care very much. He ought to grow up, be a man, accept what he's done.' She was unpinning the dress from the dummy. She said, quietly and firmly, 'One has to accept one's guilt, Daisy.'

Daisy stood up. She went to the window. She said, her back turned to Ruth, 'Do you still sleep together?' She gave a short, nervous cough. 'I mean, I know you share a bed.'

From Daisy, this was unusually delicate. Ruth smiled at her turned back. She said, 'We didn't, for about a year. He was too busy elsewhere. Now we do, rather more than before. Very agreeable it is, too. Only of course I can't help wondering if he is making comparisons and that spoils it a little. But I do enjoy it.'

'Well, at least that's *something*,' Daisy said. She turned from the window. She looked rather white but she was smiling as she unbuttoned her blouse and stood in her boned bra and tights, a tall, shapely, only slightly overweight woman, broad shouldered, big breasted, long legged. A Demeter, a corn goddess, Ruth thought, seeing in her mind's eye how the flame chiffon folds would fall from the handsome shoulders, drape the breasts. She held out the dress and Daisy stepped into it. She said, 'Ruth, you remember my mother. She did love my Dad, in spite of his being an awful old lecher. That's what it comes down to, I think in the end. I think it must have been hard for her, the first time, especially. But this could be the only time for you. I think that Joe loves you.' Her voice was husky as if her throat were constricted.

Ruth thought – if she goes on like this, I shall cry. So *unlike* her to be so sentimental! But I shall lose myself again if I cry. Be swept back into despair, into nothingness; drown in a black tide of grief. She said, in her new, light voice, 'You mean I must get things into proportion. There are worse things than an unfaithful husband. I would, for example, rather have been your mother married to your father than my mother married to my father. But that is not the choice I am faced with. I think this is going to be a lovely dress, Daisy. Look in the mirror.'

Daisy turned obediently. 'It's beautiful. God, I wish I were younger.' She slapped her cheeks and groaned. 'Washed out old hag!'

'Silly! The colour drains you a bit at the moment, but it'll look marvellous when you are tanned. Perfect for Egypt.'

Ruth knelt at Daisy's feet, turning up the hem, pinning it. Daisy said, 'Ruth, I've been meaning to say this. I don't think Bob and I should come with you.'

Ruth sat on her heels, looking at the dress in the glass. She said, 'Think of dancing on the Nile in the evenings, in this floating gin palace. That's what Joe calls the river boat. Bob used to like to dance, didn't he? I think the skirt should be a lot shorter or you'll go arse over tip down the gangway. I'll cut a few inches off and we'll try again. *Of course* you must come with us, Daisy.'

Daisy said, 'You and Joe should be alone.'

Ruth shook her head. She slipped the dress off Daisy's

shoulders and steadied her elbow as she stepped out of it. She laid it on the sewing table and picked up the shears. She said, as she cut, 'It should pack well. So should the silk print. The cotton will crease, I'm afraid, but I've got a travelling iron and a voltage adaptor.'

Daisy said, 'You can't make all these clothes for me. You know bloody well that I can't afford them.'

Ruth looked up from the table. 'Please, Daisy! It's all I can do for you. What you're doing for me, coming to Egypt, is much more important. I don't want to be on my own with Joe. If we're alone, *she*'ll be there. For me, anyway. Perhaps for him, too. A malevolent spirit, standing between us. Poisoning everything.'

Daisy was shivering, crossing her arms over her breasts and clasping her shoulders. 'You do hate her, don't you? Or is it Joe, really? I mean, I know that you're angry.'

'Not with Joe. I can't risk that. But of course I hate her. You understand, don't you? Oh, Daisy darling, when you called her a bitch, I felt so enormously grateful.' Ruth laughed suddenly, eyes shining with laughter, bright as the dressmaker's shears in her hand. 'When I think of her, that scavenging *animal*, and I do all the time, I think I'm obsessed by her, I feel more than angry, I feel really *murderous*.'

Part Three
LOVE

I

'Be careful, Joe,' Daisy said.

'What do you mean?'

He took a long swallow of beer, wiped the froth from his mouth, and smiled at her. They were sitting in a public house called The Harp and Flowers. This was one of a number of pubs Joe had found (set off with a buoyant and purposeful heart to discover) near enough to his office, a brisk trot down Fleet Street, but unfrequented by other men from the Company. To begin with, his insistence on absolute secrecy had amused Daisy. Why should he care so much that no one should see them – just two old friends having a drink at lunch time together. Now she saw that it was precisely this secrecy that had snared her. Joe had drawn a tight circle round her, leaving her no way to escape. He had planned it like that, cutting his life with her off from his 'real life' with Ruth, locking her into this closed and separate existence, binding her to him. Daisy thought – I have been lazy and stupid.

Years ago, a man at a party, an amateur palmist, had told her that her hands were extremely unusual. The left hand was the one you were born with, the right hand was the one that you made. The lines on Daisy's two palms matched exactly. 'It means,' this man had said, laughing, a little in love with the pretty girl whose large, warm hands he was holding, 'that you were born with a strong personality. Cradle to grave, nothing will change you.'

Daisy had been only mildly interested in this conversation.

It had never occurred to her that people might change. Daisy Brett, aged forty-five, was still Daisy Brown, aged fifteen, healthy, cheerful and confident – rather like a friendly golden retriever. She still liked chocolates, a good cry at the cinema, articles in magazines and television films about the Royal Family, the novels of Dennis Wheatley. She expected people to like her but wasn't much bothered if they seemed indifferent; took what she wanted unless it turned out to be awkward or difficult when she told herself she hadn't really wanted it after all. When she felt like it, she could work or play till she dropped. In between she was idle, sat about, ate huge meals, waited for something to happen. She had always believed life was simpler than most people pretended and just at the moment she was bemused by the way it had recently become so uncomfortably complicated. And slightly cross. She felt she had been misinformed. Someone should have warned her.

She said, 'Be careful with Ruth, I mean. Watch your step. She really is in a state. Oh, for God's sake, one would expect her to be pretty cheesed off, hurt and upset, and above all, bloody angry. But she says that she isn't. Not with you, anyway.'

Can't risk it, was what Ruth had said. Listening to her, Daisy had been suddenly quite deeply disturbed, almost frightened. But she was always affected by the person she happened to be with at the moment. Now, with Joe sitting there on the other side of the stained, marble-top table, so comfortable, easy, old friend and lover, Ruth's outburst and her own reaction to it seemed excessive. She said, 'I can tell you, if I'd been her, I'd have kicked your teeth in.'

'Ruth isn't like that.' He shook his head sadly, regretfully, but he sounded complacent.

'How do you know what she's like? She's changed. Oh, for God's sake, why the hell did you tell her?'

'You told Luke.'

'He told *me*. He guessed. I expect people know. You couldn't really have thought no one did? Honestly?'

But of course he had believed that. Made himself believe it. Nor had it been difficult. He had simply divided himself, seen his life as two worlds, each complete and secure. One world contained Ruth, his quiet, dark-eyed, gentle wife, his home and his children. The other, beautifully and blissfully private, held Daisy who made him feel young again; discreet meetings in pubs, happy love making – all the more joyous because it could never be as often as they both wanted. They had no safe place to go; an odd night in an hotel once or twice when Luke and Ruth happened to be away at the same time, but on the whole that was too risky for Joe. He bought the Sealyham bitch. They drove to Hampstead Heath, left the dog in the car, found a hidden hollow; met winter evenings, in the dark, in the communal gardens, clearing a space among the refuse, the litter. These occasions were the ones Joe found most exciting. Enclosed in one world, as in a transparent balloon, he could keep an eye on the other. There were several television programmes Ruth always watched with Marigold, to keep the child company. From the wild garden, from Daisy's arms, Joe could see the lights go off in one room of his house, go on in another . . .

He said, with a deep, sincere sigh, 'I never wanted to hurt her.'

Daisy knew this was true. She hadn't wanted to, either, or she would never have played it Joe's way. Her other affairs had been much more open. Not obtrusively so – she was never brazen, choosing men whose wives she didn't know and who lived a reasonable distance (she had a geographical reference for south of the river) from her own home. She had never cared if Luke knew, though she had never faced him with her behaviour deliberately, but she cared about Georgia. Now she was forced to care about Ruth. And she did care, she thought.

But there were compartments in Daisy's mind, too. Ruth was Joe's business, really.

She said, 'Well, you should have tried a bit harder, then. You shouldn't have stopped making love to her. If you wanted to keep it quiet, that was bloody stupid.'

Joe rubbed at his eyeballs, making them squeak. He muttered, 'Oh, for God's sake, I'm getting *old*.'

'Lovely old man,' Daisy said, quite affectionately but a little crisply. She was fond of Joe. She tried to measure this fondness. She loved Joe as she had, in the very beginning, loved Luke, but not as much as she had loved her father, as she still loved her brother. But she knew better than to say this to Joe. It had caused a flaming row once, when she had said to Luke, perfectly seriously, 'You can't really promise to love someone for ever, someone who isn't one of your family,' not meaning to hurt him, just trying to explain that there was a difference. It was the only time in their married life that Luke had hit her. He had slapped her across the face. Then, later on, after he had wept and apologised, he had said, 'I'm sorry, love, you can't help it. You had too happy a childhood.' What was wrong with that, Daisy wondered.

Joe said, 'I suppose what really happened, what I really thought, was, that we had grown into a different sort of relationship. Loving each other, of course, but not so much sexually. I suppose it suited me to think that. On the other hand she never said anything, never complained. I'm surprised that she told you. More than surprised – amazed, really!'

'I asked her,' Daisy said. 'It came up. Not as the most important thing.'

'I never thought she'd tell anyone, *anything*!' Joe was red in the face, growing resentful. 'I thought it was a private matter between us!'

'Well, as far as I know she's only told me. And since I knew anyway, I can't see that it's any less private now.' The girl inside Daisy wanted to giggle at this absurd situation. But she remained grave. She said, 'You'd better not tell her that you know that I know, that would send the balloon up good and proper! Though I do think you might have let me know what you'd told *her*! It was a nasty shock to begin with!'

'Sorry. I thought – well, you know what I thought. I had to protect you.' Joe put his glasses on to read the blackboard above the bar. 'Would you like something to eat? Beef, smoked salmon, chicken with F/F. What's F/F?'

'French fries,' Daisy said. 'No, I'm not hungry.'

'The smoked salmon is usually good here.'

'No thank you.'

'Are you all right?'

'Fine. I just feel a bit queasy.'

'I'm sorry.'

'Never mind about my stomach,' Daisy said.

'I do mind. I mind that you're so upset you can't eat. Ruth's off her food, too. She's lost weight. Two starving women on my hands!' He smiled miserably. 'Oh, God, I've hurt both of you, haven't I?'

'You've hurt her much more,' Daisy said. 'What I don't understand is why you couldn't have just said it was over, that you wouldn't see or speak to me – I mean to *this woman* – again.'

'I couldn't lie to Ruth altogether,' Joe said.

Daisy snorted and chuckled. She said, 'Eunice Pilbeam!'

'There was a film star called Pilbeam. She was the first woman I fell in love with, in a cinema, years ago, watching her in this old black and white film. I was about fourteen. She was exceptionally beautiful. Nova Pilbeam.'

'Why Eunice?'

'Invention, I hope. I was at my wits' end. Maybe I thought it was an unlikely name.'

'Why a physiotherapist?'

'I like nice, big, strong women,' Joe said. He touched her smooth, bare fore-arm, freckled with sun. 'I'm sorry. It's not at all funny.'

'It has its comic side,' Daisy said.

'Not for me.' Joe had finished his beer. He sat, playing with a beer mat, twisting it like a top, slapping it down hard on the marble. He said, 'I feel terrible. Mentally, obviously. But physically, too. My head aches, my eyes ache, pain *behind* the eyes all the time, as if my sinuses were filled with lead lumps. I'm beginning to wonder . . .'

'Don't blackmail me,' Daisy said. 'I'm not Ruth. If you think you've got a tumour or something, go to a doctor, ask for a brain scan. But I think it's guilt. And only because Ruth's found out. Because you've been caught. You didn't feel guilty before.'

'Didn't I?'

'It didn't show, anyway. Merry as a grig, you were. The happy little adulterer. Even when Luke . . .' She stopped. 'Oh, I'm sorry. That isn't fair.'

Joe said, with astonishment, 'D'you think I didn't feel bad about Luke? Oh, dear God.'

'There was no need if you did. Luke knew about me, what an old slag I am, he was used to it. If he chose to go over the top this time, that was his business. My business. Not yours.'

'Don't pretend to be hard. You felt terrible.'

'Only for a while, when I knew he hadn't meant to kill himself really, just drunk himself into a stupor. Of course I felt bad then, blamed myself, though it was life that had got him down, let him down, not just me. But I'm over it now. I've *buried* him, Joe.'

It wasn't as simple as that, but making things simple was one of the things Daisy was good at. At this moment she felt worse about Ruth, in the sense that she felt more responsible, than she did about her dead husband. Of course that was partly practical. Luke was dead, Ruth was alive. But it also meant there was a solution. One she could help bring about. Even if she felt, as she did, that Ruth was making an absurdly unnecessary fuss, that she was old enough to accept the fact that unfaithful, middle-aged husbands were the rule and not the exception, that had nothing to do with it. She had already made up her mind (more or less) that for her and Joe it was over. It was a pity – of all her lovers, Joe was the one she had felt happiest with, most at ease. She felt at ease with him now, sitting in The Harp and Flowers with the summer sun shafting dustily in through the windows, with the smell of beer and stubbed-out cigarettes in her nostrils. He was such a nice man, large, clean and boisterous. They had had a lot of laughs together – more important than the sex, in Daisy's view. She liked the way his eyes crinkled up at the corners; the way his face lit up like a lamp when he saw her. With Joe, she never felt dull or too fat; his love for her was uncritical, almost like her father's love. When her father was in the nursing home, Joe's approving, undemanding love had held her and comforted her through his long and difficult dying. And comforting her had been important to Joe. He had needed comfort himself. He had just missed a promotion he'd hoped for and it had depressed him, coming just before his fiftieth birthday, a time of life, Daisy thought, that was harder in some ways for men than for women. Not just the physical thing, growing old, but the way they were sometimes faced, before they were ready for it, with a sudden end to hope and ambition. She had watched Luke go through this turmoil, seeing his retirement ahead like a door slamming. Whether Joe felt as Luke did she didn't know, simply sensed he was melancholy. One evening, he and Ruth had given a dinner party and he had barely spoken all evening. Luke had cried off at the last minute, gone to bed with a stomach upset, and Joe had walked her home, still not speaking. At her door she had said, 'What's wrong with you?' and he had kissed her, then put his head on her shoulder and groaned.

That had been the beginning. To start with he had been shy, a bit gruff and uncertain, but as soon as she let him see that she knew what he wanted, he had rushed into it. There had been no guilt on his part about Ruth, or seemed to be none. He had been simply joyful. He had said, the first time they made love (on Hampstead Heath, the horrible little dog yapping like mad in the car), 'I'm so happy, this can't be wrong,' and after that 'wrong' had never been mentioned. Well, now it had been, Daisy thought, so it was time to make an end. Tidy things up, sort them out, make amends the best way she could. She felt a little weak at the prospect, she would miss Joe. It was lucky that Bob was coming. The thought of Bob steadied her.

She said, 'Look, changing the subject, I don't think Bob and I should come to Egypt. Ruth wants us to for all sorts of reasons but you could try and persuade her . . .'

Joe said, 'We're booked for October. I've paid the deposit!'

'Oh, Joe, don't be silly.'

'I want you to come.' He smiled at her. 'Like Ruth, for all sorts of reasons. Not all of them selfish. You needn't worry, I won't fall on you in some ancient tomb. But it would make things so very much easier.'

'Not for me,' Daisy said.

He seemed not to have heard this, although his eyes were watching her. He took her hand and turned it palm upwards in his own, then folded her fingers, crushing them tight. He said, 'This is going to sound pretty ridiculous. I've told this silly lie about Eunice. God knows, I wouldn't have done it if she hadn't pushed me, but there it is, a fact I can't get away from. I think, if she found out the truth, she would never forgive me. If you don't come – after all, what excuse can you give? – she might guess. She never used to be suspicious, but she's bound to be now. And it would make things so much worse – quite intolerable.'

Daisy said, 'You really do love her? You want to stay with her?'

'I think so. It would be like losing an arm or a leg. Oh, Daisy, it's all so horribly complex. There are the children. She loves me so much. I think I love her.'

'Is that what you tell her? That you *think* that you love her? Oh, yes, of course it is. What a fool you are, Joe!'

Joe said, 'I want to be honest with her. She deserves that, at least.'

'Why are you so keen on your honesty all of a sudden? You've lied to her long enough. I'd have thought you could have lied a bit longer. I think you are playing bad games with her now, keeping her hanging on, in suspense. If you want her to stay with you – and try thinking of it that way round for a change instead of your making a noble decision – tell her you love her, that it was all a most ghastly mistake, that this woman, this Eunice, is really the most God-awful tart, you see now you must have been mad! Oh, stop holding my hand, clinging on like a drowning man to an old piece of lumber. Why the hell should I have to tell you what to do, you should bloody *know*. There's nothing exceptional about the fix that you're in. You're a married man who's cheated his wife. I don't happen to think that's so dreadful, I can't see much point in all this moaning and groaning, but she thinks it is, and that is what *matters*. We've had a good time at her expense, now you make it up to her.'

She locked her hands in her lap. She was trembling.

Joe said, 'Do you want me to leave her?'

'Why do you say that?'

'Because that's the way that you're pushing me. I'd rather leave her than tell all these lies. She'd want me to leave her if she thought I was that sort of sex-crazed old idiot!' He glared at her. But there were tears in his eyes. 'I'm tired to death, Daisy. I hate seeing her suffer, I'm doing my best to go through the motions, but that's about all I can manage. If she didn't love me so much, it would be easier. But she does. It makes me feel such a shit.'

He looked really quite desperate, lips shaking, unhappy, quite suddenly very much older.

Daisy thought – my God, I feel tired, too! She said, 'Cheer up, old Joe-kins, pull your finger out, I'm trying to *help*.'

He said mournfully, 'You're being wonderful, Daisy.'

'Oh, stuff that! Just listen to what I'm trying to tell you. I don't know how to put it. Yes, I do. This is a comedy, not a tragedy. The way human beings behave. Like in *A Midsummer Night's Dream*. The only serious characters are the fairies. The people are *jokes*.'

Joe looked astonished. He said, 'Whatever made you think of that?'

'I don't know. It came into my head. Oh, thinking of Ruth, I suppose. We did *The Dream* at school. Ruth played Titania. I remember my mother thought it was an odd bit of casting. She said, "I know Ruth is dainty, but you'd have thought they'd have picked something prettier." But Ruth was perfect, of course. So small and dark and intense.'

'And so *serious*? Yes, I can see that.' He smiled – thinking of Ruth, Daisy saw, with a sudden, sharp tenderness. He said, 'What part did you play?'

'I was Bottom,' Daisy said, rather coldly. 'I tried out for Helena, but another girl got it. My mother thought I ought to be Oberon, but I was too fat. Huge thighs in black tights with spangles!'

'Oh, I do love you,' Joe said. 'We're both Rude Mechanicals. Daisy, my love. . .'

'Shut up.'

'Come to Egypt, then.'

'Shut up about that, too.' Daisy stood up. 'I'm sorry, Joe, but I really must go. What the Americans call a tight schedule today. Drinkies with my ex-lover, tea with my ma-in-law, dinner down the road with old Simon.'

'If you come to Egypt,' Joe said, 'I'll shut up. I'll do all you tell me, I promise. Do my best, anyway.'

She buttoned her jacket, picked up her handbag. *Oh, the mean bugger*, she thought. And then, *I do love him.*

She said, 'I shall know if you do, Joe, because Ruth will tell me.'

'You look well,' Stella said. 'A bit of weight suits you.'

It was hot in the flat, the electric fire on. Sweat trickled between Daisy's breasts.

'Walter is making the tea,' Stella said. 'I apologise for not being dressed to receive you. You're a bit early.'

She looked very comfortable, sitting close to the fire in a heavy man's dressing gown, feet propped up on a stool. Nice afternoon nap, Daisy thought. Did Walter share it? She wondered if she should go to the bathroom, glance in the bedroom, see if there were any signs of male occupation.

Stella said, 'I don't think Paul quite approves of my having a gentleman friend.'

'None of his business.' Daisy smiled at her mother-in-law. She had always thought her a plucky old woman. Spunky. She said, 'If I can find someone when I get to your age, I shan't worry.'

'Walter and I suit each other. We can each do different clues in the crossword. Have you heard from Paul lately?'

'He telephones – oh, about every other day, I suppose. To see how we are.'

'He's got a good wife, you know.'

'Judy?' Daisy was slightly puzzled by the intensity of the

gaze bent upon her. Those eyes were really extraordinary in such an old woman; so sharp and so blue. She laughed. 'Whether she's a good wife or not, I don't know.'

'She cares for Paul's career,' Stella said. 'She has money. Those are two very important things in a marriage.'

'Not the most important thing, I'd have thought,' Daisy said, smiling to soften this. It was impolite, her mother had taught her, to contradict very elderly people.

'Love, you mean?' Stella said. 'You get to my age, you wonder what all the fuss was about. A childish infection, like measles.'

'Most people get measles sometime or another.'

'More dangerous in middle life,' Stella said. 'I worry about Paul, sometimes. He's at a dangerous age. Ripe for foolishness. The consequences for a professional man can be fatal.'

'I should have thought Paul was the last person to do anything stupid.'

Stella smiled. 'I'm glad to hear you say that.'

'I should have thought it was obvious.' Daisy thought – what an odd conversation! She said, returning to what seemed Stella's main theme, humouring her, 'My mother always used to say that arranged marriages were much the best thing. I think she fancied herself as a matchmaker.'

Her mother had not wanted her to marry Luke. Paul was so much 'jollier'. There had been great stress on jolliness in the Brown household, on good spirits, on happiness measured in gales of laughter. Not a bad measurement either, Daisy thought now. At the time it had not seemed important. She had been seduced by Luke's thoughtfulness, by his sweet, soulful gaze. He had made her feel that there were serious things in life that had so far eluded her; things he could teach her. Luke had seen her as a girl to be moulded; a young, merry Galatea to his Pygmalion. But the teaching process had only

lasted as long as their courtship. While he held her hand in the
National Gallery, watching her looking at pictures but really,
urgently, longing to be in bed with her, she had responded to
this understandable flattery, not to what he was showing her.
Once he saw that art and music and foreign films bored her, he
was dismayed, disappointed. She was bewildered by his disappointment. She went on, chattering about the things that
did interest her, the personal lives of their friends, plans for
excursions, for parties, the choice of wallpaper and paint for
the house they were buying, but though he listened and
answered her, she began to realise that to him these were
trivialities, not worth all this eager discussion. Except in bed,
he made her feel patronised, looked down upon. No one in her
life had done that before, she could hardly believe it was
happening. She was pretty, an excellent, inventive cook, a
good *wife*, for God's sake! She looked after Luke's clothes, was
never too tired to make love when he wanted, invited his
friends to dinner. She sat at the table, watching Luke talk about
books and the theatre, his face lighting up. She tried to join in
but Luke made her nervous; she was afraid she would miss the
point, that what she said wouldn't be 'deep' enough. Sometimes Luke seemed to approve of her. 'You have a lot of
common sense, Daisy.' She read this as 'ordinary'.

She had refused to be hurt. She put Luke aside in her mind.
She wasn't unhappy. She had her little boy. She played with
him, adored him, took him out proudly, pushing his pram to
the park. She knew they looked lovely together; a strong,
pretty young mother and her beautiful son. She met men in the
park, students mostly, younger than she was, but a couple
were older; a handsome Greek waiter, a rather prim stock-
broker in his mid-thirties who shared his lunchtime sandwiches with her in the rose garden. She wanted casual
conquests, not lovers; protected by her innocent baby, she
flirted and teased; when the two older men became what she

thought of as 'tiresome', she moved on by the simple expedient of frequenting another part of the park.

She wasn't unfaithful to Luke until the child died. He got meningitis. He was three years old; his baby face wrinkled up with the terrible pain like a very old man's. She rang Luke from the hospital but he was in a meeting; she left a message and went back to the ward to watch her little boy die. She waited a little and, when Luke still didn't come, left the hospital, went to the nearest hotel, picked up the first man who spoke to her in the bar, a salesman, a traveller in agricultural machinery. That was all she remembered about him afterwards; not his face or his hands or his body, only his occupation. A couple of hours with a traveller in agricultural machinery and the pain became, not acceptable, but just about bearable. She went home, and by the time Luke arrived, frantic with worry – he had run round the streets looking for her, rung the police – she had driven the pain deep inside her. She looked at Luke with contempt – a man who could not get to his dying child's bedside. She refused to speak to him for days; locked in a shrivelling silence. Now, years later, sitting in her mother-in-law's stuffy flat, temperature well up in the eighties, she thought, we were finished then, I should have admitted it, why the hell didn't I? Oh, she had been too caught up in her sorrow, her first really deep and terrible sorrow, nothing else mattered. She didn't care enough about Luke to leave him, he was nothing to her, why should she bother? And once she no longer cared, once he could no longer in any way hurt her, he had become kinder, less critical. They got along well enough, Georgia was born, they both loved her. No point in brooding, Daisy thought. She looked at her mother-in-law, who had lost a son, too, and said, 'I suppose arranged marriages would deal with things like money and suitability. But Luke and I were fond of each other.'

Stella sighed. 'Yes,' she said, 'well.' And then, with another of her sharp looks, rather briskly, 'You've got a lot of life still ahead of you, Daisy. Don't waste it.'

Walter came in pushing a trolley. He was wearing a grey roll-necked sweater, somewhat too large for him, leather patched at the elbows, that Daisy recognised as belonging to Stella's dead husband; she had sewn on those leather patches herself, years ago. Walter had moved in all right, Daisy thought, as he poured the tea, handed round plates, and then sat primly on the edge of a chair, eyeing her shyly, wondering how she was going to take it. Nervous, poor bloke! Daisy smiled privately, thinking of Paul. What a facer for him! She was suddenly hungry, she ate a huge wedge of cake, feeding crumbs to Walter's dog who sat at her feet, and talked away cheerfully, about the weather, about Bob who was coming 'home' from Australia. They must both meet Bob, she would bring him to see them. She told a few silly jokes. At least there was something she was good at, she thought, seeing Walter relax; I can always put on an act, chatter away, smile till my face cracks. When she went she kissed both old people – a light kiss on the surprised Walter's face, a warm hug for Stella.

'You're a nice girl,' Stella said, with unusual, grateful affection. 'Walter and I will always be glad to see you.'

Outside in the street, she felt suddenly quite exhausted by her social endeavours, the spirit gone from her, an empty shell walking, a large, empty body with nothing inside it. But as soon as she thought of this image, she found it ridiculous, put her shoulders back, lifted her chin. She would go home, have a long, hot bath, wash her hair, dress up for dinner with Simon, that would make her feel better. Treat herself to a taxi, even though she couldn't afford it.

She gave the driver the address of Ruth's shop. Not much of a diversion from Chelsea, and if Ruth was there today she would be leaving just about now. Cheaper to get a lift in Ruth's car than pay the fare all the way home. The traffic was

slow; cars parked either side of this fashionable, small shopping street, and from the idling taxi she saw Ruth some way
ahead, on the pavement. She was standing outside the shop
with a rosy-cheeked, youngish man who was wearing a velvet
suit and a huge, flowing, silk cravat, a riot of flowers. He was
talking to Ruth very earnestly, holding her hand to his chest,
eyes fixed on her face. Ruth seemed to be listening equally
earnestly; then, as the line of cars began to move and Daisy's
taxi jerked forward, she lifted her free hand and touched the
man's tightly curled hair. A playful touch only, but Ruth was
smiling with glowing ease and a kind of relief as if something
this obviously old and close friend had said had given her
comfort or pleasure. A lover? No, not Ruth! The bloke who
ran the money side, probably. Daisy had never met him but
she had heard Joe's snide remarks about his fancy appearance.
Still, queer or not, he was clearly what her mother would have
called 'smitten', Daisy thought, as she tapped the driver's
window and gave him her home address. No mistaking that
look – as Mrs Brown used to say, proud of her daughter's
ability to produce it on the faces of so many young men.

Sitting well back in the cab, out of Ruth's view, Daisy was
seized by an acute attack of nostalgia. Oh, to be going home –
really 'home', especially in winter with the curtains drawn, the
banked up fire blazing fiercely, tea on the table and her
mother's voice running on, wondering whether the Princess
Elizabeth was really in love with 'her Philip'. In spite of a
philandering husband, Mrs Brown's happy obsession with
love had been an unbroken thread on which her whole life was
strung, convincing Daisy throughout her girlhood that it was
the only prize really worth seeking. And yet here I am now,
Daisy thought, and felt her eyes stinging.

Naked, Simon looked much younger than he did clothed. His chest was surprisingly broad and muscular, tapering down to a narrow waist, a flat belly. His erect penis rose like some sturdy, succulent plant from thick, curling, coppery foliage. Naked herself, lying on his wide, comfortable bed, Daisy looked at the taut, elderly face, the grizzled head perched on the trim, young man's body, and thought – with hair that colour, he must once have been beautiful.

He sat beside her. They had had a small sherry each before dinner, and then half a bottle of wine. Presumably Simon thought that too much alcohol would affect his performance. Well, from the look of him, there seemed little fear of that. Daisy half expected him to hurl himself on her immediately. (And why not? It was what she had come for.) Instead, he began to stroke her feet, then her ankles and legs, quite firmly and purposefully. He had some kind of oil on his hands faintly scented with a sharpish, clean smell – orange or lemon? – that made his careful massaging extraordinarily pleasant. He seemed to be giving it his complete attention – no sly glances at her face to see how she was taking it – moving discreetly from the outer side of her thighs to her arms, long, sweeping, unhurried strokes. It was very soothing. Daisy had a sensation of being lovingly tended, taken care of, no need to respond, to do anything. A sense of social responsibility made her murmur, 'That's lovely, no one has ever done that to me before what a cunning old devil you are,' but he didn't answer, simply pressed his thumbs into the palms of her hands and smiled without looking at her face. He turned her over and massaged her neck, her shoulder muscles, the small of her back and her buttocks, until she gave a low, moaning cry. She felt a sudden release, a gentle, relaxing sadness. When he lifted her, gathered her into his arms and rocked her, holding her against his warm shoulder, she found herself weeping for the first time for years, a voluptuous torrent. She wept for Luke, for herself,

173

for their loveless marriage, for her dead little son. She wept while Simon made love to her, their bodies moving together, slippery with sex, oil and tears. She clung to him, weeping, 'Oh, I'm so sorry, so silly to cry,' and he said, 'Don't be brave with me, Daisy.'

She drifted into sleep while he was still inside her. When she woke he was dressed, sitting on the bed, watching her. She smiled at him sleepily, stretched herself, yawning. She felt like a great, soft, lazy cat. She thought – well, that's one kind of love, pity it was only old Simon. She said, 'Why have you got all your clothes on?' and he took her hands and pulled her up off the bed. He patted her shoulder blades briskly, and said, 'Musn't be greedy! Time to go home, little one. Nearly midnight.'

He was grinning at her, very bright and alert. She thought – goodness, he's pleased with himself! The lovely warmth she had woken with left her. She smiled at him, feeling a chill creeping through her, and said, 'Yes, of course. Georgia will be wondering where I have got to.'

Part Four
THE ICE HOUSE

I

Flying from Cairo to Aswan, looking down from the aeroplane, they have seen the wide, muddy river, a green serpent flowing from south to north, the source of religion and life, feeding the people, creating the gods. The Nile god is a man, wearing on his head a bundle of papyrus or lotus flowers, his woman's breasts symbolising fertility. Once a year the god summons the rising river, bearing the rich mud in its tumbling waters, greening the banks, keeping alive the precarious, thin strip of civilisation in the middle of desert. Though (as Bob, the engineer, tells them) since the High Dam was built, this annual miracle has been less effective. Unlike the old Dam, the British Dam, the High Dam holds back the greatest gift of the gods, the evil smelling Nile silt. A natural fertiliser cannot altogether be reproduced by chemical means and artificial fertilisers are, anyway, too expensive for the poor peasant farmers. All they have gained from the High Dam is electricity. Televisions flicker at dusk on the banks, in the mud villages. Otherwise not much has changed since the Pharoahs, Bob says. The ibis, sacred in Ancient Egypt, is still a protected bird and probably for the original reason: it eats the insects that feed on the crops. This may or may not be true. Bob is a lecturer in civil engineering who sometimes wishes he had read an arts subject at university. He has read up a bit in preparation for this expedition and got a few things wrong, probably; he admits it quite cheerfully. Although he is keen on what he calls 'doing his homework', he also enjoys speculation.

From the river boat, designed for the comfort of tourists, the desert cannot be seen; only the yellow banks gliding by, the mud villages, men in clean cotton shifts, women washing clothes in the river or carrying water pots on their erect, graceful necks, donkeys and oxen, palm trees silhouetted as in a child's picture book against a blue sky, hard as iron. Standing on the decks of the slow, comfortable boat, the tourists take photographs with elaborate, expensive cameras, look through binoculars at the bird life. There are the white ibis, the duck. Sometimes the lucky ones see a pair of blue herons.

Most of the tourists are not interested in the desert or in the present day life of the people. They have come to visit the burial chambers of the once wealthy dead, the Pharoahs and Nobles who believed in eternal existence and prepared for it from the moment of birth, embalming their bodies, building their tombs. Death was part of life, a continuing, adventurous journey in which all the elements of a man must take part; his earthly body, his abstract personality that can leave or unite the body at will, his spirit, his double, his shadow, his form and his name. To keep the whole man together required complex rituals, the assistance of many gods, and careful provision in his burial chamber of the things he enjoyed in his life: food and wine, incense, cooking pots, jewels, gold and silver. Many of the tombs were robbed thousands of years ago by the common men, the peasants who built them, but the records of their dead owners' lives, how they ate and drank, worshipped their gods, hunted game, ploughed their fields, took their harvests in, remain on the walls of their tombs, and it is these carved, painted pictures that the tourists have come to see. To look at, and marvel.

They have come for other things, naturally. To take photographs, sail on the Nile in feluccas, ride camels, buy post cards and souvenirs, acquire an impressive holiday tan. This morning, the third day of October, Daisy and Bob, Ruth and Joe, are sunning themselves on the deck of the river boat, taking it easy between one ancient tomb and another. Also on deck are a party of Japanese students, a large group of Germans, two young French couples (hairdressers from Paris, Bob has discovered), a doctor from Surrey and a man from the BBC with their wives. Daisy is stretched on a sun bed, wearing a white bikini, a straw hat shading her eyes. She is only half listening to Bob, recumbent beside her, reading out extracts from The Egyptian Book Of The Dead, and commenting on them. He is amazed by what he calls the 'psychological depth' of this old religion. 'Amazing,' he says, 'all those thousands of years before Freud, they knew it all, didn't they?' Daisy smiles at him fondly. Though she likes the sound of Bob's voice (if he read out a laundry list it would give her pleasure) she is really only interested in living people. She is happy Bob is here with her, so close that if she stretches out a lazy hand she can touch him, but it is the other passengers she is watching.

And, of course, Ruth and Joe. She is glad, for Bob's sake, that Ruth, sitting in a wicker chair, hands folded in the lap of her cotton dress, appears to be giving her full attention to the information about Ancient Egypt that Bob is enthusiastically offering. Although Ruth's loss of weight has made her look older, something about her (the way she is sitting perhaps, ankles crossed, head on one side, so still and attentive) reminds Daisy of a much younger Ruth, a schoolgirl politely anxious to please, patiently listening. From time to time this young Ruth nods gravely, asks an obviously interested question, smiles at Daisy or Bob. Not at Joe. In the last half hour or so she has not once looked at Joe. Well, Joe is busy birdwatching. Binoculars hide his eyes. He is hiding behind them. Believing himself unobserved, he looks morose and unhappy.

His own bloody fault, Daisy thinks. He has brought this about, willed this situation, why the hell can't he pull himself together? Here we all are, on this expensive holiday, why can't he relax and enjoy it? Oh, I know all about the suffering and shame he says that he feels, but he's *wallowing* in it, a real ego trip, that is boring and selfish.

At this point, Joe puts down his binoculars, blinks, rubs his eyes, smiles at her. Daisy frowns and turns on her stomach and opens her paperback thriller.

Once Bob had come, it had all seemed so easy. For a moment, meeting him at the airport, he had seemed like a stranger, much older, lines round his eyes, blond hair streaked with grey, then he had dropped his bags, put his arms round her, and he was Bob again, quite unchanged, her laughing and beautiful brother. She was so happy to be with him; these last two months in his happy company she had grown back into herself again, become the old Daisy, no more miseries, doubts, everything simple, straightforward. She had had an unwise love affair but it was over, she had done the right thing, there was no point in moaning over spilt milk. She did not comfort herself with this platitude; it rang perfectly true to her. She had given Joe up, sent him back to Ruth with some good advice, he had accepted it, that was the end of the matter.

Or she had thought that it was. Otherwise, in spite of her promises to Ruth and to Joe, she would not have come on this trip. She would have made some excuse to Bob, even though he was looking forward to Egypt, the high spot of his holiday. Not the truth, no need for that. He might understand and not blame her but it would complicate his relationship with Ruth and Joe, cast a cloud on the pleasure he took in their company. She had found it easy enough to treat Joe in her old, comradely fashion, as she always had done in public, and it had begun to seem, as the weeks passed, that nothing of any real importance had happened between them, or at least that it was safely over, forgotten.

Until yesterday in Aswan. Bob had carried Ruth off with the main party from the boat to see the High Dam. Joe and Daisy had ducked out of this dull expedition and gone with the Japanese students, riding on camels to an old monastery in the hills. Clinging to their absurdly uncomfortable mounts, isolated by language (none of the Japanese spoke any English) they laughed at each other, exhilarated as children, as they rode out of the oasis into the desert, saffron yellow in the sun, purple in shadow. The same boy led both their ungainly camels; from time to time, they lurched together, knees touching. In the monastery ruins they held hands, slipped away from the Japanese, kissed and clung to each other.

'Oh, Daisy, I've missed you.'

'Missed you too, you old goat.'

'I'm so glad. This is the first time we've been alone – oh God, for so long! Don't laugh at me Daisy. I love you.'

'What about Ruth?'

'I love her too, I suppose. Love you both, I can't help it.'

'Stop it, Joe. We agreed. Don't be so feeble.'

'I try not to be. I really do try. And I honestly believe that it's working. Ruth's being so good and sweet, I think she really is getting over it. Things are not quite back to normal, of course, I wake up sometimes in the night and she's crying, but she lets me comfort her. And we don't have any more of those dreadful, draining discussions.'

'No more Eunice Pilbeam?'

'She's not mentioned her – oh, for ages. I really think she has put it behind her. Does she talk about her to you?'

'Not recently.'

'Does she talk about me?'

'That would be betraying a confidence.'

'Oh, for heaven's sake, Daisy! Don't tease me. I hate this female conspiracy. Whenever I see you together. . .'

'I know. It makes me laugh, seeing you sweat.'

'Pig. Lovely Pig-Daisy.'

'As a matter of fact, it it comforts you, she hasn't talked to me much at all since Bob came. We've been busy, there hasn't been much opportunity. I don't think she wants to talk anyway. I did answer her – oh, several weeks ago, that night we all went to the theatre and you and Bob were getting drinks at the bar. I said, is old Joe behaving himself, and she said, with one of those funny, prim smiles, "he's trying hard to be dutiful".'

'Oh, God!'

'She was putting *me* down, don't worry. Telling me to mind my own business.'

'I'm doing my best. I suppose it'll never be good enough. I thought she'd forgiven me.'

'Maybe she has. Have you told her you've finished with Eunice?'

'I told you, it hasn't come up. Not since she told you what had happened, I think. I suppose getting it off her chest like that may have helped her get the thing in proportion, though it seemed to me pretty disloyal at the time. Made me bloody angry, in fact.'

'That must have eased your own guilt a bit. She hasn't given you much else to complain of.'

'I wish she had. Oh, that's wicked nonsense, I don't really mean it. But it's bloody hard to be so much in the wrong. Her goodness diminishes me in a way, makes me feel worthless and mean. I can't hold my head up. I know I shouldn't resent it, but sometimes I do.'

'Perhaps she'll let you off the hook. Would you feel better if she found someone to nip into bed with? How do you know that she hasn't? What about that man, what's his name, Danny? Opportunity there. All those trips they go on. They've been to Paris a couple of times these last few weeks, haven't they?'

'That funny little Jew? Don't be ridiculous. Queer as a coot.'

'Can't be sure, can you?'

'Pretty sure.'

'Well, okay. But he isn't the only fish in the sea. Perhaps she'll take up with Bob. Look how keen she was to rush off to that boring old dam.'

'She was just being obliging.'

'I wouldn't be so certain of that. Ruth's much sexier than I am, you know, even if she has hang-ups about talking about it. How do you know she wouldn't be happy to get a bit of her own back? Tit for tat. I would, in her place.'

'Because she isn't that kind of person.'

'Not coarse and vulgar like me, you mean? Thanks very much.'

'Idiot Daisy. Silly girl. You're not vulgar at all. You're good, brave and strong. Much stronger than I am. When you said we must stop, I admired you. But your goodness isn't the stifling kind. You're a free person, you go your own way, make no demands, it makes me feel, oh, I don't know, more at peace with myself. Whole again, not some sort of shameful, grovelling sinner, just an ordinary man who fell in love in a perfectly natural way, without meaning to hurt anyone. Just to be with you makes me feel better.'

'If I'd said *I* was hurt, if I'd moaned and clung, you'd have found it easier to give me up, would you?'

'I don't know. It would have torn me in pieces, I couldn't have borne it. I might just have gone away on my own. Disappeared altogether. Sometimes I think it might have been the best thing for everyone.'

'How heroic!'

'No. Just that I feel so confused. I keep hoping that something will happen, something miraculous, like the Red Sea parting and showing me the way clear. I look at Ruth and I want to love her as she loves me, as she deserves to be loved, as

I think I could love her if only she didn't know how shabby I am, and then I see you. . .'

'*How happy could I be with either, were t'other dear charmer away.* It's me that ought to clear off.'

'Rubbish. Oh, Daisy. Do you still love me a little?'

If the Japanese had not been around, gargling and gurgling at each other, they might have made love in the sand and the dust of the ruins. In fact, Daisy thought, lying on her stomach in the hot sun and feeling irritated suddenly, if it were not for Ruth's silliness they could all have a merry old time. A bit of switcheroo might cheer them all up. Even Ruth. Bob was so jolly and kind, really much fonder of women in general than Joe, a little affair with him would do Ruth a power of good. Help Joe, too, to find out Ruth wasn't a saint. Joe was really in a worse mess than anyone, such a simple, masculine man, quite at sea in all these awful, romantic complexities. He had had his bit of fun on the side; if he had persuaded Ruth to see it that way instead of allowing her to turn it into a great, roaring tragedy, he could have put it behind him, after a proper display of contrition – bunches of flowers, a few presents – and recovered his pride, without all this fearsome self-torture. Daisy wanted no part of it. Did she want Joe? Oh, perhaps, at this moment, lying here, feeling randy, but she didn't want to be dragged into the despairing mess and muddle he seemed to be making. Could she keep out of it? Oh, of course she could, she wasn't a puppet. She was fed up with the two of them, Joe and Ruth. If they wanted to make themselves miserable, wring their hands, freak their minds out, that was their business.

She raised her head and said, 'Nearly feeding time, isn't it? Anyone ready for drinkies?'

Joe sprang to his feet. The sudden movement made him

cough – a noisy, wheezy cough, reddening his face, watering his eyes. He thumped his chest. 'Sand. That was the desert. Gets in the tubes. Sorry. Beer, everyone?'

'Whisky,' Daisy said.

Bob slapped her bottom. 'Expensive slut. You'll drink the good beer with the rest of us.'

'Gnat's piss,' Daisy said, twisting round to peer at her buttock. 'You *hurt* me, you sod.'

'Nothing to how you'll hurt if you lie in the sun any longer. I've been watching that pretty French girl broiling slowly like a little pork sausage.'

'Bet that's not why you've been watching her.'

'Not altogether.' They grinned at each other. Bob said, 'Put something on, cover your shoulders, at least. There's a good girl.'

'Can't be bothered to go down to the cabin.'

'Lord above! Lazy tart! Hey – take my shirt, then.'

He threw it at her, knocking her hat off. She sat up, laughing. Ruth and Joe were watching this exchange with indulgent expressions. Daisy put her dark glasses on and smiled up at them. 'I'll have a beer then, since Bob's being so mean.'

'It's better for you,' Ruth said. 'Stops you from getting dehydrated. I'll give you a hand, Joe.'

Propped on his elbow, Bob watched them go. 'What a nice pair,' he said. 'Ruth's not changed a bit, has she? Still the cool little princess. Some of the temple carvings remind me of her. Those graceful goddesses. Lucky old Joe.'

'D'you wish that you'd married her?'

'Nope. Why on earth should I?'

'Mother thought of it. When she was eighteen, nineteen, and it seemed that you fancied her.' Daisy giggled. 'The little heiress! Mother thought it would set you up nicely.' A mild velleity floated through her mind, a thin wisp of smoke. *Joe loves Daisy, Bob loves Ruth.* She sighed and dismissed it.

'Mmm. I remember. A bit formidable for me, though.'

'Formidable? Ruth?'

'Oh, I dunno. Something about her. Gentle on top, underneath a bit steely. Bet old Joe has to watch his step. Wouldn't do for me, would it?'

'Don't you wish you'd got married?'

'I'd have liked kids. Half a dozen. Sometimes I dream of my children.' Bob sighed quite deeply. 'It's the rest of it – locked up for life in a breeding box with a strange woman.' He looked at Daisy and laughed. 'Pity we aren't Ancient Egyptians. Isis and Osiris. In Ancient Egypt, brothers and sisters married each other.'

'Incestuous brute,' Daisy said.

Bob rolled on his stomach and gazed at her solemnly. 'It's the mirror image thing, nothing to do with sex, really. I can see myself in you. Several times, on the brink with some girl, I've thought, it won't work, she isn't like Daisy, she'll never know me. When you think of it, the first fifteen years of your life are the most important. It's only the people who knew you then you can really count on.'

Daisy looked at him through her dark glasses. She shivered and pulled his shirt round her.

He said, 'What's the matter?'

'Nothing.'

'Come *on*! *Joke*! Half a joke, anyway. I didn't mean to upset you.'

'You haven't. It's just that we haven't much longer.'

'You could come to Australia. What's to stop you?' He paused. 'It's a decent size house. Room for Georgia, too. We could be a family.'

Daisy said nothing.

'No one else around, is there?'

'I don't know. No, there isn't.'

'You sound a bit doubtful. Sad.' He took her hand. 'Can't you tell me?'

She shook her head and laughed. 'There's nothing to tell. I'm fine, really.'

In the afternoon of the following day, a little bleary with too much local wine at lunch on the boat, they walk round the crocodile temple. Leaning over a stone parapet they look down into the pit, at the pool of opaque, slimy water, and the stone steps cut in the circular sides; the stair for the crocodile god. 'The old croc bathed down there and came up for his meals on the altar,' Bob informs Daisy. 'Doped, I imagine. Come and look at the mummies.'

Behind the grille of a small temple piles of mummified crocodiles give off a sour, dry smell, only mildly unpleasant. The Japanese adjust their light meters, click cameras, pose for each other in front of this charnel house. Daisy says, 'Ugh! All this *death*.'

It has begun to oppress her. The cold tombs fill her with a queer sense of foreboding. All this frozen eternity, fixed and still for such a vast stretch of time, seems to hold out its icy hands, trying to touch her. She is amazed that no one else seems to feel it. She spends as much time as she can in the sunlight outside the tombs, buying beads, little gods made of agate or sandstone; Horus, the falcon-headed god, a painted head of King Tut; fly whisks, flimsy dresses covered with sequins. On board the boat she drinks more than usual, flirts openly, harmlessly, with the man from the BBC, with the nice doctor from Surrey; chats to their wives; swims furiously up and down the small pool, dances in the saloon with anyone who asks her – with Bob, with a fat Egyptian in a white robe who never speaks, only rolls his handsome dark eyes at her, shaking his vast belly in a comic belly dance, with the doctor, with Joe. . .

Dancing with Joe, late that evening, she watches Ruth, sitting on a stool at the bar watching Joe, smiling a sedate, thoughtful smile. When Joe stops dancing, out of breath with a spasm of coughing, and goes to talk to the BBC man and an elderly German, the editor of a West German newspaper, Ruth continues to watch him with an expression Daisy finds hard to read. Considering? Contemptuous? Oh, surely not, Daisy thinks, joining Ruth, ordering whisky. At the other end of the bar Joe's voice booms out loudly. Daisy says, 'Laying down the law about something or other.'

Ruth smiles at her. She says, 'The thing about Joe is that he really prefers masculine company. Sometimes I think he only comes really alive when he's talking to other men. Do you know your hem is torn, Daisy? You must have caught your heel in it. If you give it to me tomorrow morning, I'll mend it.'

Perfectly poised, perfectly natural. An untroubled, good wife, a kind friend. Daisy says, 'God, it's hot, isn't it? Sultry. Like before a storm.'

'Unlikely in October, in Egypt,' Ruth says. 'It'll be cooler on deck.'

The deck is empty of people. There is a pleasant breeze, a faint stink of Nile mud. They are moored near a village; on the banks, white garments glimmer, a few small lights twinkle. The throb of music is comfortably distant from where they sit in the stern of the boat. There is no music from the sister ship, moored a few hundred yards downstream, only the blue flicker of the television in the darkened saloon. '*Death on the Nile*, I expect,' Daisy says. This is the film they were shown the previous evening, while the band played on the other ship.

Coloured lights, strung haphazardly along the boat rail, turn Daisy's flame chiffon to purple. Ruth's dark grey shift appears almost black. She seems to melt into the darkness behind her. Only her pale face, turned to Daisy, is visible.

Daisy says, after what seems a long silence, 'You're very quiet, Ruth. Are you all right?'

'I've been thinking. Oh, yes, I'm all right. I'm so glad you're here. And Bob, too. He's so nice, so easy to be with. Even if you haven't kept Eunice away as I hoped that you would.'

Apart from the girls in the Japanese party, there are only two unattached women on the boat; a middle-aged mother and her gawky daughter with lank hair and acne. Daisy says, 'How stupid, Ruth, of course she's not here.'

'Not physically, I didn't mean that. But she's here in Joe's mind. When he's sitting still, staring at nothing. And I think about her. Every evening when I write in my diary, particularly. It's a five year diary, I'm on the third year, and each day I look back at what happened the other years and it all falls into place like putting a jigsaw together. Last year, for example, on the fourth of October, Joe went to Cambridge for the night. He said he was giving a lecture. He rang me from the hotel, very late. I was in bed. She was probably in *his* bed when he spoke to me. And three weeks before that, he'd been on another trip, a conference, two days in Manchester. I made the call that time. Marigold was ill, she had a high fever, and I was worried. I rang several times, the last time after midnight, but he wasn't in the hotel. I expect they were out to dinner.'

Daisy sits very still in her wicker chair. She had not been with Joe in Cambridge. She had not gone to Manchester.

'All these last two years,' Ruth says, speaking very lightly and coolly, 'I thought I was married, that Joe and I were together, sharing our life. I see now that wasn't true, or not in any real sense. He was living two lives, and the one he was living with me, with me and the children, must have seemed boring and shabby to him, a sort of second-class life. I see that the evenings we spent, the family meals, watching television together, that I thought were comfortable, safe, happy evenings, were simply dull times of waiting for him, infinitely tedious because she wasn't there. And because he found our life so boring and shabby, it seems like that to me now. A grey waste.'

Daisy said nothing. What can she say to this nonsense?

Ruth says, 'She knows everything that happened to us during that time. He would have told her. All what I thought was our private life. I wonder how he spoke about me. Did he call me *Ruth*? Or, *my wife*? My dull wife.'

Daisy draws a deep breath. 'You said you weren't angry with him. But you are.'

'I don't know,' Ruth says. 'I don't know how I feel about him. I don't know how I feel about myself, either. You are what other people make you, I think. To take a simple example. If you removed one of those men we can see on the bank from his village, put him down some place where no one knew him, he wouldn't know who he was. One doesn't exist except in relation to people to whom one is of importance. What they think of you, how they see you, is what you *are*. I wasn't important to Joe all that time, or not in the way I believed that I was, as his wife, as his love, and so the part I was playing was a false one. He made me act falsely, and so *I* don't exist.'

Daisy longs for her whisky. But she doesn't dare move to pick up her glass from the table.

Ruth says, 'You know, Bob was telling me, when a Pharoah died, the first act of the new Pharoah was often to remove his predecessor's name from his tomb. I feel Joe has done that to me. He has struck out my name, so I am nothing. I have no purpose, no place anywhere.'

'You're still married to Joe,' Daisy says. 'You're Joe's wife.'

'When I hear the word *wife* I want to weep,' Ruth says. 'It doesn't apply to me any longer.'

Daisy says, carefully, 'Have you told Joe how you feel?'

'I may have tried once. It's no use, he can't understand. He thinks he's come back to me, or that he never left me, I don't know.'

'That's true in a way, isn't it?'

'Only in the way that he chooses to see it. That isn't my way.'

'Are you going to leave him. Divorce him?'

'If that was what he wanted, I suppose that I would. I haven't thought about it. I don't feel real enough to myself, solid enough, to make that kind of decision. Of course I am free now to do what I want, Joe has freed me, but I have to find out who I am first. Gather the bits of me up, the way Isis recovered the scattered pieces of her brother Osiris that were buried all over Egypt.'

'Oh God,' Daisy says. 'That old tale! Bob's been telling me, too.'

Ruth laughs. 'Of course Isis had a pretty hard time of it, and she had a bit of help, anyway. The Jackal god – Anubis, isn't it? – the god of embalmment came to her rescue. I don't think I can hope for that kind of divine assistance. My case is more like poor Humpty's.'

'Humpty?'

'Humpty Dumpty sat on a wall,
Humpty Dumpty had a great fall,
All the King's horses and all the King's men,
Couldn't put Humpty together again.'

Ruth sings this nursery rhyme in a high, cracked, tuneless voice. Then she laughs again, breathlessly. Daisy can see her eyes shining. *Mad* she thinks. *Cracked and crazy.*

She says, 'Ruth this is a bloody silly game, isn't it? I know that you're jealous and that's bloody painful. But you're making too much of it, aren't you?'

Ruth has stopped laughing. She turns her face away, with-draws into darkness, becomes an unmoving, dark shadow against the starry vault of the sky. Still as stone. *A temple goddess*, Daisy thinks, and feels a chill strike her. As if she were in one of those horrible tombs. Well, of course the temperature drops in the desert at night. She says, 'I'm cold, Ruth. You must be cold, too.'

'I quite like the cold,' Ruth says. 'It calms me down. Perhaps my father was right when he used to shut me down in the ice house. I really do have a terrible temper. And of course I am jealous. My father was, too. While he was in the Japanese camp, my mother's cousin used to come and visit us. You met him once, his name is Alistair, he came to my wedding. My mother's parents never spoke to her after she married my father, they disapproved of him, hated him, really, but I think they sent Alistair to see if we were all right. He was funny and nice, it was always very jolly when he came. I don't know if my mother had an affair with him but my father believed that she did. When he came back after the war he never let her forget it. He used to call her a dirty whore. He said, *If that man ever comes near this house again, I'll shoot his balls off.* I used to think that was incomprehensibly wicked. Now I still think it was wicked, but I understand better.'

'What do you understand?' Daisy asked, shocked. She is really very cold now; she drains her whisky glass and stands up, wrapping her arms around her, tapping her foot, anxious to get back to the music, the dancing.

Ruth stands too, shrugging her shoulders, spreading her hands out palm upwards. 'Oh,' she says, 'my father, of course. Perhaps I'm more like him than I had thought.'

Daisy was frightened. She couldn't put a name to her fear. Ruth had been just 'acting up' she decided, a bit of pure self-indulgence. Perhaps she had needed to blow her top, get the dirt out of her system. Certainly, the next afternoon, in the great temple at Karnac, wandering hand in hand with Joe among the huge, reddish stone pillars, and later, sitting beside him, opposite Daisy and Bob, in a gaily be-ribboned, clattering calèche, driving from the boat into the town of Luxor, she seemed her usual calm self again, looking about her with interest, at the black-veiled women, the roadside markets. She smiled her thanks at Joe when he helped her down from the calèche, asked his advice in the bazaar where she was buying presents for Marigold, Mark and Georgia, for Mrs Costello and the girls in her shop. Ruth had an introduction to the owner of this bazaar from a man in Cairo who was a friend of a jeweller she knew in London. 'You will give me a good price, I know, Mr Hashid,' she said, when they were all sitting round a low table in a back room, drinking tiny cups of black, bitter coffee, and Joe looked at her proudly. 'My wife is the expert,' he said, and after that it was to Ruth the bazaar owner talked, showing her one tray of jewellery, and then, when she shook her head smiling, bringing out what he called his 'serious pieces', all very old, all very genuine. 'This is from a very ancient tomb,' he said, holding up a string of turquoise and amber beads, 'about four thousand years old.' Ruth picked the beads up and examined them; then she looked at the man's face for a moment and he laughed and took them away from her. 'Perhaps not quite so old,' he said. 'Perhaps, in my safe, I will have something that will interest you more?'

Ruth shook her head. Her brown eyes were bright, like polished nuts. She was in her element, Daisy saw with amusement, watching her pick over gold and silver chains, some with semi-precious stones, others with a pendant, the Egyptian life symbol. 'I am not buying antiquities,' she said, 'only pretty things for my family and my friends. This, if the price is right, is what I would like for my daughter.'

She bargained delicately but decisively. A little frown, a little nod, putting a piece aside as if it had no interest for her, and then returning to it with a gravely considering expression. She bought a silver life symbol for Marigold, rings and chains for her shop assistants and Mrs Costello, an ivory paper knife for Mark, and, at what seemed a ridiculously high price to Daisy, the turquoise and amber beads for Georgia. 'Too much,' Daisy protested. The bazaar owner spread his hands in despair. 'It is almost a gift.' Ruth said, 'Not absolutely, Mr Hashid,' and they smiled contentedly at each other.

Joe was playing with a gold chain made of little, linked, golden fishes. He held it out on his palm. 'Ruth, this is nice, I think. Do you like it? You've bought all these things for everyone else. Let me get this for you.'

She looked at the chain for a second, then at him. She had gone quiet and still suddenly, mouth pinched, face screwed up, witch-like. 'No thank you, Joe. It's very sweet of you but I'd rather not, really.'

Bob looked at her curiously. 'Why not, Ruth? Let the man buy it for you if he wants to.'

'Not if she doesn't want it,' Joe said. He smiled as he put the chain down but he had gone white. *That was cruel,* Daisy thought. And then, fairly, *though why shouldn't she be if she feels like it?*

She felt confused and unhappy. Bob took her wrist and stroked it with his thumb. She turned to him gratefully and he wrinkled his nose at her, knowing that she needed cheering up, though not why, and said, 'Back on board ship, I think. Long day tomorrow, up at the crack of dawn, ready for a big slice of culture. The Valley of the Kings, where all the real nobs were buried. Tombs again, I'm afraid, Daisy.'

'This is sacred soil,' Bob says, as they disembark from the ferry that has taken them across the river to the west bank. 'Everyone who doesn't live on this side of the Nile has to leave it by sundown.' Pleased with this romantic notion, clutching his guide books, he bounds up the steps from the landing stage to the waiting coaches. Daisy, following slowly, is surrounded the moment she reaches the top of the steps by pedlars offering beads, little statues of gods, wooden heads of King Tutankhamen. When she waves them away, they jostle her, thrusting their dark, alien faces close to hers, shouting angrily. A lone woman is a good target for touts. She has lost sight of Bob. By the time she reaches the coach, there are only two seats still vacant, one next to the BBC man, the other next to his wife who smiles at Daisy and pats the place beside her invitingly. Bob is at the back of the coach, is talking to one of the French girls, leaning confidingly towards her with his arm on the back of the seat, his fingers brushing her shoulder. So that was why he was in such a hurry, Daisy thinks, noting sourly that in his eagerness to please this pretty, young girl he looks younger himself, tanned face smoothed out and smiling. Though it is absurd to be hurt by this, she is hurt, staring mutinously out of the window as they drive out of the oasis of palms and sycamore trees, through fields of cotton and sugar cane, up into the red hills of the desert. A small village clings to the side of a steep, barren slope, mud walls decorated with flowers and geometric designs. 'Those paintings on the houses show that the owners have been on a pilgrimage to Mecca,' the BBC man's wife tells her. 'How interesting,' Daisy says, twisting round, looking for Joe. He is sitting with Ruth, several seats back, both their heads bent over the book they are studying. Their shoulders are touching.

'The tombs of the Nobles are supposed to be fascinating,' the BBC man's wife says. 'The paintings are more lively and natural than in the big tombs, wonderful scenes of everyday life, I believe, but I suppose we shall only be seeing the chief ones, the tourist run of the Valley. Not that one would wish to miss old King Tut, of course, or Ramses the Sixth, but it would be nice to get off the beaten track sometimes, don't you think?'

'I don't know that I really mind terribly.' This is rude. Daisy smiles her apology. 'It's so hot.'

'Cool enough in the tombs,' the woman says, rather briskly, dismissing Daisy it seems as a sympathetic travelling companion and turning round to smile at her husband behind her. They had both wanted window seats, that was why they were sitting separately, Daisy realises. The man leans forward and touches his wife's cheek and Daisy feels abandoned and desolate – a widow alone. No one to count on. Even Bob, for all his sweet talk about brotherly and sisterly love, has abandoned her for a hairdresser. She thinks – maybe I should have grabbed old Joe while I had the chance. Ruth doesn't want him, they are never going to be happy together. Poor Joe! She feels a sudden, immense, aching longing for him that is partly sexual but more for the easy joy of their secret meetings, the comfort of loving and being loved, of knowing she came first with someone. She had come first with Joe for a long time. If she had hung on, wept and wailed, he would have been agonised, torn, but he would have left Ruth in the end. Why the hell hadn't she made him? Sitting in the bus, Daisy feels leaden with misery and loss. How pointlessly altruistic, pious and po-faced, she had been! And for what purpose? No one cared or gave her any credit, she had simply lost out all round, they had all lost out, no one was going to be any happier for it. If Joe didn't know how Ruth felt, he would find out soon enough. He thought she was behaving well, did he? So 'good and sweet'. If he'd heard her the other night, he might think again! Should she tell him that Ruth doesn't consider herself his wife any longer? But if she did tell him, would he believe her? Playing the scene back in her mind, Daisy hardly believes it herself – what Ruth had said was so weird! Really quite batty! You couldn't take that kind of wild raving seriously.

And yet Ruth had not spoken wildly but with a cold, stony calm. *Steely* was what Bob had called her – and old Bob wasn't a bad judge of women. Ruth will make Joe pay for what he has done, Daisy thinks, she will take her revenge, he won't know what's hit him. *Ruth* – well, that was a misnomer. *Ruthless* would be more to the point. Oh, not at first, in her first surge of shock and unhappiness, but now she has altered. Almost as if, in the last two months, she has become a quite different person.

The coach has stopped. They troop out into heat that strikes like a furnace, into a desert of stone. 'That is the natural pyramid, the Theban mountain,' the BBC man's wife informs Daisy politely, pointing to a pale gold peak high above them. A hot wind blows little spirals of red dust in the air. Daisy hears Joe coughing dryly behind her. She turns and he winks at her. His expression is innocently jovial. He is holding Ruth's elbow in what seems to Daisy an unnecessarily proprietary fashion. As if he were carrying a purse full of money, or some precious object.

The Egyptian guide is gathering his party around him. They are to visit the tomb of Tutankhamen, discovered by Carter in 1922 with its treasure complete, safe from the grave robbers because it had been concealed beneath another tomb. This tomb, the great tomb of Ramses the Sixth, was the one they would enter first, leaving cameras at the entrance, please, where they would be safely guarded, and proceed down the wooden stairway through a series of chambers, examining the painted, carved friezes and taking special note of the brilliant colours which have been exceptionally well preserved. There are many tourists here today and they must not crowd the stair, keeping in single file on the right, leaving room for those who are coming up on the left. 'Forward now, keep together,' the Egyptian cries, waving his arm and striding ahead like a white, graceful bird in his long, flowing robe. They all shuffle after him meekly, queuing at the entrance, leaving their camera equipment – some of them rather reluctantly, suspicious of the scruffy appearance of the official guardian, or annoyed because they are not allowed to record their visit to this particularly beautiful tomb. 'It is not forbidden to photograph,' the guide explains patiently. 'Only that this morning there are so many people, it is for your own safety that no one should hold up the line on the stair.'

The Japanese party are putting on cotton masks, covering their noses and mouths. One of the young men stands aside to let Daisy pass, accompanying this courtesy with a neat little bow. She smiles at him – he is very good looking – but his eyes remain distant and solemn. Daisy is an old woman to him – old enough to be his aunt or his mother. She sighs at this depressing thought and looks conscientiously at the friezes as she moves step by step slowly downwards. They really are very pretty, she ought to be interested, she tells herself, as she had told herself years ago when Luke had taken her round exhibitions and picture galleries. She had wished then that she could see what other people appeared to see – though sometimes she thought they only pretended, she had a sense that in some vital way she was missing something. It had not seemed to matter too much, but now she was alone, growing older – too old to strike a spark in a handsome young man – it would be nice to have other interests. I shall take up bridge like my mother, she thinks. Or good works. She yawns, scratching her ribs where her brassiere is too tight, cutting into her, decides that when she gets home she will go on a diet, giving up butter, perhaps, and wondering how long it will be before they have lunch, how long they will be stuck in this tomb. The slow procession down the stairway, tunnelling down and down into the hill, seems unending. Although the air is surprisingly fresh, she begins to feel suffocated, claustrophobic. Suppose the lights should go out? Everyone will go mad, these stairs, with their double queue, are a death trap. There will be a stampede; trying to get out, people will knock each other down, tread on each other. . .

But she has reached the bottom of the wooden stair now and there is more room to move. Here, the tomb opens out into a number of vaulted chambers on different levels with walkways between them. She catches sight of Bob for a moment but he is talking to the French girl whose husband (or lover) is not here. At least, Daisy can't see him. Stayed behind on the boat, she thinks enviously. Sensible fellow. Where is Joe? Oh, for God's sake, forget him! Plenty more fish in the sea. If she wants a fuck, old man Simon is better. But she feels an obscure pain, a kind of emptiness mixed with resentment. Why had he taken his dismissal so readily? Abandoned her with a few regretful kisses and sighs? Oh, she could answer that for herself, couldn't she? It had been almost insultingly clear at Aswan, in the monastery. He was grateful that she had tidied up his life for him! Good old Daisy, the brave girl, the strong one, stepping down so conveniently, making way for weak little wifey who needed him more. Oh, stuff that, Daisy thinks, I need him too. Ruth is stronger than any of us, doesn't he know that? After what she went through, she is a survivor! Oh, of course Joe didn't know that, no one knew it but her. 'Poor little Ruth,' her mother had said, pitying the fatherless girl after the 'tragedy', fussing over her, reproaching Daisy for not being 'kinder', sensing a reserve in her daughter that bewildered her. Daisy had said, 'You needn't be too sorry, Mum, *she*'s not sorry, her father was horrible to her.' And her mother had said, 'That can't be true, darling, of course the child loved her Daddy.'

She hears Joe coughing. Somewhere below her. She couldn't see him but she recognised that cough. A strained, whooping sound. She runs down a few steps into a rough stone chamber painted with blue birds and boats and finds him alone there, leaning against the painted wall, one hand clasping his throat. He is spluttering, wheezing, crimson patches on his cheeks, white as flour round his mouth. He is trying to breathe but each attempt produces a fresh spasm of that dry, desperate coughing. Daisy feels a sympathetic tightness in her own chest. She can smell the dust; the air, so agreeably fresh on the stairway, is thick with it here. She says, 'Joe! Oh, my darling!'

He grasps at her shoulder, digging his nails in. He can't speak; his eyes, bulging and bloodshot, look beyond her, above her. She looks where he looks and sees people standing on a wooden platform, a walkway along the top of the chamber; a couple of strange women, several strange men, the doctor from Surrey, one of the Japanese, wearing his cotton mask, Ruth in a blue linen dress, a blue scarf round her hair.

Joe doubles up, gasping, and lurches against Daisy. She can't hold him, he falls like a tree, lies on his side at her feet, knees drawn up to his chest. His hair is pink with dust from the ground, there are marks on his throat where his fingers have clutched it. Daisy kneels, trying to lift him, seeing the whites of his eyes rolling up. She thinks – the kiss of life, how do you do it? Someone pushes her away, bends over Joe; the Surrey doctor, lifting his limp wrist, feeling his pulse. The Japanese is beside him, tugging at his mask, holding it out to the doctor. But not Ruth. Ruth isn't here. She has disappeared from the platform. The doctor says, 'Better get him out of here.'

He and the Japanese are struggling with Joe's heavy body, dragging his arms over their shoulders. Daisy cries, 'Ruth!' She stumbles up the steps to the platform, sees the blue dress at the end of the gallery, at the foot of the wooden stair. A lot of people are milling about; Ruth is ducking, wriggling, pushing her way through them, climbing the stair. Running away, Daisy thinks, leaving him. Oh, dear God, how wicked! She is seized by terror and outrage as she follows Ruth, shoving people aside, shouting into uncomprehending, foreign faces, 'Sorry, let me pass please, it's urgent.' How slow they all are, how stupid, don't they know a man is dying down there, in the cold tomb? She is so afraid. She thinks, cold as the ice house, and recognises the source of her fear like a blinding light, a revelation. When she catches up with Ruth outside the tomb, by the stone shelf where they have all left their cameras, she falls upon her, twisting her round, screaming at her, 'You won't get away with it this time, you murdering bitch, what the hell do you think you are doing?'

Ruth says, 'Joe's camera.'

'His *camera*?'

'A Leica in a brown case. His inhaler is in it. Let me go, Daisy.'

Daisy lets her go. She leans against the wall, shaking and sweating. Ruth is diving into the pile of cameras, the guardian is protesting, trying to stop her. Shouts echo up the wooden stairway, hollow cries from the burial chambers. Ruth turns, white faced, a leather case in her hand. Daisy says, 'Oh, my God, Ruth, I thought. . .'

Ruth looks at her. For a second she is quite still, dark eyes staring at Daisy without any expression. Then she smiles – amazingly, she *smiles* – and she says, as she pushes past, 'I know what you thought. Oh, poor Daisy!'

II

Daisy said, 'You don't have to tell me anything. I was off my bloody head. Please forget it. I don't know what got into me. I was just being bloody ridiculous.'

It was after lunch. They had left the main party in The Valley of The Kings and returned to the boat by taxi and ferry. Joe was resting in his cabin. Ruth was sitting with Daisy in her cabin next door. If Joe needed her, he would knock on the wall. She was sewing the hem of Daisy's dress, her dark hair bent over the bright, flame coloured chiffon.

'A little melodramatic, perhaps,' Ruth said. She lifted her head and smiled. A little smile of private amusement. This was cool Ruth, Daisy thought, composed, secret Ruth. Her voice was light – a girl's voice, young but controlled. This Ruth said, 'You know how my father died, of course. That day, when I came down to breakfast, that Sunday morning, he wasn't there. He had already eaten, my mother said, and gone out with his gun. I ate my breakfast and went to my room to finish my homework. I left my door open and I could hear my mother playing the gramophone – sometimes she did that when he went shooting, she didn't like to hear him banging away, killing the little grey squirrels. She didn't mind about the pigeons so much for some reason. I think I was a bit surprised that she had the gramophone on so loud. I think – that is, I *think* I thought – that she wanted to hear it in the kitchen while she was washing the dishes and getting lunch ready. Then she came up with her hat and coat on and asked

me if I would go to church with her. When I came down the
dining room door was wide open and the table was already laid
with three places. My father's study door was closed. I
suppose I thought he was there. We went to church. We came
back. I went upstairs to the bathroom and when I came down,
my mother told me that he was dead. She was still wearing her
hat and coat. She had gone to look for him in the wood, to call
him for lunch, and found him dead in the ice house. She said he
must have slipped on the damp leaves and fallen in. She said
she was sure he was dead, but we must telephone for an
ambulance before we did anything else, all the same. She said,
'Our troubles are over,' and put her arms round me. I suppose
now that she must have known all the time. Perhaps she heard
him cry out, early on, before she called me for breakfast. Or perhaps she just guessed, when he didn't come back. She'd often
told him the ice house was dangerous, that he ought to fix
something across the entrance. I don't know. But she did close
the study door so that when I came down I would assume he was
there. She played the gramophone. She took me to church.
We didn't often go to church. That's absolutely all I know,
Daisy. My mother never said anything. I couldn't ask her.'

Daisy wondered if she believed this. She thought of Ruth
and her mother, that silent pair, alone in their big, gloomy
house. This suffocating secret between them.

She said, dry-mouthed, 'It must have been terrible for you.'

'No. I was a bit scared for a while that someone would ask
difficult questions. I mean, I was afraid for my mother. But
after the inquest, you know what they said at the inquest, that
he had broken the long bone in his thigh and bled into it, dying
quite quickly, I wasn't afraid any longer. I was glad he was
dead. She was glad he was dead. It was like being set free from
a prison. We burned all his clothes, all his papers, his shaving
things, everything. An enormous bonfire one evening. We
opened the windows and cleaned the house, scrubbing the

floors, washing the paint. My mother started to sing again. She had a pretty voice – not much volume, but true. I remember the first time I heard her sing. It was the day after his funeral. I was in my bedroom with the door open and she was downstairs somewhere. I remember I thought – *we're safe now, my life can begin.*' She looked at Daisy and smiled. 'You know the rest. When my mother got ill, your mother asked me to stay with you. I felt as if I'd been born again, into some kind of fairy tale. You were all so wonderful to me, you and Bob, your mother and father. I felt like an ordinary girl. So happy. . .'

She snipped a thread, examined her work, and folded the dress. She looked out of the cabin window that was just above the water line, at the rubbish bobbing by, trapped between the boat and the bank. She stood up and peered out. 'The coach party is coming back.' She waved. 'That's Bob, on the gangplank. . .' She turned to Daisy and sighed. 'That's all. Nothing else. I never thought I'd tell anyone. I couldn't, of course, while she was alive. And after that I had no reason to. Until now.'

Daisy said, 'Doesn't Joe know?'

Ruth shook her head.

'He should know. You ought to tell him.'

'Why? I don't want him to look at his children and think, they're tainted, their grandfather was a brute, their grandmother a kind of murderess. Even if she didn't actually do anything, I suppose you could call her that. I don't want Joe to know what my childhood was like. I don't want him to pity me. There are some things it's best not to talk about.' She paused for a moment. 'I should never have told you about Eunice Pilbeam. It was disloyal to Joe.' She sat down on the bed close to Daisy, and looked at her with wide, rueful eyes. 'Oh,' she said, 'I've been such a fool.'

'Telling me?'

'Not only that. Fussing over that stupid creature as if she were someone important. Poor Joe. I thought, when we were getting him up out of that tomb, oh, how silly I've been! Carrying on so you actually thought I wanted him dead! That was my fault, not yours. Though in a way I am grateful, Daisy. You made it all clear to me. My own *evil* folly! And then, in the taxi, I was holding his hand, and he tried to smile at me, and I thought, this is real, this is now, what's happened is gone, in the past. *She*'s in the past!'

'Are you sure of that? Have you asked him?'

'I can't ask him, he'll think I don't trust him. I'm almost quite sure.'

'Do you trust him?'

'No. Well. Not absolutely, how could I? After all the lies he has told me? But I try not to think of that, tell myself this was just something that happened, that there was a time when he was unhappy, couldn't talk to me for some reason, or was just bored with me – it really doesn't matter. He needed something he thought I couldn't give him and he took it from her, whatever it was that he needed – sex, conversation, he made *use* of her for *his* comfort, not hers. And now he's discarded her. Chucked her. Even if he hasn't quite done it yet, I think he is trying to. She's become a nuisance to him, an irrelevance.'

'Poor old Eunice!'

'Don't sneer at her, Daisy. I want to be kind when I think of her, not jealous or spiteful.'

'Do you think you can keep it up? You'll be a real saint if you can.'

'I don't know. I try and tell myself – perhaps Joe was the only real love of her life and she's lost him.'

'And you've got him back?'

'Perhaps. I don't know.'

'Do you want him?'

'I think so.'

'*Think*?' Daisy snorted disgustedly. Ruth was as bad as Joe, all this *thinking*!

'Well. I *hope* so. That's the most I can say. Such a lot has gone, trust and security. There are the children, but they're growing up. I have my work, I'm independent financially, Joe doesn't have to support me. We have to find out what's left. *I* have to find out.' Her eyes shone – it seemed to Daisy that they shone with a cold light. 'What's in it for me?'

'Oh, I see,' Daisy said. 'You pay the piper, call the tune, old Joe has to dance. Is that it?'

'No. I meant, what's in it for both of us? That's what we have to start from. There's no point in being sentimental over the past, that's over and done, we aren't the same people. We've changed. Eunice Pilbeam has changed us. The first thing we have to do before we start over, is to get rid of her. Kill her off.'

'Oh, my God,' Daisy said.

'She's dying already for me. If you like, if you want to be fanciful, she began to die in that tomb. I shall never know if she's dead for Joe, there's no point in asking him, because I shan't know if he's answering me truthfully, shall I? But perhaps, once *I'm* rid of her, we have a chance to pick up the pieces. I think, when we get back, I shall try to exorcise her out of my mind. I might even employ a private detective to find out about her. I would like to know where she lives, who her friends are, what she looks like. Of course, if she turns out to be beautiful, it will be depressing, but I'm halfway prepared for that. I mean, I know she is quite a lot younger.'

'*Younger?*'

'Younger than we are, that is. In her thirties, Joe said. Why do you find that surprising?'

Daisy said, 'Oh, the bastard!'

Ruth smiled. But her eyes were no longer cold. They were thoughtful, and waiting, and tender.

'Oh Christ,' Daisy said. 'You know it all, don't you? There never was any Eunice Pilbeam. Only me.'

Ruth started to laugh. She laughed till the tears came. When someone knocked on the cabin door, she was still laughing, wiping her eyes on her skirt, whooping and spluttering.

Joe opened the door. He looked pale and amazed. 'What the hell are you laughing at, Ruth? There's nothing to – oh, of course you don't know. Something frightful. Sadat has been killed. President Sadat. Assassinated by some Moslem fanatics. The BBC chap heard it on his radio. Bob's just been to tell me. God knows what's going to happen.'

The door to the gangway was locked. People were arguing with the boat manager. 'I am sorry,' he said, 'but no one must leave. You will be safe here. But no one must go to the town, to Luxor. There may be trouble between the religious elements.'

'The Copts and the Muslims,' someone said. An authoritative voice from the back of the crowd. A man's voice. Daisy looked round but she couldn't see who was speaking.

The manager said, 'The bar is open. There are refreshments. Since the expedition to the Luxor temple and the museum has to be cancelled, there will be an extra entertainment this evening. Games, and a fancy dress competition. The shop on the upper deck has pretty dresses for sale to the ladies.'

Several people laughed. Ruth tugged at Daisy's arm. She stood on tiptoe to whisper, 'If we could find some white coats, we could both go as physiotherapists, couldn't we?'

'Shut up,' Daisy hissed. Bob and Joe were standing behind them. But they couldn't have heard; there was too much noise now. People were beginning to argue, to shout. A confusion of languages.

Bob pushed his way forward. He said to the manager, 'Can

we telephone the airline? Some of us might like to alter our reservations.'

'I regret we have no telephone line to the shore,' the manager said. 'There is no need to change anything. You must all keep calm, everything is under control, you are tourists, no one will harm you. To stay on the boat is an extra precaution. I am responsible for you.'

He was sweating. He mopped at his forehead with a white cotton handkerchief. He wore a dark European suit, a white shirt. Either side of him, two of the bar tenders, in red uniform robes, stood silently, guarding the door.

Bob said, 'No point in arguing. We can get off, no hassle. Only we'll have to be quick.'

He was rolling up his shirt sleeves, jutting his jaw. Man of action. He said to Joe, 'If there's going to be revolution, sooner we get out the better.'

On the river side of the boat, the glass door was open. The BBC man was there, and, bobbing against the side of the boat, a felucca. 'Two pounds,' the BBC man was saying. The young Egyptian laughed and held up five fingers.

'Oh, come on,' Bob said. 'Whatever he wants. Coming, Joe?'

They dropped into the narrow felucca. They grinned up at Daisy and Ruth, excited as boys. Joe said, 'We'll be back, soon as we've found out what's happening. Don't worry, Ruth.'

'I'm not worried,' she said. 'But if you want to get us on a flight home, I've got the plane tickets here in my bag. Catch me, Joe.' He shook his head but she jumped, and he caught her. Daisy hesitated. The manager was shouting and people were pushing behind her. She jumped, with the BBC man, and the felucca rocked and swayed under them. The Egyptian pushed off from the river boat with his pole, shipping it in midstream, holding the tiller with one hand, loosening the tall, single sail with the other. His passengers lurched about, settling on the seats, laughing at each other self-consciously. Absurdly, this seemed like an adventure. The BBC man said, 'There's an afternoon flight from Luxor. You might get on it but I'm not sure I'd trust the connection. I want to get to Cairo, see what's going on with our man there, but the last thing you people want is to get stuck in the crossfire. All hell breaking loose.'

'No harm in finding out,' Bob said. 'We'd be all right at the airport, there'll be army and police everywhere. If it looks really dicey, we can always go back to the boat. I can't think there's really much danger.'

Peaceful enough on the river. Another felucca passed them, its sail full, racing them to the shore. It was laden with other passengers from the river boat. The German newspaper editor waved at them, shouting, 'We are the last to escape from our guardian. The rest are now under lock and key!'.

'There were other people killed, too,' Joe said. 'On the stand at the parade. I wish you'd stayed on the boat, Ruth.'

Except for a smiling glance, Ruth didn't answer him. She was sitting with one arm along the side of the boat, the wind blowing her dark hair loose from its chignon, watching the river. She looked cool and neat; Daisy, seeing her mouth twitch with amusement, felt suddenly hot with anxiety. She thought, if she tells Joe I've told her, Joe will never forgive me. On the other hand, it may bring it all to a head. There may be some tremendous explosion. All out in the open, no more stupid secrets and lies, all of us free at last. Free to choose. Though events had their own momentum, sweeping you along like a helpless twig in the current, you could always, if you made a real effort, strike out for the shore. She said, looking at the bank of the Nile, at the pink town drawing near, 'It looks very quiet, nothing seems to be happening,' and thought, here, on this boat, is the real action.

Bob said, 'I think you and Ruth should stay in the felucca. If there's any trouble the man can take you back to the boat.'

Ruth was already standing. She said, 'I want to telephone home if I can. If the children have heard the news, they'll be worried.'

She was first out of the felucca, running up the steps of the landing stage. Children were playing on the mud bank below her. A little girl with a smaller child on her hip scrambled up, holding her hand out. Ruth opened her bag, gave her a coin, and she ran away giggling.

They walked into a dusty square, the buildings honey coloured in the bright sun. Two old men sat on mats outside a shuttered shop, two bundles of ancient rags with bare feet sticking out. They were sharing a hubble-bubble pipe. Otherwise this square was empty.

Joe said, 'It looks as if everyone is indoors watching the telly. Perhaps the airline office will have a telephone you can use. Though I should think the local exchange will be pretty busy.'

'We could go to the bazaar,' Ruth said. 'If Mr Hashid can ring Cairo, his friend might be able to get through to London.'

'Worth a try,' Joe said. 'First things first, though. We must change the plane tickets. The kids are all right, it won't hurt them to worry.'

He took her hand, and then, as they entered a street at the side of the square, put his arm round her. Down this street, people were suddenly running and shouting, cries echoing from high, blank walls either side. A calèche clattered towards them, thin horse cantering, the driver standing up, using his whip like a charioteer, the German editor behind him on the flowered, plastic seat. As the calèche passed them, he shouted, 'The airline office is closed, I am going to the airport.' Behind the calèche came more people, Egyptians in cotton robes, waving sticks, screaming. Joe was pushing Ruth in front of him; he turned to grab Daisy's wrist, dragging her into a lane that opened beside them. This was a narrow alley with dark, open-doored hovels either side, and dark eyes peering out. Chickens ran, cackling, under their feet. The centre of the alley was a muddy stream of water and sewage. Joe said, 'Ruth, can you remember how to get to the bazaar? It was in one of the smaller squares, wasn't it?'

Bob was no longer with them. Daisy said, 'Joe, please wait. . .' But he and Ruth were hurrying on. She hesitated, looking back, and a man came out of one of the hovels, an old, thin man with a head like a skull, hairless, almost fleshless, gummed up eyes hardly visible. He held out his hand – for money, she supposed, like the child on the bank of the Nile. She shook her head and he laughed, toothless mouth wide, touching her breast with his fingers, twisting the nipple. She slapped his hand away and ran, splashing in the filthy water. Joe said, turning, impatient, 'For Heaven's sake keep up with us, Daisy.'

The lane led into another lane. In one of the mud houses a woman was wailing. The mob had already passed this way; they waded through the debris of a street market, smashed stalls, vegetables and clothing trampled into the mud and the dust, and came to the square they were looking for. The bazaar was closed. The shutters were up. Joe thumped on the shutters. Nothing happened. Ruth stood back. She said, 'There's someone up there, looking out of the window. I think it's Hashid. I think that he's seen us.'

They waited. It was still quiet in this square but they could hear shouting, some way away still, an undifferentiated wild howling. Joe said, 'It's coming closer, I think.' He pushed the two women into the doorway of the bazaar and stood in front of them. Then the door opened. Joe said, 'Mr Hashid, may my wife shelter here?' A curiously pompous choice of words, Daisy thought.

Joe was pushing them both, hustling them in front of him as if they were recalcitrant children. They went down a passage into the small room at the back of the bazaar where Ruth had bargained for trinkets. Hashid said, 'I am sorry I did not open immediately, but I have to take care for my family. We are Christians.' He was fingering a silver cross at his throat. He said, 'I apologise for this foolish disturbance. It is bad for the tourists.'

Ruth said, 'We have had riots in England this summer. So for us it is nothing unusual. We aren't frightened. But thank you for taking us in.'

'You are my sister,' Hashid said formally. 'You must stay until it is over. I do not think it will be very terrible. President Sadat is popular abroad but not here, in Egypt. He has not cared for his people.'

Joe said, 'I will leave the women here, if I may, Mr Hashid. I must go and search for my friend.'

He was still speaking oddly, it seemed to Daisy. As if he were translating from some foreign language. She said, 'Don't be a bloody fool, Joe. Bob can look after himself. He's a big boy.'

'All the same.' Joe was looking remarkably cheerful, squaring his shoulders for battle, enjoying this masculine situation, his role as fighter, defender. Damn sight easier, Daisy thought irritably, than sorting out his domestic life. Leave that to the women! That sort of muddle was their job. Like sorting odd socks into pairs!

He kissed them both. A peck on the cheek for his wife and his concubine, Daisy thought, turning her face away. When he had gone, she said, 'Bloody *men*.'

'Don't worry about Joe. He'll be all right.'

'Aren't you worried?'

'Not much. I think, at the moment, he needs to do something.'

Hashid brought coffee and left them alone. It was very quiet in the little room. They sat on a low bench covered with carpets, a table in front of them, gold and silver dimly gleaming in locked cabinets against the four walls. Daisy waited. Surely Ruth would speak soon? But it seemed that Ruth was waiting, too. Silently, patiently, sitting quite comfortably, hands in her lap, waiting for Daisy.

At last, Daisy said, 'How long have you known?'

'I'm not sure. Oh, I realised, of course, in the tomb. I thought – how stupid, I've been. But now it seems I must have known for a long time. I was put off, you see, by a number of things. Your mother-in-law, to begin with. Stella thought – she told me she thought – you were having an affair with Paul.' Ruth looked shy. 'I'm sorry. I didn't really believe it.'

'She's a wicked old thing,' Daisy said. 'Well, I wasn't. What else?'

'The Tate Gallery. Joe said you met there. It wouldn't be his choice. So I thought she must be. . .'

'A cultured lady?'

'I suppose so. I knew so little, he told me so little, it was part of the picture, I was trying to *see* her.'

Daisy said, 'The Tate Gallery is close to Stella's flat. There is a restaurant. We used to have *tea* there, for God's sake!'

Ruth nodded. She picked up her coffee cup, looked at it, and put it down again.

Daisy said, grimly, 'There wasn't all that much of the other. Not much chance, was there? We're both too old and too large for the backs of cars. Parks and open spaces.'

Ruth said, 'I wondered why he bought that horrible dog.'

She smiled at Daisy. She seemed very composed; unnaturally composed, rather as if she had retreated into some quiet, safe place where no one could touch her. She hasn't changed, Daisy thought suddenly. It was as if she had gone back in time, become a girl again, little Ruth Perkin, watchful and secretive.

Daisy said, 'You must think me the most frightful bitch. Why the hell don't you say so?'

'Because it's more complex than that.' Ruth's eyes looked at her with a dark, thoughtful sheen. Wondering if Daisy was capable of understanding? Oh, how smug, how superior! Then Ruth said, 'In a way, you see, I'm glad it was you. It makes everything different.'

'Better or worse?'

'Better, I think.'

'Why on earth . . ?'

'I'm not sure. I think I know why. It's somehow less frightening.' She gave a small, breathless laugh. She wasn't so composed after all. She was twisting her hands in her lap. She said, 'Ever since he told me about her, I've been so afraid. I used to look out of the bathroom window, sitting on the lavatory, or just standing and staring, looking out at the city, at the gardens, and think, *she*'s lurking out there. This un-known woman, this faceless creature, this thief. I don't know how she is, what she's like, what she's said to him, what he's said to her! What lies he has told both of us! Does he wish I would die, so they could get married? Is she nicer than me, funnier, cleverer? Or has she some frightful extra power over him? I even thought – is she having his baby? But, as you said, it was only you, Daisy. I couldn't be frightened of you.'

'Thanks very much,' Daisy said. 'What a compliment.'

'I didn't mean to hurt you,' Ruth said.

'Yes, you did. I'm not beautiful or witty or clever, just old tarty Daisy, that amiable fat slut, nothing but sex on her tiny mind. Doesn't ever cross yours, I suppose? You must have fancied other men sometimes? What about Danny? I expect Joe's wondered about him, hasn't he? Bit of a fool if he hasn't, even if he does think he's queer. Swanning off round Europe together, jet-setting about. Such a good alibi. I don't say there's anything in it but some people might look at it dif-ferently. And what about *Fergus*? Oh, God, Ruth, I've seen how you look at him, *ooze* round him at parties.' She saw Ruth was blushing. She said triumphantly, 'There you are, look at you!'

Ruth said, 'Oh, of course, I've sometimes half wanted. . .' She swallowed, frowning, looking at Daisy timidly, 'I mean, I do understand some of it. It must be lovely to have an affair, or at least in the beginning, to feel new and strange and young again and desirable. But it can't be like that with you and Joe, can it? You've known each other too long.' She sighed. A long sigh. 'So he must love you. You must love him. And that means he's behaved – still is behaving – quite dreadfully badly towards you.'

She spoke in a low, reverent tone. It seemed to Daisy to lay a heavy weight on her. The terrible burden of the serious world Ruth inhabited. She thought, if I say yes, I do love him, she'll *give* him to me, hand him over like a bloody parcel!

She said, 'Love? Oh, I don't know about love! It's just a word, isn't it.'

'Words usually mean something,' Ruth said, more crisply. 'If you mean that all this fuss we are making just now about who loves whom and how much is an irrelevant luxury when men and women may be dying around us, then I agree with you. It's the careless chatter of privileged persons. The life that we lead, our comfortable houses, the food on our tables, the clothes we put on our backs, this expensive holiday we are taking, is the life of privileged persons. But it's the life we've been given to lead, and the only way not to make it hopelessly trivial is to lead it within some kind of discipline. I could say, I love Joe, I want him to be happy, so if he loves you, I ought to let him go. I'm tempted to say that. In some ways I would find it much easier. I want to be happy with him, but I'm afraid to be happy. And a lot of the time, I'm in *torment*! He holds my hand, smiles, makes love to me – and it makes the pain worse. I think, oh, you false friend! But then I think, he's being kind, partly because he does love me, but mostly because he wants to behave well. He wants to hold on to our marriage because he thinks that's the right thing to do. If I break it up because I'm angry and jealous and hurt, out of spite, out of silly pride, then I'll do him more damage than he's ever done me.'

'Horse shit,' Daisy said. 'Oh, not altogether. It's the way that you put it. For God's sake, whatever happens, we'll all get over it, all the same in a hundred years. I'm sorry you're miserable, *I'm* bloody miserable, I daresay he's miserable too, if he isn't bloody well *dead*! Here we sit, yammering away, he may be out there, dead in a gutter! That would bloody sort things out, wouldn't it? Two of us, merry old widows!' She glared at Ruth, feeling tears of rage burn her eyes. 'Listen,' she said, 'you've been happy with Joe, years and years you've been happy with Joe, doesn't that count for something? The poor bugger loves you, what are you trying to do, pull the house down round his ears? For God's sake, he doesn't want me. Oh, maybe he did for a bit, and good fun it was too, I'm damned if I'll pretend that it wasn't. A bit of fun wouldn't do you any harm either.'

Ruth said, 'You really do care for him, don't you? Don't pretend, Daisy. I'm being so selfish. If you really do care, if you want to go on, well seeing each other. . .' Her face was painfully crimson but her eyes watched Daisy gravely and steadily. 'I mean, I wouldn't make scenes, I would try. . .'

'What had you in mind, dear? Friday evenings, every fourth Sunday?'

'I don't know.' Ruth covered her crimson face with her hands, hid her eyes. She whispered, 'I wanted to be the only one, the only person he loved, that was wicked and selfish, I'm sorry, I'm *sorry*. . .' She began to sob, rocking backwards and forwards. 'My father was right, he was right about me, he knew me better than I knew myself, he knew I was *wicked*. . .'

Daisy said, 'You don't have to play that trump card, my duck, not with me.'

She sat very still for a moment. Then she leaned forward and took Ruth's hands from her face, noting with interest that her eyes were quite dry. She said, pressing Ruth's fingers gently, 'I can't tell you what to do about Joe. That's up to you. How you feel. But I'm out of the running, believe me. And not just for your sake, I'm not being noble. Eunice Pilbeam is in her *thirties*, remember? That flight of fancy was a dead giveaway, wasn't it? Bloody male vanity! A woman of my age, practically menopausal for God's sake, wouldn't have been nearly so flattering! Well, that finished him for me. Put the tin lid on it.'

Ruth murmured, 'Perhaps I shouldn't have told you. If I'd known. . .'

'You did know,' Daisy said. 'Cunning bitch. Never mind, I don't hold it against you.'

She saw, with immense relief, that Ruth was beginning to smile. Daisy laughed herself, rolling her eyes. 'Of course,' she said, 'he may have been cheating on both of us, have you thought of that? Some dinky little chick, physiotherapist, masseuse, maybe a doctor. Bound to be someone in the medical line, with his hypochondria.' Not very funny, she thought, but the best she could manage.

'Oh, poor Joe!' Ruth giggled suddenly, a high, childish sound. 'Oh Daisy, you are so absurd, I do love you.' Her eyes, solemn again, searched Daisy's face. She sighed. 'I wish I was like you.'

'Work at it,' Daisy said. 'You never know your luck.'

They were still holding hands. Bob said from the doorway, 'Having a seance, girls? Break it up now. All quiet on the western front at the moment. We're going back to the boat.'

There was a bruised lump like a large plum above his left eyebrow. As they looked at him, his fingers went up to it, gently exploring. 'Just a stone,' he said, and then, quickly, 'It's all right, Joe's all right, he's outside, standing guard over the taxi.'

III

Marigold, thumping up the stairs from the kitchen with a tray of coffee and sandwiches, making a lot of noise so that Mark and Georgia should know she was coming, heard her brother say, 'What they do is nothing to do with us, Georgia. Absolutely none of our business.'

Although they were sitting with perfect propriety on two separate Habitat cushions, several feet of carpet and the Sealyham bitch lying between them, Georgia leapt up when Marigold entered, and blushed. Innocence Surprised, Marigold thought. Or perhaps Innocent Guilt. (She had recently been with her art class at school to an exhibition of Victorian painting.) What on earth would Georgia do if she and Mark were caught actually holding *hands*, or even, God save the mark, *kissing*? Swoon away, probably. Marigold said, 'What is none of our business, Mark?'

'Nothing.' He shrugged his shoulders and sighed, over-elaborately. 'Oh, parents. That sort of thing. A general discussion.'

He looked guilty all right! 'Oh, never mind, don't bother to tell me, no one ever does tell me anything!' Marigold spoke fairly cheerfully, used to this situation just lately. Georgia and Mark, mutter, mutter in corners, leaving her to clear tables, wash dishes, make coffee. Secrets. Lovers' talk. None of her business. But she did resent it a little. She said, 'Don't worry, I'm not staying here, in your way, I've got loads of homework.' She was amused to see Georgia blush even more deeply. She added, 'I mean, I know that two's company.'

'Don't tease,' Mark said sharply. 'Georgia's upset.' He stopped, colouring up a little himself at the sight of Marigold archly raising her eyebrows. Georgia was always 'upset'. Sex upset her, eating meat upset her, baby lambs being slaughtered upset her. A grunge, Marigold thought, a real whinge! Did Georgia really imagine she had a monopoly of tender feelings? Mark knew what his sister was thinking. He said, ineffectually, 'She's worrying about Daisy.'

Marigold's eyebrows disappeared into her fringe of hair. 'They're on the Nile. Not in Cairo. Miles away, Georgia. Don't be such a ghastly old worringe.'

Georgia shook her head. She was incapable of subterfuge. Marigold saw the look she gave Mark, an intimate, anguished look, almost feverish in its despair. So it was more than that! Marigold said, this time with more irritation, 'If you want to talk privately, don't leave the door open. I'll always knock.'

Georgia sank gracefully down, arranging her muslin skirt round her as she sat crosslegged on the cushion. Head bent, she stroked the Sealyham's woolly back. The bitch began to snarl, a low, idly menacing rumble.

'It wasn't really private,' Mark said, speaking to Marigold but watching Georgia, preparing to dive to the rescue if the snarls grew more animated. 'We were talking about marriage. Why people stay together, that sort of thing. If you marry the wrong person, it can't just be put right by leaving. Mistakes grow into your life.'

The discussion had not been as general as that. Marigold knew when her brother was lying.

She said, 'Our parents are all right.' A carefully flat statement, denying the question that she preferred not to ask. The unthinkable question.

Mark said, with relieved heartiness, 'Yes, of course.' He

smiled at Georgia, on easier ground now. 'Marigold still loves her Mum and Dad.'

'Why shouldn't I?'

'No reason. It's just that the way that you love them, the way you're hung up on them, is something you grow out of.' He looked at Georgia meaningfully. 'When you fall in love.'

Love was an inconvenient obsession in Marigold's view. She had seen sensible girls made silly by it, using up time and energy when they had examinations to take. She intended to put it off until a suitable moment. Perhaps after she had finished with university, begun her career. She said, 'I shan't fall in love until I'm at least twenty-six, and I shan't get married unless the man promises to do just as much house-work as me.'

'Suppose you have babies?' Georgia said. 'He can't have the babies, can he?'

'I don't want babies,' Marigold said. 'If you and Mark get married, you can have babies, Georgia, and I shall be a simply super aunt.'

Georgia wrinkled her nose with disgust. Though not at this unnatural remark. An evil smell filled the room.

Marigold said, 'God! What a pench!'

Georgia looked puzzled. 'Mixture of pong and stench,' Mark interpreted. He took a sandwich and said, to his sister, 'The dog keeps on farting. Did she have liver or something?'

'Whatever there was in the tin. *You* don't feed her, do you? Have you walked her this evening? No, of course you haven't. It's not fair. I took her this morning. Oh, you're so lazy, I really could gouge your eyes out.'

'Goneril!' Mark put his head on one side, coaxing her with his prettiest smile. 'No, you're a *noble* girl, really. Can't you let her out in the garden? I want to watch the nine o'clock news.'

Georgia said, 'Must we? I don't think I can bear to see it again.' She shivered. 'That poor man, poor Sadat, all those others too, just mown down, it's so horrible.'

'You can shut your eyes,' Mark said – with rather less tenderness than one might have expected, Marigold thought. Was he getting bored with this bleeding heart nonsense at last? The possibility cheered her.

She said graciously, 'All right then, as long as you let me know if there's anything new. I'm just as worried about the old folk as Georgia!'

She stirred the dog with her foot. It turned to snap, but only half-heartedly, rose to its stumpy legs, stretched – with another poisonous fart – and pattered after her. She went down the stairs and opened the kitchen door. The dog ran out. It was raining. Marigold stood in the doorway, feeling cold and disconsolate. 'Mark used to talk to me, now he talks to Georgia, they shut me off, it's like being behind a glass wall,' she said silently, addressing the unseen friend about whom she had never spoken to anyone, believing she was the only person to have thought of this device to ease loneliness. This familiar knew a great many things about Marigold, some of them deplorably childish, like her fear of the dentist, of large savage animals; and about other, more shameful feelings, the dark jealous anger that seized her whenever either of her parents looked at Mark lovingly, the even darker suspicions that had grown in her these last months about her mother and father.

She said now, 'There are these terrible, echoing silences, it's awful when we're having supper, I don't dare look up from my plate. They try and talk to me, but they don't talk to each other, and sometimes it's almost . . .' She couldn't quite formulate what she meant. 'As if there were someone else in the room, someone they're both afraid of, a sort of invisible presence standing between them,' was the best she could manage, but it seemed somehow too fanciful. She said, 'I could ask Mark, I'm sure he knows something, but I don't want to ask him. Once you talk about a thing that's only half there, like a ghost, it might become solid.' That was fanciful, too. She said, peering out into the rain, wishing the dog would hurry up, empty its beastly bowels and come back, 'I'm not imagining it. If I were younger, I'd think it was all my fault, that I'd done something wrong, but I'm too old for that. Mum got drunk at Luke's funeral, she talked to herself like a drunken old woman. I didn't imagine that, did I? Perhaps she was just sad about Luke, but she's gone on ever since looking sad. As if a light had gone out inside her. I can't bear it. I wish I could go away and not see it, live with some people who were laughing and happy and friendly. I thought it was Dad's fault at first, that he'd done something dreadful to hurt her, but I'm not sure now. He's been kind to her, much kinder than usual, it's she who's pushing him away, closing against him, like shutting a door. Perhaps she's fallen in love with someone else. She's not all that old, younger than Dad. That might make her sad, falling in love always seems to make people sad, though it isn't supposed to. Oh, I do hope she hasn't, what would we all do if she went off with this man? I don't want to be left behind with Dad and with Mark, always having to clear away by myself after supper, both Dad and Mark are so lazy. I'd rather go with her, really, but the man might not want me. Perhaps I could go to boarding school, a Sixth Form college or something like that, and just come home in the holidays. Only it wouldn't be home if they weren't both here, would it? Perhaps they'd try and make up for it somehow, like buying me a car for my seventeenth birthday. Oh, I wish they'd come back and get on with whatever horrible thing it is that they're going to do, get it over. No, of course I don't wish that. I just wish they'd come back.'

Confusion and pain overcame her. She said, aloud, 'At least Dad walks the foul dog sometimes,' and laughed with sudden bravado. She clapped her hands so hard that they stung and shouted, 'Dog, come here, Dog,' thinking how stupid it was to call the creature just that, affected in a way, really. But no one had found a name for it that had stuck. Mark sometimes called it Wilkie because Wilkie Collins had written a book called *No Name*, but that had seemed more affected than anything. So now it was Dog. 'Blasted Dog,' Marigold called again. There was no answering scamper, no flash of white in the dark. It had escaped through the gap in the holly hedge at the side of the iron gate that led into the communal garden.

IV

Over Egypt, over the Nile, the clear night sky hung like a theatrical canopy. Beneath it, on the lit, enclosed stage of the river boat, the entertainment arranged to divert attention from trouble ashore was in full, noisy swing. Bob, sketchily attired as a pirate (black patch over bruised eye, red scarf and white shirt) was pointing to the sky and trying out his French on the pretty hairdresser from Paris. 'La déesse Nut a avalé le soleil. Demain matin – la naissance.' The hairdresser smiled at him willingly but without comprehension. 'La mythologie ancienne,' Bob began, and then laughed. 'Oh, hell, forget it, come and look at the stars. La belle nuit.' Winking at Daisy with his visible eye, he draped an arm round the girl's shoulders and led her purposefully towards the stern of the boat.

Daisy said, watching him, 'Hopeful old goat. Shouldn't think he's got much chance with her really. Still, full marks for trying. What's happened to her husband, he hasn't left, has he?'

As far as they knew, only the German editor and the BBC man had managed to get away. Either by air, or the overnight train from Cairo.

'Sick?' Ruth shrugged and smiled. 'Tummy bug? Perhaps he's been drinking the water.'

They were sitting on deck outside the saloon, recovering from a game organised by the boat manager; a race between two teams of passengers, passing an orange from chin to chin. Daisy's neck was still red and sore from the enthusiastic embrace of a bristly German; Ruth, placed between two smoother skinned Japanese students, had escaped with less damage. Both women wore skimpy tubes of thin cotton covered with sequins that Daisy had bought outside the temple at Karnac. 'We will be all-purpose temple maidens,' Ruth had said, showing less creative interest in their fancy dress than Daisy expected. Well, it was pretty weird, she thought now; grown men and women putting on silly clothes and playing silly games while God alone knew what mayhem and murder was going on elsewhere, on the darkened banks of the Nile, in Luxor. Earlier, there had been a fire, a red glow in the sky over the town. The tourists had lined the boat rails, watching and speculating.

Now most of them were in the saloon. Several men, Joe and the Surrey doctor among them, were being encased in white lavatory paper, rolled up into mummies by small, female partners. The tall Surrey doctor swayed, helpless with laughter, as an exceptionally tiny Japanese girl attempted to reach around his broad chest. Ruth said, 'Do look, Daisy. It really is rather funny.' She giggled unaffectedly like a child at a party.

Daisy said, 'A bit crass, isn't it? I know it's only a game, and we have to pass the time somehow locked up in this bloody boat, but it seems out of place. I mean, here in *Egypt*, for God's sake. Like mocking their dead.'

'We've been out of place all the time on this boat.' Ruth reached out and manacled Daisy's wrist, lightly, affectionately. 'Haven't you felt that? Those people out there scratching a living on the edge of the desert and us here, sailing by. Two worlds that don't touch each other.'

'Fancy talk,' Daisy said. 'There is only one world.'

Ruth released her wrist and leaned back in her chair. A mosquito buzzed round her. She flapped at it vaguely, then lit a cigarette, inhaled deeply, and coughed. 'I know, darling,' she said. 'That can be so awkward, sometimes.'

To Daisy's ear, this innocent sounding remark had an uncomfortable resonance. She wasn't keen to examine it, preferring to try and hold on to her old habits of mind; keep things simple. The situation was *bloody* awkward, no point in denying it, and Ruth had a perfect right to put the boot in now and then if she wanted to. But she seemed to be treating the whole stupid mess as some kind of *joke*. That was where the discomfort lay. Ever since they had returned to the boat in the taxi, Ruth had seemed to be trembling on the edge of wild laughter. Not hysterical laughter, understandable after the events of the day, but something cleaner, more bubbling, more joyful. At dinner she had glittered – there was no other word for it – turning from Joe, to Bob, to Daisy, bright as a diamond, bestowing on them all a benison of pure, sparkling happiness. Oh, just putting a bold face on it as I would do in her place, Daisy thought, and yet, shifting her buttocks restlessly on her creaking wicker chair, she couldn't shake off the sense of unease. What was Ruth up to? She said, cautiously, 'You're being remarkably cheerful.'

'Am I?'

'I would say so.'

Ruth stubbed out her cigarette. She said, 'After we got back to the boat, while we were changing, Joe told me he'd finished with Eunice. All over, he said, it had never meant very much really, a sexual flutter without any sentimental attachment, but he had been too ashamed to admit that before. He should have admitted it, he saw that now, he was sorry. And so on and so forth.' She paused. 'It was really quite a handsome apology.'

'Sounds like it. What did you say?'

'Nothing. What could I say? I just smiled,' Ruth said, smiling at Daisy. Then, reflectively, 'I shall miss Eunice. She had become quite a companion. I used to talk to her, write her letters in my head. Rather unpleasant ones, naturally, but that was a good release in a way. Like a spring clean, turning out cupboards, all the dark nooks and crannies. I've never had anyone I could vent my spleen on before. Too anxious to please, or too scared. I wonder if Joe will miss Eunice too? She must have meant something to him, he made her up, after all. Someone he could talk to who was always on his side, saw his point of view. Children have imaginary friends. She must have become a bit like that to him, don't you think?'

'Don't be malicious,' Daisy said. 'Don't enjoy it too much.'

'But I am enjoying it, darling. It's all so wonderfully silly. You and Joe – oh, I'm sorry, but I'm allowed a bit of fun, aren't I? You said it would do me good!'

She laughed. Daisy recognised the source of her unease in this laughter. Several hours ago, in Hashid's little parlour, looking at Ruth's withdrawn, wounded face, Daisy had felt for the first time a shock of horror and shame as if she had been party to some kind of murder. If Ruth had attacked her, reviled and reproached her, she would have accepted it meekly, almost with gratitude, felt healed and forgiven. But this cold, amused teasing was new and alarming. There was an element of heartlessness in it that could bring them all down. If Ruth were to tell Joe she knew the truth, tell him *now*, after his pathetic 'confession', it would break him. Oh, of course Ruth knew that, she wouldn't tell him. Or would she? In this mood, Ruth might do anything.

Daisy said, 'For God's sake, Ruth, do be serious!'

'I am being serious. Aren't I always? This is just a new style.' Ruth beamed at Daisy. 'If you're fond of Joe, you won't want to hurt him. We shall both have to be tremendously cunning and clever.' She looked beyond Daisy, lips curving sweetly. She said, 'Hallo, darling.'

Joe was joining them, carrying drinks. He was wearing a red robe he had borrowed from one of the boat crew. Flecks of white lavatory paper adhered to the robe, to his thick eyebrows, his crisp thatch of hair. He said, 'Drinks are free. I won the mummy game. My partner was that girl with huge glasses. Plain, but swift and determined.' He seemed pleased with himself, at ease and expansive. He said, 'Naked knees next. Men sitting with their trousers rolled up and blindfolded wives identifying their husbands.'

Ruth looked at Daisy – a sly look – and laughed. Joe was eyeing her too, with a quizzical grin. Both inviting her, separately, to share this comical secret: would Daisy know Joe's knees if she touched them? Oh Christ, it's me they will break between them, Daisy thought, seeing the months ahead – *years* of such amiably conspiratorial glances. She said, 'If the two of you think that's funny, I must be the only sane person left in the world.'

Ruth got the message. She sent, with a rueful smile, a kind of apology. Joe, less perceptive, laughed. 'Spoilsport! Though I admit I've had enough too. Not that I've been playing the fool altogether. I bought the tour guide a very large drink. It's not announced yet but there is an extra charter laid on for tomorrow. No stopover in Cairo. I know you wanted to see the museum, Ruth, but I think we'd be pushing our luck. If it's all right by you, I'll have a word with old Bob and confirm our seats before the rush starts.'

'Don't bother with Bob,' Daisy said. 'I want to go home.'
'Ruth?'

He looked at her earnestly, almost anxiously. As she nodded and smiled her assent, it seemed to Daisy that her eyes searched his face in an odd, lingering way, learning his features, fixing them in her mind as if she were saying goodbye to him, withdrawing into herself, into some inner fastness. But this could be an act too, Daisy told herself, an act put on for her benefit. A warning.

She said, when Joe had gone, 'I don't underestimate you, my old duck, don't you ever think it.'

Ruth widened her eyes, looking young and perplexed. 'What makes you say that?'

'I know you,' Daisy said, rather roughly, sensing in Ruth's shining gaze, bent thoughtfully upon her face now, the completeness of her withdrawal and the power that it gave her. Ruth held the ace in her hand. If pushed, she would use it.

'Of course you know me,' Ruth said, with a soft, candid look. 'You're my oldest friend, aren't you?'

V

Marigold stood in the communal gardens, whistling and calling. Behind her, the terrace shone with comforting light; from windows, from her own kitchen door, left wide open. Before her the woodland, beyond the first trees, was dark.

As a little girl, Marigold had been frightened of tigers. Running through these gardens at dusk, heart in mouth, hearing the pad of great, soft feet in the undergrowth, other dangers, warnings from parents, even her own experiences with boys from the tenement who had jeered and thrown stones, had not really troubled her. Since she was eight years old she had grown up in the city, learned to walk to and from school discreetly, avoiding unlit alleys, groups of yobs idling on corners. The riots this summer, fights with the police, petrol bombs, burning cars, pavements covered with broken glass, boarded up shops, had merely increased her sensible caution. In her opinion, it was only adults, accustomed to travel in cars, unused to the life of the streets, who were frightened of people. The only danger she felt in the gardens this black rainy night was her old fear of tigers, returning to make her knees weak, her pulse race.

'Idiot,' she said sternly, aloud. '*Baby*. Idiot baby!' Contempt dismissed her fear temporarily. She marched forward into the trees, wet leaves blowing cold round her ankles, wind cracking and groaning in the branches above her, shouting, 'Dog! Come here, *good* dog' – hoping to coax it with this false suggestion of love. The filthy creature had probably found something to scavenge in the garbage that littered the gardens; decaying fried fish, an old chicken carcase. Or worse. Last year a dead baby had been dug up from its shallow grave, rotting, half-eaten. Vomit rose in her throat. Two minutes, she thought, fighting panic. If it didn't turn up in two minutes, it could bloody well stay out all night. Perhaps, with a bit of luck, it would disappear altogether. But Dad would be upset. 'Dog. Come here, *nice* dog.'

She thought she heard something. So much stormy noise from the big trees above her she couldn't be certain, but it seemed to come from the ground. A rustling, snapping of twigs, fallen branches. Not the Sealyham, something larger and heavier. She stood still, eyes and ears straining, and then saw it briefly as it passed from one tree to another, a dark, flitting shape against the light from the terrace, cutting her off from safety and home, bounding towards her. She knew what it was, heard its bark, but recognition, though almost immediate, came too late to halt her instinctive terror. *Tyger, tyger, burning bright.* She fled from it, fleeing her old, childhood fear, stumbling, sobbing, snatched at by brambles, tripping at last over a tree root and falling. A sharp pain in her hands, then a sharper pain in her cheek, searing anguish, as the big Labrador crashed down on her back, trampling on top of her, shoving her face down hard into the rubbish beneath her, rusty tins, slimy leaves, broken bottles. *Bones,* she thought, sick with horror, dead people's bones cutting into her, and as the frightened dog leapt away and Simon ran up, brandishing his stout stick and shouting, she rolled over, screaming, hands pressed to her bleeding face, trying to brush the dead bones away, and driving the jagged shards of glass deeper.

VI

'Well, I'm glad to be out of that, I can tell you,' the fat woman in the window seat said, not speaking it seemed to anyone in particular, addressing this remark, pugnaciously, to the air.

Daisy, sitting next to her, saw a red face, small blue eyes hard and round as a baby doll's, small mouth pursed tight with aggression. Fear, Daisy supposed. She said, 'At least we were lucky to get on this flight. Though as far as one can tell, there hasn't been much trouble in Cairo.'

'Oh, that!' the woman said. 'You expect that sort of thing abroad. Killing each other like animals. Not that it's much better at home, decent people can't walk safe in the streets anymore. I meant the *filth*. Did you go on the Nile? I can tell you, I left the boat once, and that was quite enough, thank you! I don't know when I've been so disgusted.'

'Your memory must be failing you, dear.' The man on Daisy's other side, who until now had appeared to be dozing, pressed his seat button and sat upright. His eyes met Daisy's with a glazed, thoughtful look. 'My wife doesn't much care for foreign travel. It's the dirt, you see, and the flies.'

'Malta,' the woman said. 'I wouldn't give you twopence for Malta. As for Athens, that's not a place I would ever go back to, not if you paid me a thousand pounds. Noise and pollution.'

'The islands. We went to the islands,' her husband reminded her, returning his seat to a reclining position and folding his hands over his stomach as if settling back into slumber.

'Don't give me the islands!'

'How could I, my dear? They are not mine to give, I'm afraid.'

'You know what I mean.' The woman leaned across Daisy. Her hands were clenched on her knees.

'Hydra,' he murmured. 'Hydra is beautiful.'

Goading her, Daisy realised, seeing his eyes gleam under his lower lids, his mouth twitch.

She gave a deep sigh. 'No bath in that miserable pension, not even a washbasin, sharing a toilet with Tom, Dick and Harry. How would you like that?' she asked, hurling this question at Daisy like a challenging gauntlet. 'Not everyone is particular. Used paper thrown into a plastic basket instead of put down the bowl.'

'Greek plumbing leaves something to be desired,' the man said, opening his eyes again and smiling with secret pleasure at Daisy. He had a narrow, pale face – unlike the other returning tourists on this packed charter flight he seemed untouched by the sun – and he was dressed as if for a business board meeting in a dark suit and tie. He looked much younger than his wife. Spite kept him young, Daisy decided. 'Do you know Greece?' he asked her. 'What always surprises me is not the inadequate lavatories, but the lack of visual sense. The Ancient Greeks built like gods, now their descendants litter the landscape with hideous boxes like blind children playing with concrete. Hydra is an exception, even if my dear wife doesn't think so.'

'I was constipated in Hydra,' the woman said. 'Not once did I open my bowels and we were there for a fortnight.'

'Better than the other way. Remember Morocco?'

His wife seized this cue with an enraged, hissing sound. 'In Morocco,' she said, 'I caught dysentery.'

Daisy heard Ruth give a stifled giggle behind her. She craned round and met Ruth's amazed, laughing eyes. Daisy frowned. All right for Ruth to laugh, out of the line of fire. *She* was trapped on this battlefield. On the other side of the aisle Bob was sleeping, snoring with his mouth open. Joe was somewhere at the back of the plane.

She saw with relief that the steward was offering drinks. The man took a whisky, Daisy a gin and tonic. The woman accepted an orange juice. 'Tinned, of course,' she said with contempt.

'Better than fresh,' her husband said. 'Infection from dirty fingers is always a danger. In fact, dear, that plastic glass may not be as pure as it should be.'

The woman stood up. Her doll's eyes were washed with tears suddenly; the dull crimson flesh sagged either side of her mouth. As she pushed past Daisy's raised knees, she said, her voice shaking, 'Sometimes you go too far, Harry.'

He laughed. As she made her defeated way up the aisle, flabby and clumsy, skirt rucking up as she squeezed past the drink trolley on her way to the toilets, he said, with quiet hatred, 'Travel is supposed to broaden the mind. For my wife, it is a constant battle with hygiene.'

Daisy stared straight ahead. She felt (as she had felt once before, years ago, facing Ruth's terrible father) that she had witnessed a scene of such exemplary cruelty that she could not encompass it. She stretched her mind out to the years that must have led up to it and shrank back with dread. She thought of her own marriage, running through flickering sequences; silences, disappointments, brighter moments of intimacy, and a phrase Ruth had used came to her. The careless chatter of privileged persons. She thought of Luke without regret or desire, but to think of him comforted her. It wasn't so bad, we were not after all so unlucky, she said to his shade, and laid him to rest at last, without anger.

As they land at Heathrow, through thick cloud that turns into rain as the plane thumps down on the runway, Daisy is happy. She doesn't wonder why, simply accepts it in comfortable, immediate terms of getting off this cramped plane, going home, soaking in a hot bath, seeing Georgia. Tramping up the

long ramp from the aircraft with two plastic bags containing little gods, alabaster ash trays, and other useless, last minute purchases, she sees the fat woman lumbering ahead of her, weighed down by more luggage than she is carrying. For a split second Daisy has an impulse to help her. She checks it. The woman might think she is offering more than a helping hand and Daisy had no wish, at this moment, to befriend or console such an obvious victim. When Ruth comes up beside her, Daisy nods at the fat woman's back and says, only half as a joke, 'I hope you have counted your blessings.' Ruth smiles and takes one of Daisy's bags from her.

Joe is waiting at Passport Control. Bob has already gone through, in urgent search of a lavatory. Gyppy tummy. Joe says, to Ruth, 'Do you want to ring home?' She shakes her head – what's the hurry? – and he raises his eyebrows. Returning from holiday, Ruth is usually full of foolish anxieties. But not now, apparently. So it is Joe who goes to the telephone in the baggage hall, fumbling in his pocket for English coins; Joe, who turns a few minutes later, with a white, ravaged face, looking for his wife. Then Ruth is gone, running, and Daisy is left (no sign of Bob yet) to rescue four suitcases from the carousel. The next time she looks (rather crossly, heaving heavy cases on to a trolley) they are still by the telephone, arms entwined, clinging together like people caught in a shipwreck.

Marigold will be scarred for life. Although most of the cuts will fade with time, the wound on her cheek where the neck of the bottle laid open the bone, will always be visible. But for a strong, confident and beautiful girl, a whitening scar is not a great handicap, providing at least a talking point, and occasionally an added sexual piquancy. It has also given her, Joe considers – or rather, months of painful plastic surgery have given her – something of her mother's remoteness, her air of amused detachment. This is a not unattractive quality in a

woman, though not one he remembers his serious Ruth possessing before. If it puzzles him sometimes, he tells himself that people change as they grow older, and Ruth has not changed so much otherwise. She tucks her small hand into his as she always did, digs her chin in the same old way into his shoulder; is friendly, confiding, telling him when she comes home from her travels, from Paris, from Rome, from New York, all the comic or interesting things that have happened, the funny stories Danny has told her. Some of these are rather coarse and Joe is faintly surprised that Ruth should repeat them, but he is glad she enjoys Danny's company. Ruth has few close friends and he knows that she misses Daisy.

When Daisy's monthly letters arrive from Australia, Ruth falls on them eagerly and reads out the news with a smile. Daisy is busy running a voluntary organisation concerned with old people's housing about which she writes with an enthusiasm that strikes oddly on Joe's ear. This is not the Daisy he remembers, but then the Daisy he remembers has become mysteriously confused in his mind with Eunice Pilbeam. That illusory figure materialises rather too often, a dark shape on the edge of his vision that he recognises for what it is; the lie that has somehow worked its way into and distorted his life. There are moments (usually when he has been drinking) when he longs to exorcise this uncomfortable phantom, tell Ruth, put things straight between them. But she seems to be happy. He believes he is happy. Since he stopped committing adultery, his blood pressure, that had become worryingly high, has reverted to normal. So why open old wounds? It would hurt Ruth, spoil her friendship with Daisy. It might even hurt him. Daisy is a long way off – in every way, another country. The only time she comes to him, unencumbered by Eunice, is when he and Ruth make love. Ruth laughs more often than she used to on these occasions and sometimes when she laughs (though not always) she reminds him of Daisy.